"INCOMING TORPEDOES, BEARING TWO-FIVE-FIVE!"

In the *Rickover's* control room, John Walden reached for a microphone and secured a direct line to sonar.

"Chief, do you have a definite on those torpedoes?"

"That's affirmative, Captain. They're still outside the twenty-thousand-yard envelope, but both appear to be emitting."

"What the hell's coming down, Skipper?" the XO asked.

Walden scanned the instruments above the helm. "Looks like whoever lashed us didn't appreciate it when we returned the favor. Now he's expressed his displeasure by taking a potshot at us. If we're living right, our decoy will take care of the threat."

"But what about that guy out there who's responsible for this unwarranted attack?" the XO said.

"We've got one hundred and forty lives to get out of harm's way," Walden replied evenly. "First we'll neutralize those incoming torpedoes. *Then* we'll take care of that cowardly bastard!"

Zebra titles by Richard P. Henrick:

Silent Warriors
The Phoenix Odyssey
Counterforce
Flight of the Condor
When Duty Calls
Beneath the Silent Seas
Cry of the Deep
Under the Ice
Sea Devil
The Golden U-Boat
Sea of Death
Dive to Oblivion

RICHARD P. HENRICK

DIVE TO OBLIVION

Zebra Books
Kensington Publishing Corp.
http://www.zebrabooks.com

ZEBRA BOOKS are published by

Kensington Publishing Corp.
850 Third Avenue
New York, NY 10022

First Printing: January, 1993
10 9 8 7 6 5 4 3 2

Printed in the United States of America

This story wouldn't have been possible without the invaluable assistance of my friend and editor, Wallace Exman, and the crew of the USS *Hyman G. Rickover* (SSN-709), who taught me what it means to be "committed to excellence."

"Nothing in life is to be feared. It is only to be understood."

— Marie Curie

"The universe is not only queerer than we imagine, it is queerer than we can imagine."

— Lord Haldane

"A man should look for what is, and not for what he thinks should be."

— Albert Einstein

One

Commander Pete Slater awoke from his restless slumber long before his alarm clock was due to ring. The forty-two-year-old Annapolis graduate never slept well while at sea, and this current patrol proved no exception. His weary eyes scanned the darkened stateroom, stopping on the collection of softly glowing, luminescent-lit instruments mounted on the bulkhead before him. With a practiced glance he saw they were travelling on a southwesterly course, at a speed of fifteen knots, two hundred and eighty feet beneath the sea's surface.

Without referring to a chart, Slater visualized their position. A little less than twenty-four hours ago, the USS *Lewis and Clark* had left its berth at Charleston, South Carolina to begin a high-speed sprint into the Atlantic. Their initial course took them to the southeast, into the Bahamas. Here they skirted the eastern coast of Great Abaco Island, and entered Northeast Providence Channel. Nassau lay to the south, and soon they'd turn back to the southeast, to penetrate the deep, relatively narrow expanse of water bordered by

Andros Island to the west, and known as the Tongue of the Ocean.

The *Lewis and Clark* had been ordered into the Tongue of the Ocean to undergo sea trials in a specially designed U.S. Navy underwater test range. Pete Slater was no stranger to this state-of-the-art facility, though this would be his first visit as the commanding officer of a nuclear-powered, ballistic missile submarine.

To command such a vessel was a privilege, and Slater took his responsibility seriously. The *Lewis and Clark* was a Benjamin Franklin class submarine, that had been recently retrofitted to carry sixteen Trident C-4 missiles. Each missile could carry up to eight 100-kiloton, MIRV'd warheads with a range of over 4,000 nautical miles. Because of this vastly increased range, vessels of the *Lewis and Clark's* class were being withdrawn from forward-basing in Europe.

Though there were newer ballistic missile submarines in the fleet, the *Lewis and Clark* could still hold its own as a potent fighting platform. Originally commissioned on December 22, 1965, the vessel was outfitted with a variety of sophisticated electronics and weapons systems, making it a capable, first-line man-of-war. Four hundred and twenty-five feet long, the sub displaced over 8,250 tons. An S5W pressurized water-cooled reactor powered a single shaft, allowing for speeds in excess of twenty knots.

A crew of one hundred and forty officers and enlisted men manned the vessel. Their mission of deterrence made the avoidance of hostile submarines a number one priority. Therefore the boat's sonar outfit was designed for long-range detection rather than fire control. Yet should the *Lewis and Clark* need to defend itself, it could readily do so with four bow-mounted torpedo tubes capable of firing the high-performance Mk 48.

An electronic tone sounded routinely in the background. Slater sat up, yawned, and after rubbing his hand over his stubbled jaw, decided that a shave was in order. His quarters included a private head, certainly a luxury on a vessel as cramped for space as a submarine. Ever grateful for this convenience, he washed his hands with warm water in the Pullman-style washbasin and brushed his teeth before reaching for the hot lather machine. As he spread the aloe-scented cream over his face, he caught his reflection in the mirror, and took a second to appraise his tightly muscled upper torso that he managed to keep firm with frequent visits to the boat's Universal machine. His stomach was still flat, and the only evidence of the passing years was the white that increasingly colored his short blond hair and the crow's-feet around the outer corners of his deep blue eyes.

After soaking his razor in hot water, he proceeded to scrape the lather off his face, being careful not to cut the deeply dimpled skin of his chin. This distinctive feature had been inherited from his father, and according to his wife Mimi, was only one of the qualities that made him almost an exact look-alike to the actor Kirk Douglas. Others made the same comparison, and Slater had long ago gotten used to hearing such comments.

After completing his toilet, he pulled on a pair of dark blue coveralls and crossed over to his bulkhead mounted desk where a thick stack of paperwork awaited. Before tackling it, he looked at the calendar.

Tomorrow would be his wife's thirty-seventh birthday, and he reread the familygram that he had sent earlier in the day.

Happy B'day, Mouse. May all your champagne wishes and caviar dreams come true. C.Y.K. Dutch.

Because communications with a submerged submarine were kept at an absolute minimum, the familygram was the submariners' only contact with the outside world. Limited in length and content due to security concerns, such personal dispatches were broadcast only when conditions permitted.

To ensure privacy and to get around the ever present shore-based censors, a personal code was often created. Pete Slater's latest familygram utilized a variety of terms that would only have meaning to his wife.

Slater began calling her Mouse twenty years ago, on the night they first met at a Naval Academy costume party. Mimi had made an adorable Minnie Mouse at that time, while Slater earned his nickname by wearing the costume of the little Dutchman, complete with wooden shoes that he had carved himself.

The rest of his latest familygram was equally symbolic. On those rare occasions when he was home, they often watched Robin Leach chronicle the lives of the rich and famous on television. Both were painfully aware that this would be as close as they would ever come to sharing the carefree lives of a jet-setter, and Slater teased his wife with his best Robin Leach imitation whenever the situation warranted.

C.Y.K. had a different source. Short for consider

yourself kissed, it was originally coined by Mimi's great-aunt. It was a term of endearment, but it also meant that all was well.

Satisfied that his familygram would be well received, Slater's thoughts were redirected by the inviting scent of fresh-perked coffee. He took another look at the stack of paperwork that sat before him, and decided that he'd be much better prepared to dig into it after a quick breakfast.

In the nearby wardroom, Slater found two officers seated at the large, rectangular table. One was his XO, Lieutenant Commander Tim Bressler, who was polishing off a stack of hotcakes. Seated beside the XO, a detailed bathymetric chart spread out before him, was the *Lewis and Clark*'s navigator, Lieutenant Todd Ferrell.

"Good morning, Skipper. How'd you sleep?" greeted Bressler between bites.

Slater answered while seating himself at his customary position at the head of the table. "I believe that I managed to get a couple of decent hours of shuteye in, XO. How soon until we make our next course change?"

"At present speed, we've got another quarter of an hour to go until we leave Northeast Providence Channel, Captain," volunteered the navigator, as he pointed towards the chart and outlined the narrow channel lying between Andros Island and Nassau. "As planned, we'll be entering Tongue of the Ocean by way of the Andros Trench."

A tall, lanky sailor entered the wardroom carrying a thermos of coffee. He nervously cleared his throat upon spotting the newly arrived officer seated at the table's head.

"What can I get for you, Captain?" managed the sailor, whose soft voice had a southern drawl to it.

"Some coffee for starters," replied Slater. "What kind of hot cereal do we have this morning?"

"I believe it's oatmeal, sir," said the redheaded sailor, whose hand slightly shook as he filled Slater's ceramic mug with piping hot coffee.

"That will be fine," said Slater, who looked the young sailor in the eye and continued. "Say, you're new aboard *Lewis and Clark,* aren't you, son?"

"That I am, sir," replied the seaman rather sheepishly.

"Well, what's your name and where are you from?" asked Slater as he warmed his hands on the sides of the mug.

"I'm Seaman Second Class Homer Morgan, sir, from Eureka Springs, Arkansas."

There was a look of fondness on Slater's face as he responded to this revelation. "That's beautiful country, Seaman Morgan. My wife's family is from Little Rock, and several years ago they took me on a float trip on the Buffalo River. Boy, did we ever have a wonderful time."

"Why I practically grew up on the Buffalo," revealed Homer Morgan with a bit more enthusiasm.

"I envy you, son," said Slater dreamily.

Not certain what to say next, Homer Morgan shyly diverted his glance downwards and turned for the galley to get the captain's oatmeal. Around the wardroom table, a moment of introspective silence followed. Slater sipped his coffee, and visualized his week spent with Mimi and her mother and father in the magnifi-

14

cent wilds of northwest Arkansas. Tim Bressler finished off his hotcakes, while Lieutenant Ferrell folded up the chart and stood.

"I'll be in control monitoring our course change, sir," said the navigator.

"We'll join you there," instructed Slater, who caught his navigator's glance and added. "The key element in this whole approach will be locating the Andros Trench, and then following it straight into the test range. Can you handle it, Mr. Ferrell?"

"No trouble, sir," returned the navigator as he turned for the forward doorway and just missed colliding into Seaman Morgan, who had been rushing into the compartment with the captain's breakfast in hand.

Slater sweetened his oatmeal with honey, and was in the process of pouring in some skim milk, when the intercom rang. It was Tim Bressler who alertly picked up the nearest telephone handset and spoke into the transmitter.

"XO here."

"Officer of the Deck, sir," replied a steady voice on the other end of the line. "We've got an unidentified submerged contact, designated Sierra three."

"Have the tracking party initiate a TMA," returned Bressler. "I'll be right with you."

The XO hung up the handset and addressed Slater. "Sonar contact, Skipper. Suspected submarine."

Pete Slater hastily swallowed down a mouthful of oatmeal and stood. "It never fails to happen right at mealtime. Lead the way, XO."

It took them less than a minute to reach the control room, where they joined a bespectacled, blond-haired officer beside the fire-control console.

15

"What have you got Officer of the Deck?" greeted Slater.

The OOD pointed towards the ceiling-mounted repeater screen. "Sierra three is bearing three-two-five, at approximately five thousand yards, sir."

"How many ranges do you have on it?" quizzed Slater.

"Two, Captain," answered the OOD.

"And how many legs?" asked Tim Bressler.

"This is our fourth, sir," returned the OOD.

"Why don't we take a look and see precisely where we are," offered Slater, who led the way over to navigation.

Todd Ferrell was draped over a detailed bathymetric chart of Northeast Providence Channel, and barely looked up with the arrival of the three newcomers.

"Where are we, Mr. Ferrell?" questioned Slater.

The navigator picked up a blue grease pencil and made a small *x* in the waters off the northeastern coast of Andros Island.

"Our latest SINS update puts us right here, sir," he reported. "We're scheduled to make our turn to the southeast and enter Tongue of the Ocean in another seven minutes."

"This is one hell of a time to have a bogey in our midst," reflected Bressler.

Pete Slater thoughtfully rubbed his dimpled chin, as he studied the chart. "We've still got plenty of room. Let's maneuver and get another leg on him."

"Will do, Captain," responded the OOD as he turned for the helm to carry out this directive.

With his gaze still centered on the chart, Slater quietly expressed himself. "If it is indeed another submarine out there, you can bet the farm that it's not one of ours. These waters have been cleared for our use only."

"Do you want to sound battle stations, Skipper?" asked Bressler.

"Let's hold off until we get a definite tag on it," answered Slater. "Who knows, maybe Sierra three is nothing but a wayward whale."

"And what if it turns out to be a hostile?" asked Ferrell.

Slater looked up and directly met the navigator's concerned glance. "Then the *Lewis and Clark* will do what she does best, Mr. Ferrell. And afterwards, we'll be able to attain our destination as planned, this time with the waters of the Andros Trench all to ourselves."

Back in the boat's wardroom, Homer Morgan was surprised to find the compartment completely empty. The captain had barely touched his oatmeal and his coffee. As the sailor cleared off the table, he wondered if the food was at fault, and he made certain to pass on his suspicions upon returning to the galley.

"It seems the CO doesn't like our chow, Chief," commented Homer to his immediate superior, Petty Officer First Class Vince Cunnetto.

The *Lewis and Clark*'s portly head cook barely paid this observation any attention as he completed a minor repair to the trash compactor.

"That's news to me," managed Cunnetto, who studied the gasket that he had just installed on the compactor's inner lid.

"Well I just returned from the wardroom and the captain left behind a bowl of oatmeal and most of his joe," added Homer.

Cunnetto held back his response until he was certain that the gasket was properly fitted. "Most likely, he was called away by an emergency of some sort, Homer. The old man enjoys his hot cereal in the morning, and I've yet to hear a complaint out of him."

To make certain that his cooking wasn't the cause, Cunnetto walked over to the stove and sampled the remaining oatmeal. It tasted fine to him, and after diluting it with a cup of hot water, he readdressed Seaman Morgan.

"If you're gonna make it here in the galley, you can't take leftovers so seriously, Homer. The crew is frequently called back to work at unexpected times, and you'll be encountering your fair share of waste that has nothing to do with poor quality."

"I hear you, Chief," said Homer apologetically. "It's just that this being my first day servin' the wardroom and all, I wanted things to be perfect."

"What do you think of Captain Slater, Homer?" quizzed Cunnetto as he returned to the compactor and pulled open its upper lid.

"He sure seemed like a nice fellow, Chief. He even noticed that I was new, and took the time to ask my name and where I was from. Did you know that his wife was from Little Rock, and that he once floated the Buffalo river with her parents? Why I practically grew up on that river!"

"You don't say," mumbled Cunnetto, whose attention had refocused itself on double-checking the fit of the gasket. Satisfied that all looked well, he sealed the lid shut and reached over to turn the unit on.

The compactor activated with a low-pitched, grinding hum. Several seconds later, it turned itself off and

Cunnetto anxiously opened the lid. A satisfied smirk painted his moustached face as he lifted out a heavy, black plastic bag filled with tightly compacted trash.

"Did you know that this is the second repair that I successfully completed this morning, Homer? Sometimes I think that I should have been a mechanic."

"What else did you fix?" questioned Homer.

"The TDU," responded Cunnetto as he handed his shipmate the garbage bag. "Follow me and I'll show ya."

It took both hands for Homer to lift the bag and carry it across the galley to an adjoining space where the TDU, or trash disposal unit, was located. It was through this opening to the sea beyond that the sub's trash was ejected. Several more plastic bags of garbage lay on the deck here, and Cunnetto opened the TDU's main chute and pointed inside.

"Remember yesterday when we went to shoot the trash and we couldn't get the unit to seal properly," commented Cunnetto.

Homer nodded that he did as Cunnetto continued. "Well I thought about the problem all night, and figured that it couldn't be anything too serious. Sure enough, this morning when I went to take a closer look I found a can caught in the ball valve. I cleared it in time to start breakfast. Load it up and let's give it a try."

Homer managed to drop each of the plastic bundles into the chute, noting the sickening ripe scent that emanated from the garbage bags that had been stored on the deck. With great relief he torqued shut the hatch and backed away.

"Homer, you look a little green around the gills," observed Cunnetto with a wink. "Now you can just imagine what this whole boat would have smelled like if the TDU were inoperable during the rest of this patrol. Stand by to shoot the trash, while I get permission to unlock from the Chief of the Watch."

"Receiving hull popping noises from the contact, Captain," reported the OOD. "Sonar classifies Sierra three a hostile submerged contact by the nature of this sound."

"Man battle stations!" ordered Slater forcefully.

A steady electronic tone began warbling in the background as Slater and his XO gathered behind the fire-control console, where they were met by Ensign Lockhart, the head of the tracking party.

"Captain," said Lockhart, "Sierra three appears to be in the first convergence zone, with a range of two-one thousand yards. Its course is westerly, at a speed of seven knots."

"Has sonar been able to run a signature I.D. check on it?" questioned Slater.

Ensign Lockhart nodded. "That they have, sir. Preliminary data show Sierra three to be a Russian fast-attack sub."

Bressler winced with this revelation. "Great, just the type of vessel we want to lead into our underwater test range."

"I doubt that they've got a definite on us, XO," offered Slater. "Ensign Lockhart, inform sonar to initiate a self-noise check."

Slater and Bressler were in the process of returning

to navigation, when Ensign Lockhart's voice spoke out tensely. "Captain, sonar reports that we're making noise aft."

"What?" retorted Slater, who vented his rage on the nearest intercom handset. "Lieutenant Worth, what the hell's going on back there?"

The *Lewis and Clark's* reactor officer answered directly. "Water pump failure, Captain. We're switching over to the auxiliary unit, and I'll have us buttoned down as soon as possible."

Slater disgustedly hung up the handset and addressed his XO. "Murphy's law strikes again. We've got a malfunctioning water pump."

"That bogey will have us for sure now," said Bressler. "Maybe we can lose them in the layer."

"Good idea," said Slater as he turned towards the two seated planesmen positioned forward in the control room. "We're going up through the layer. I've got the conn. Make your depth nine-zero feet."

"Nine-zero feet, aye, sir," returned the diving officer. "Helm, five degrees up on the fairwater planes."

"Five degrees up on the fairwater planes, aye," repeated the helmsman as he pulled back on his control yoke.

The sub's rounded bow angled upwards, and as it crossed into the layer of relatively warm water near the sea's surface, Lieutenant Worth informed them that the auxiliary water pump was now online. Seconds later, sonar reported that the *Lewis and Clark* was no longer making unwanted noise, and Slater's relief was noticeable.

"They've lost us now, XO. No way could they follow us with all this surface noise topside."

"Now where to, Skipper?" asked Bressler.

Slater answered while scanning the instruments mounted before the helm. "It's time to take us back beneath the layer and get on with our mission. The *Lewis and Clark* has got a date to keep in the Andros Trench."

As both of the boat's senior officers turned for navigation, neither of them paid attention to the chief of the watch as he picked up the intercom and fielded a question from Chief Cunnetto in the galley. Without a second's hesitation, the watch chief denied Cunnetto's request to shoot the trash, instructing him instead to concentrate his efforts on preparing his compartment for a deep dive.

Homer Morgan was the only one in the galley whom Chief Cunnetto failed to inform of the dive. Still waiting in the tight space reserved for the TDU, Homer reached out for a handhold when the bow unexpectedly pointed downwards at a steep thirty-degree angle. It took a total effort on his part to remain standing, and he breathlessly listened as several implements went crashing to the deck outside in the food-preparation area.

Unwanted sound was every submariner's worst nightmare, and Homer knew that a can crashing to the deck could reveal their position to an enemy. Ever since being assigned to the galley staff, Chief Cunnetto had emphasized this fact to him, and Homer could picture the mess crew as they frantically struggled to stow away the rest of their gear. He wasn't surprised when the chief forcefully called out to him:

"Homer, get the hell in here and give us a hand!"

"Should I shoot the trash?" asked Homer before abandoning his post.

Before Cunnetto could answer him, the pot holding the oatmeal went sliding off the stove, and one of the cooks caught it just before it tumbled to the floor.

"Empty that damn thing, sailor!" ordered the chief angrily.

Thinking that Cunnetto was responding to his question, Homer reached out to activate the TDU. He flooded down the chamber, and adjusted the pressure until it was equal to that of the surrounding sea. Then he opened the outer hatch and depressed the button that was supposed to launch the trash into the depths beyond. Strangely enough, the trash remained in the tube, and when he depressed the button once more, the interior hatch sprang open and Homer was sprayed with a shower of icy seawater. As the torrent intensified, Homer was thrown to the slippery deck by a pressurized column of water that had the force of a fire hose.

"Flooding in the galley! I show the TDU open to the sea!"

The watch officer's words of alarm filled the control room crew with instant dread, and prompted an immediate response from the sub's captain.

"Blow all ballast! Emergency surface!"

Before the diving officer could convey this directive, Ensign Lockhart frantically called out for all to hear. "Sonar reports that Sierra three has broken the layer directly above us, Captain. If we ascend now, we'll smack right into them!"

"Belay that order to surface!" cried Slater. "Secure all watertight doors and get those pumps working. XO, I want you to get down to the galley and size up the situation. The TDU hatch has a manual backup that can be closed if all else fails."

"Aye, aye, Skipper," said Bressler, who quickly rushed out the aft passageway.

Slater turned his attention back to the helm. "How's she handling?"

"Sluggishly, sir," reported the senior planesman as he struggled to pull back on his control yoke.

Immediately beside the helmsman, the watch officer anxiously surveyed the gauges of his console. "If we take on much more seawater, we'll never be able to pull out of this dive, Captain," he warned.

"Stand by to blow emergency," instructed Slater. "If the TDU can't be sealed in the next couple of minutes, we'll just have to take our chances with a collision."

Back in the galley, Homer struggled to pick himself up off the soaked deck. The water was halfway up to his knees, and continued to pour out of the ruptured hatch with a frightening velocity.

"Damn it, Homer! What in the hell did you do?" shouted Chief Cunnetto from the flooded galley.

To be heard over the crash of the onrushing seawater, Homer had to scream his response. "I'm sorry, Chief. All I did was shoot the trash."

"You idiot! I never gave you permission to activate the TDU," returned the enraged chief. "And now we're gonna pay for your incompetence with our lives!"

A knot formed in Homer's gut as he realized the se

24

riousness of their predicament. Though he could have sworn that he had heard his superior order him to empty the TDU, excuses meant nothing now. All that mattered was stopping the flow of water before the chief's grim prediction came true.

While Homer was wondering what he could do to dam the flow of water, the XO arrived in the galley. Lieutenant Commander Bressler carried an emergency breathing apparatus and headed straight for Homer. The ever-deepening water made his progress difficult, and his knees were covered by the time he reached his goal.

"I'm sorry, sir," said Homer, his voice cracking from both fear and the cold.

Tim Bressler ignored this apology, focusing his attention instead on the column of seawater that poured through the ruptured hatch. The TDU itself would soon be covered, and the XO looked over at Homer and asked a single question.

"Can you swim, sailor?"

Homer shook his head that he could, and Bressler continued. "There's a hand crank located alongside the right wall of the TDU. By turning it clockwise you should be able to close the ball valve and reseal the hatch."

"I can find it, sir," said Homer anxiously.

"Then go to it," returned the XO, who handed Homer the emergency breathing apparatus.

Known as an EBA for short, the device was comprised of a rubber mask that was connected to a small oxygen tank by a hose. It was designed to provide up to thirty minutes of air, and Homer readily strapped it on.

"I'm going to call in an update to the captain. Good luck, sailor," offered the XO.

Thankful for this second chance to prove himself, Homer proceeded at once to the ruptured hatch. With the assistance of the EBA, he ducked beneath the wildly spraying water and reached the bulkhead where the TDU was located. Trying his best to ignore the water's numbing chill, he extended his right arm into the hatch and blindly groped for the hand crank.

Pete Slater received his XO's optimistic update while perched beside the sub's helm. Bressler estimated that the opening to the sea could be closed in another couple of minutes, yet Slater wondered if they could hold out that long.

The depth gauge had fallen below seven hundred feet, and continued to drop. Though the *Lewis and Clark*'s hull was designed to survive over twice this depth, Slater dared not put it to such a demanding test.

"I've got the results of our latest sounding," informed the navigator. "We've got a good thousand feet of water below us, putting us well within the mouth of the Andros Trench."

"The pumps are operating at full capacity," reported the officer of the watch. "They just can't handle all that volume."

The hull seemed to moan in protest as they dropped below seven hundred and fifty feet. Slater's grip on the ceiling-mounted handhold instinctively tightened. Their angle of descent was well over thirty degrees now, and he could feel the pull of gravity pulling them ever downwards on this dive into oblivion.

26

"To hell with that Russian sub!" cried Slater. "Blow emergency ballast! We're heading topside no matter what lies above us."

It seemed to take an eternity for Homer to locate the hand crank. By the time he did so, he was completely submerged. As instructed, he turned the crank in a clockwise direction, and slowly but surely the valve began to close.

The current of water that had been surging from the hatch lessened, and Homer turned the crank until the flood ceased. He was in the process of pulling himself out of the water when the deck began vibrating wildly beneath him. Thrown backwards by this unexpected movement, he sank beneath the five feet of seawater that had accumulated on the deck below.

The forceful vibration continued to affect him even underwater. By tightly gripping a submerged portion of pipe, he was able to keep from being smashed up against the madly shaking bulkhead. Fearing that his mask would be jarred loose, Homer listened as a bubbling roar sounded in the background. It got louder and louder, until it was almost deafening. The wildly shaking waters, and this ear-shattering sound, had an almost delirious effect on Homer, and his thoughts went back in time to his adolescence, and the day he had almost drowned while in the midst of a float trip.

His canoe had overturned in the middle of a particularly nasty set of rapids, and he had found himself pinned beneath the aluminum vessel, with his body jammed up against a huge, partially submerged boulder. This was as close to death as Homer had ever

27

come, and he survived only through an unwavering faith in a Lord he was just discovering, and a strong will to live.

Only by summoning these same qualities did Seaman Second Class Homer Morgan regain his senses. And as his thoughts returned to his present predicament, he fought off the urge to let go and die. Oblivious to the gut-wrenching vibration, and the demonic shriek that penetrated the very depths of his soul, he managed to reach upwards and grasp the iron rail that encircled the TDU. And he began the short journey out of his watery sarcophagus.

TWO

It took the better part of two days for the *Hari Maru* to reach the rich fishing grounds off Iwo Jima. Soon after setting sail from Okinawa, the crew of nineteen began sewing together a drift net, over three miles long. Stored on a pair of massive, stern-mounted rollers, this translucent, monofilament net was fitted with a series of corks on the top and with weighted line on the bottom. The net would create a floating barrier thirty-five feet deep, whose sole purpose was to catch squid.

The sun had yet to rise on the third day of their voyage, when the ship's air horn sounded three times. This signal called the fishermen from their bunks. Hurriedly dressed in blue oilskins and white boots, they assembled on the foredeck, where the vessel's fishing master, or *sendo*, instructed them to release the net.

The net itself was assembled in one-hundred-foot sections called *tans*. One hundred and sixty *tans* had been sewed together to create a single *nagashi-ami*. A white buoy marked the beginning and end of each separate *tan*. Positioned beside each buoy was a red num-

29

bered flag, a miniature battery-powered strobe light, and a radio antenna that signaled a direction-finder located in the *Hari Maru's* wheelhouse.

A thick, grey fog shrouded the calm sea as the net was tossed overboard. Deployment took over an hour. To insure good fortune, the *sendo* made certain to soak the net with sake, which was stored beside a small Shinto altar near the bridge.

The youngest fishermen currently aboard the *Hari Maru* were a pair of seventeen-year-old twins — Toshi and Yukio Tanaka, born in Naha, Okinawa. They came from a long line of squidders, among whom was their uncle, the ship's present *sendo*. This was only their second working cruise, and both impressionable teen-agers looked at this event as a great adventure. This was especially the case when the net was fully deployed, and they anxiously stood at the rail, waiting for the first squid to be pulled in.

"This is some morning," observed Toshi as he gazed out to sea. "The fog is so thick that even the sunrise will be veiled from us."

Yukio seemed uneasy as he voiced his reply. "What did you expect, brother? The sea here is perpetually shrouded."

"I hope that you still don't think that this portion of the sea is haunted by demons?" asked Toshi lightly.

Yukio's serious tone did not falter. "You may laugh all you want, Toshi. But for me, this area will always be *Mano Umi,* the sea of the devil."

"Oh come now, Yukio. You're beginning to sound just like a superstitious old woman."

"Then why are the other fishermen so somber this morning?" questioned Yukio. "Even Uncle seems affected. Never before have I seen him bless our net with an entire bottle of sake."

"I blame it all on the Americans and Canadians," reflected Toshi. "If it wasn't for their unfair protectionist laws, we'd be fishing in safety off the coasts of California or British Columbia, instead of in these treacherous waters."

"Then how do you account for the hundreds of ships and planes that have mysteriously vanished while traveling over this portion of the Pacific?" asked Yukio.

"One only has to look at nature for the answer to that question, Yukio. The floor of the ocean beneath us is ringed with underwater volcanoes and deep trenches scoured by powerful currents. This region is also no stranger to sudden storms and freak waves, that can swallow a ship in the blink of an eye. All of these naturally occurring phenomena could be responsible for the disappearances that you speak of."

Before Yukio could respond to this, their uncle joined them at the rail. The *Hari Maru*'s *sendo* was a powerfully built man, with a full, black beard and gentle brown eyes. A veteran mariner, he intently scanned the fog-shrouded seas, centering his gaze on one of the blinking strobe lights, just visible in the near distance.

"Well nephews, what do you think of this glorious morning?"

Toshi was the first to answer him. "My brother fears that there's a demon lurking below these waters, Uncle, just waiting to swallow us up at the first opportunity."

"You don't say," replied the *sendo*, whose kind glance turned towards Yukio. "Have no fear of the *Mano Umi,* nephew. When I was your age, I too heard

31

the frightening tales of the sea demons that supposedly inhabited these waters. Many a horrible nightmare has since been filled with visions of a ferocious dragon, which comes to the ocean's surface to seize my fishing boat, and drag me and my crew down to the dragon's underwater lair. But here I am an old man already, and still this tragic prophecy has not come true. So set your mind at ease, Yukio, and know that the only monsters in these parts are right here in your head."

Yukio managed a slight smile. Satisfied that his message got through, the *sendo* looked to his watch and added. "The sun will soon be breaking the eastern horizon, and with its arrival the squid will swim up to the surface to feed. If I were you, I'd go below and get some hot tea and rice in your bellies, for all too soon there will be no time for such a luxury."

Quick to follow their uncle's advice, the twins climbed below deck and joined the other fishermen in the galley. They were in the midst of enjoying a large bowl of fish soup, when the *Hari Maru*'s air horn sounded twice. This was followed by the shrill blast of a whistle and the *sendo*'s booming voice.

"Come on, lads. To the nets with you!"

Gulping down a last mouthful of soup, the twins rushed from the cabin and gathered on the stern. The net was already in the process of being pulled aboard. Its corks and weighted line were drawn through separate rollers, so that the four-and-a-half-inch mesh could be grasped by the fishermen and yanked onto the main deck amidships.

Toshi and Yukio took their positions beside the rail and watched as the first squid was pulled in.

"Ika! Ika!" shouted the excited *sendo*, who brought his whistle to his mouth and blew out a series of spirited blasts.

The squid plopped down onto the deck beside Yukio. Its sleek, oblong body was over two feet long, and as it brushed up against Yukio's boot, it shot out a spurt of jet black ink, this being the creature's primary defensive mechanism.

"My, that one's a beauty," observed Toshi as he bent down to pick up the squid by its head. "It must weigh a good five pounds!"

Both the twins admired its purple, tubelike mantle. The squid's head had a pair of clearly discernible eyes, and a beaklike mouth, with two long tentacles and eight shorter arms protruding downwards. One of these shorter arms attached itself onto Yukio's arm, and he quickly yanked the sucker free.

Hundreds of similarly sized squid soon covered the deck, that was awash now in black ink. The *sendo* seemed particularly pleased and as he passed by the stern, Toshi breathlessly addressed him.

"What species of squid are these, Uncle?"

"We call them neon flying squid," he answered.

"Why's that?" asked Yukio.

The *sendo* grinned. "Believe it or not, these creatures give off a bright flash of light while pursuing their prey of small fish. I've once seen this miraculous sight myself, while watching a hunting squid break the surface of the sea and leap through the air."

"Aren't they in danger of being overfished, if we continue taking them in these numbers?" asked Yukio.

"Not this species," replied the *sendo*. "I've been told that each female produces as many as half a million eggs during their one-year life span."

A sudden grinding noise broke from the stern, followed by the rending sound of tearing net.

"Stop the rollers!" shouted the *sendo*, his tone filled with concern. "What in the world is going on back there?"

"We've hit some sort of snag!" replied the crew member who operated the roller mechanism.

Both the *sendo* and his nephews quickly joined this individual, who was positioned on the aft-most portion of the *Hari Maru*'s stern. As the roller ground to a halt, they collectively examined the torn net, whose shredded remnants extended well out to sea.

"There's a good mile of net still out there," said the roller operator as he pointed towards the fog-enshrouded waters at their stern.

Even though the sun had long since risen, the thick fog completely veiled the horizon in all directions. A ghostly, milky white radiance hinted that a new day had dawned, with the only evidence of the surrounding ocean being the occasional slap of a passing wave.

"Perhaps we've caught a whale out there," offered Yukio.

"Or maybe it's a sea serpent that we've snagged," joked his brother.

"A whale could very well be responsible for this entire mess," observed the *sendo*. "Since this fog veils even our strobe lights, the only way that we're going to be able to recover the rest of the net is by tracking it down with the radio-direction finder. Join me in the wheelhouse, Nephews, and we'll get on with this task."

The wheelhouse was located on the ship's foredeck. A short flight of steps took them up into an equipment-packed compartment dominated by a wraparound window.

"Yukio, switch on the radar," instructed the *sendo*. "Toshi, have you ever used a radio-direction finder before?"

"Not in a fog like this one," replied the wide-eyed teen-ager.

"Well, stick close then, and I'll give you a quick lesson."

The *sendo* led his nephew over to a large console where he switched on a green-tinted monitor screen. After inputting a series of commands on the computer keyboard, the elder looked as the screen beeped a single time before going unceremoniously silent.

"That's certainly strange," he thoughtfully observed. "We appear to have lost our data link with the rest of the net."

"But how can that be, Uncle?" asked Toshi. "Aren't those direction-finders on the net battery powered? They couldn't have all failed to transmit at the same time."

"Uncle, what do you make of this?" interrupted Yukio.

The *sendo* was quick to join him beside the radar screen, as Yukio added. "There seems to be another vessel out there."

"I'll say," reflected the surprised *sendo*. "That return that you're getting shows an immense ship, over four hundred feet long, floating in waters less than a half mile off our stern."

"So that's what snagged our net," supposed Toshi.

"Switch on the foghorn and activate our running lights," ordered the *sendo*. "It's time to see for ourselves just what it is besides squid that the *Hari Maru* has managed to catch this morning."

Yukio's stomach tightened as he studied the radar screen. Then he looked up and peered out the window. From this vantage point, he could see several crew members gathered on the foredeck. Their lower torsos were completely hidden by the swirling fog, and Yukio could only pray that the *Hari Maru* wouldn't be the victim of a collision.

His uncle readily engaged the throttle and expertly steered the trawler in a broad, circular turn. With the foghorn mournfully crying out in steady warning, they cut through calm seas, blind to that which lay before them.

"The contact lies dead ahead of us, Uncle!" warned Yukio, whose eyes had returned to the radar screen. "Approximate range is 10,000 yards."

"Yukio, I want you to climb up on the flying bridge and activate the spotlight," ordered the *sendo*.

"But Uncle, who will monitor the radar screen?" countered Yukio.

"Don't worry, lad. Our spotlight will illuminate any traffic out there, regardless of this damn fog."

Though he was all set to argue otherwise, Yukio held his tongue, and after meeting his brother's concerned gaze, proceeded outside to the exposed bridge. A gust of cool, damp air greeted him as he began climbing the ladder that would take him up to the ship's flying bridge. This compact, elevated platform was supported on a base of four steel poles. During normal daytime conditions, a lookout would be stationed there to scan the surrounding ocean for signs of feeding squid. Yukio regularly volunteered for such duty, though in this instance, he sincerely wished that his uncle had chosen another in his place.

Try as he could, Yukio couldn't shake a feeling of unease as he climbed onto the flying bridge and peered down below. Except for the ship's red and green running lights, the main deck was all but invisible, effectively veiled by the thick, ghostly mist. Adding to the eerie atmosphere was the persistent, lonely cry of the foghorn, and the muted chugging whine of their diesel engine.

His uncle had yet to cut back the throttle. This meant that the danger of a collision increased with every second. With this fear in mind, he reached up and pulled off the spotlight's canvas cover. As he turned on the spotlight, there was a loud clicking noise. Yukio swung the swivel base so that the powerful beam of light was focused on the waters immediately ahead of them.

As he expected, the fog veiled even the ocean's surface. A supertanker could be out there and they'd never know it, and Yukio angrily cursed their predicament.

Visions of slithering sea serpents formed in his mind's eye. Such terrors of the deep had been well documented in these parts for centuries past. He had actually seen grown men shake in horror upon describing their terrifying experiences in the *Mano Umi*. And here they were today, foolishly challenging the fates, in the sea where the devil stalked.

Yukio's pulse quickened as he spotted a brief flash of greenish light in the distance. Several more quick flashes followed, and Yukio wondered if they could be from a group of flying neon squid.

As he slightly angled the spotlight upwards a bone-chilling, fetid breeze hit him full in the face. Fighting back the urge to retch, Yukio watched as the flashing green lights intensified, until it almost appeared as if a miniature electrical storm was occurring in the seas before them. Seriously doubting that such a phenomenon could be caused by squid, he looked on in wonder as the fog slowly began to part.

Never would Yukio forget the immense, black-skinned object that his spotlight next illuminated. At first he thought that it was a whale. But then he spotted the distinctive conning tower of a surfaced submarine. It lay dead in the water, with seaweed hanging from its sail-mounted hydroplanes. Strangely enough, it had no running lights on, and its deck was vacant of sailors. Puzzled by this fact, Yukio excitedly called down, to share this amazing discovery with the others.

Three

Commander Thomas Moore stood outside the USS *Iwo Jima*'s infirmary — where the captain's mast was taking place — still dressed in the uniform of a petty officer first class. He had been outfitted in this manner for three long weeks, and no one on board knew his real rank, except the ship's commanding officer.

A freckle-faced seaman, whom Moore readily recognized, walked stiffly down the passageway escorted by a pair of burly marines. Barely nineteen years old, the youngster noted Moore's presence beside the hatchway and spoke out with a high-pitched, strained voice.

"I'm scared to death, Chief. What are they gonna do to me?"

Moore looked the youngster straight in the eye and replied directly. "Just tell the truth, son. And don't be afraid to take your punishment like a man."

This proved to be the extent of their conversation, as the marines quickly led the terrified enlisted man into the infirmary. A captain's mast was never a pleasant experience. While at sea, this was how justice was handed out for a variety of infractions ranging from consistent tardiness, to petty theft and assault.

As an investigator with the Naval Investigative Service, Thomas Moore knew very well that this afternoon's session signaled the end of yet another successful mission on his part. Once again, he had gone undercover, this time to expose a group of illegal drug users aboard the amphibious assault ship.

This had been his first extended stay on a "gator freighter," and Moore was ready to be airlifted to a more comfortable location. Originally built over three decades ago, the USS *Iwo Jima* was the first assault ship exclusively designed to carry helicopters. Six hundred feet long, and displacing over 18,000 tons, it currently held in addition to its crew of 684, an entire Marine battalion landing team, their weapons, equipment, a reinforced squadron of transport helicopters, and various support personnel. Thus space was at a minimum, with normal creature comforts sorely lacking.

Moore was very fortunate to find a spare bunk in the ship's three-hundred-bed hospital. This allowed him some privacy, and kept him from having to mix too closely with the crew. As it turned out, an unsuspecting member of the infirmary staff provided him with his first real clue in the case.

Moore's "official" job on the *Iwo Jima* was as a clerk in the hospital's supply department. He did his best to fit in as one of the gang, and to not call any undue attention to himself.

One of the primary assets that allowed him to make a success of this undercover assignment, was his rather bland physical appearance. Thomas Moore's average looks fit his role perfectly. He was the type of person who could blend into a crowd. Of average height and a bit overweight, he could readily pass as the typical guy next door.

For as long as he could remember, he had kept his brown hair in a crew cut. He had his father's chubby face, and could easily go several days without needing a shave. Like his mother he had blue eyes, capped by thick, blond brows, that merged together on the bridge of his flat nose. By habit, he tended towards the sloppy, and it was an effort for him to keep a clean uniform, or for that matter, even to keep his shirt tail securely tucked in place.

When not on assignment, this tendency often got him in trouble with his superiors back in Washington. Far from being the perfect example of an officer and a gentleman, he was more like the U.S. Navy's version of detective Columbo. And much like Columbo, his ability to crack a difficult case where others had failed, forced his superiors to overlook personal traits that they found distasteful.

The door to the infirmary opened from the inside, and out walked the two marines, with a single, balding individual between them. This sailor wore handcuffs, and as he passed by Moore, he said, "I didn't mean any harm, Chief. The guys needed something to stay awake, and the captain came down on me like I was a heroin dealer."

Before Moore could reply, one of the marines forcefully intervened. "Keep your mouth shut and those eyes straight ahead, sailor! And no more talking until we reach the brig."

The prisoner did as ordered, and Moore silently conveyed his pity with a solemn shake of his head. Two weeks ago, Moore had learned that this sailor was stealing amphetamines from the hospital pharmacy. As a pharmacist's mate, his job had been to dispense potent drugs for the treatment of such maladies as hay fever and severe head colds.

By faking the symptoms of a bad sinus infection, Moore sought treatment. His prescribed medication, an amphetamine derivative, had been replaced by a simple aspirin compound. In such a manner, the pharmacist's mate had been able illegally to accumulate hundreds of pills, which he efficiently resold on the ship's black market.

It took Moore fourteen days to uncover the distribution network. It extended to almost every department on the *Iwo Jima*, including the embarked marine battalion. Misuse was especially prevalent amongst the engine-room crew and the helicopter mechanics. Often called to duty for exhausting twelve-hour shifts, they used the amphetamines to help them stay awake.

Also known as speed, the amphetamines could have dangerous physical side effects including dizziness, dry mouth, and increased pulse rate. Such drugs could also lead to dangerous mistakes in judgment, a disruption in normal sleep patterns, a decrease in one's appetite, and even paranoia and other serious psychotic behavior. Although the military often used speed to keep pilots and combat soldiers alert during long missions, this was an exception rather than the rule, and such use was always closely monitored by attending physicians.

When drugs were misused, Moore knew that there

42

was almost always an increase in the accident rate. Carelessness prevailed in such an atmosphere, and untold lives could be endangered. Thus, with a minimum of misgiving on his part, Moore sought out not only dealers, but users as well.

All told, his list implicated over three dozen men. They ranged in rank from lowly seamen second class, to an ensign in the air wing. All would receive severe reprimands from the *Iwo Jima*'s commanding officer, who per Navy tradition served as both judge and jury. Sentences would be issued to fit the crime, with the dealers being hit the hardest. They could look forward to actual jail time, while the users would be punished by a loss of rank and privileges.

Recently, the Navy had instituted a treatment program, whereby all those convicted of substance abuse would be required to undergo therapy in a support group environment. This novel program showed great promise, and Thomas Moore sincerely prayed that the sailors that he had busted would take this opportunity to get their lives in order, before they were ruined for good.

It was with this hope in mind that Moore looked at his watch, then returned to his bunk to pack up his belongings. He didn't have to go far to reach his locker. The hospital ward where he had been sleeping was currently empty of patients. It reeked of disinfectant, and he couldn't wait to return to shore and enjoy the luxury of a real bed.

The *Iwo Jima* was currently transiting the Ryukyu Islands, and he hoped to spend the night at Sasebo Navy base, on the Japanese island of Kyushu. Tomorrow, he planned to take the bullet train to Tokyo, and begin a long-anticipated five-day leave in the capital city, before having to return to his office at the Washington Navy Yard.

He was in the process of stuffing his seabag with socks, when the ship's supply officer entered the ward. Lieutenant Roger Samuels had been Moore's division officer while on the *Iwo Jima*, and a pain in the behind from the very beginning.

Known as spic-and-span Samuels to his subordinates, the supply officer demanded that proper naval etiquette be applied when in his divine presence. He was the type of stuffy, abusive, know-it-all officer that Moore couldn't stand, and he braced himself for the worst as Samuels greeted him with his nasal voice.

"So, you're leaving us already, Chief. I can't say that we're going to miss you. Hell, half the time you were out on sick leave. And from what I understand, when you were on the job, you depended upon others to do the work for you. Who gets the honor of your company next?"

"I can't really say, sir," answered Moore without emotion. "My new orders merely send me as far as Sasebo."

There was a look of disgust on Samuels's pinched face as he inspected Moore from head to foot. "Put a shine on those shoes in the meantime, and tuck in that shirt! Take some pride in that uniform, sailor, and perhaps the Navy can make something out of you yet."

"Yes sir," returned Moore, who practically had to bite his tongue to keep from revealing his true rank.

"I understand that we have a fink in our midst," commented Samuels as he eyed Moore suspiciously. "Though I certainly don't condone drugs, a little speed

44

never hurt the Navy. Why we practically run on caffeine as it is."

Moore kept packing as Samuels continued. "In my department, I like my men coming to me first with their suspicions, before running off to tattle to the CO. Do you read me, sailor?"

Moore shook his head. "I'm afraid that I don't know what you're talking about, sir."

"Come now, Chief," said Samuels. "Scuttlebutt has it that you were seen talking with the captain in private on three separate occasions. Unless the old man's a long-lost uncle of yours, I'd say that's a bit unusual."

With great relief Moore packed away his last item of clothing, sealed shut his seabag, and slung it over his shoulder.

"If you'll excuse me, Lieutenant, I've got a helicopter to catch," he managed, as calmly as possible.

Not to be denied, Samuels stepped in front of Moore. "Not so quick, sailor. In the U.S. Navy that I serve, we've learned to take care of our problems amongst ourselves. The way I hear it, too many good men have had their service records irrevocably blemished during that captain's mast, and all for consuming a little stimulant to help keep them working harder. We're a family here aboard the *Iwo Jima*, and we don't take lightly to outsiders coming in and sticking their noses where they don't belong."

Moore reacted to this accusation with an icy stare, and he attempted to step around his accuser. Samuels stepped sideways to block him.

"Do you hear me, sailor?" he questioned as he poked Moore's shoulder with his right index finger.

Instinctively, Moore reached up and slapped away

45

the supply officer's hand. Yet before Samuels could react to this unexpected movement, the deep, authoritative voice of the ship's CO, Captain Andrew Ritter, boomed out in the background.

"Chief, can I see you a minute?"

Lieutenant Samuels instantly went at ease. He backed away, and after leaving Moore with his best "I'll deal with you later" sneer, strode past the captain with a crisp salute, and exited the compartment.

"What was ole spic 'n span's problem?" asked Ritter as he walked over to join Moore.

"I guess he just didn't like the shine on my shoes, Captain," answered Moore with a wink.

"Come to think of it, they could use a bit of polish," said the captain, who warmly smiled and added, "Commander Moore, I just wanted to thank you again before you left us."

"I appreciate that, sir," returned Moore, who accepted Ritter's firm handshake. "But the way it looks, I'll be getting off the ship just in time. It seems that my cover's been blown."

"Well, no matter, Commander. Your work here is over, and I'll be certain to pass on word of a job well done to your superiors back at NIS."

"I hope that I haven't caused a lot of hard feelings among your crew, Captain. These sting operations can be painful."

"Nonsense," replied the captain. "In fact, all of them owe you their gratitude, especially the men that I just got through sentencing. Hopefully, we got to them in time to break their habit. And with a lot of hard work and luck, we'll get them back on the clean and sober path to normalcy once again."

Moore transferred his seabag to his other hand and looked down at his watch.

"What time's your flight?" asked Ritter.

"The chopper's supposed to leave in another ten minutes, sir."

"Then I won't keep you any longer. Have a safe trip, Commander, and make certain to give my regards to our shore-based shipmates inside the Beltway."

Moore flashed the senior officer a thumbs-up, and headed out the forward hatch. A series of passageways and ladders took him through the bowels of the ship and up onto the flight deck.

The fresh air topside was cool and refreshing, and smelled of the sea. The sun was high overhead in a clear blue sky, and Moore realized that he had almost forgotten how good it could feel on his pale skin.

Six CH-46 Sea Knight helicopters were parked forward of the ship's island. The rest of the *Iwo Jima*'s flight deck was empty, except for a single SH-60 Seahawk parked by the stern. This sleek chopper was painted white, and had several crewmen congregated beside it. It was obvious that this platform would be his transport to Sasebo, and he proceeded over to it without delay.

"I bet you're our passenger," greeted a bright-eyed airman dressed in a green flight suit. "I'm Petty Officer Michael Knowlton, the ATO."

Without bothering to introduce himself, Moore got right down to business. "How soon until we get to Sasebo?"

The air tactical officer beckoned towards the open fuselage door. "We'll have you there in time for early evening cocktails at Mama San's. Hop in, grab a helmet, and make yourself at home."

Helicopters were definitely not one of Moore's favorite methods of transportation. They were cramped, noisy, and frequently leaked hydraulic fluid. Yet the Seahawk did offer him a quick, convenient way to make good his exit from the *Iwo Jima*'s crowded confines, and he gratefully settled inside the chopper's main cabin without further complaint.

Five minutes later, they were airborne. True to form, the helicopter's twin turboshaft engines produced an incredibly loud racket. And by the time the *Iwo Jima* faded in the distance, his khakis were stained with a foul-smelling substance that constantly dripped from the ceiling above. Oblivious to these distractions, Moore wrapped himself up in a blanket and nestled into a vacant space situated beside the sonobuoy launcher. In a matter of seconds, he was sound asleep.

In his dream, he was back home in Alexandria, Virginia, on his favorite ten-speed, taking the bike path to Mt. Vernon. His wife Laurie was beside him on her mountain bike, and together they sped through the swamps and forests that George Washington once explored. The Potomac flowed beside them, and in a heartbeat, he was transferred to a compact racing sloop, running before an angry thunderstorm. Strangely enough, Laurie had disappeared, and there was genuine fear in his heart as he vainly scanned the flooded cabin searching for her.

A jagged bolt of lightning exploded from the black heavens and struck the sailboat's mast with a thunderous crack. Temporarily blinded by the ensuing flash, he suddenly found himself back on his bicycle. He was coasting down a steep hill, with Laurie a good distance ahead of him. The wind felt cool on his face, and as he reached for the brakes, he was shocked to find them totally inoperable.

Heedless of his own safety, he cried out to Laurie to slow down. Yet she couldn't hear him. Nor could she see the fully loaded tractor-trailer that was approaching from a side street at the bottom of the hill.

Thomas Moore's dream turned to nightmare as he tried with all his might to catch up to Laurie. With his legs weighted down by inexplicable fatigue, he could only watch in horror as the truck continued speeding towards the bike path, on a certain collision course with his wife, who remained totally unaware of the tragedy that would soon befall her.

"Commander Moore," spoke a concerned voice in the far distance. "Commander?"

It proved to be a gentle hand on his shoulder that awoke him from his deep slumber, and Moore looked up into the searching eyes of the ATO. Quickly now, his nightmarish vision faded, to be replaced by the steady chopping roar of the Seahawk's rotors and the deep voice of Petty Officer Knowlton.

"Excuse me, Sir, but the pilot would like to talk with you."

Knowlton pointed towards the cockpit. Moore acknowledged him with a curt nod and stiffly sat up. The cabin was wildly vibrating around him as he carefully made his way forward.

"Commander Moore," greeted the pilot, who sat on the left-hand side of the equipment-packed cockpit. "We just received a top-priority, scrambled transmission from CINCPAC, ordering us to an alternative destination."

"But I've got to get to Sasebo," countered Moore, his thoughts still partially clouded by his dream.

"Afraid not, sir," replied the pilot. "My new orders specifically state that you're to be transferred to these new coordinates at once, sir."

"I hope they're not sending me back to the *Iwo Jima*," said Moore.

The pilot answered while unfolding a chart on his lap. "Not unless that gator freighter's travelled a hundred nautical miles in the last hour."

He circled a portion of ocean off the west coast of the Bonin Islands and added. "We'll be dropping you off here, sir."

"But that's in the middle of the damn ocean!" exclaimed Moore.

The pilot shrugged his shoulders. "All I can tell you is that these are the exact coordinates that CINCPAC relayed to us, sir. If you can just hang on another quarter of an hour, we'll soon enough find out what this is all about."

Moore was in an irritable mood as he returned to the main cabin and sat down in front of a plexiglass window set into the closed hatchway. From this vantage point, he could view the sea rapidly passing five thousand feet below them. A two-masted sailboat could be seen cutting through the water, and his thoughts went back to his recently concluded nightmare.

It had been a long time since he had dreamt of Laurie. And it seemed like yesterday that they were together, sharing the best that life had to offer.

Just thinking about her again brought back a kaleidoscope of memories, some pleasant and some painful. They had practically grown up together as neighbors, and what started out as a childhood friendship blossomed into adolescent love. There was never a doubt that they would be married, and after attending college together at the University of Virginia, they made vows of eternal love.

Laurie's father had been in the Navy, and she knew very well what she was getting in for when her husband picked this same branch of the military for his profession. They decided not to have children until Thomas returned from his initial sea duty, and secured a permanent shore-based position in intelligence or investigative fields.

His first assignment after getting his commission was on a sub tender in Holy Loch, Scotland. Though Laurie remained in Alexandria at this time teaching elementary school, she visited him whenever their budget and her own schedule allowed.

It had been hard being away from her at first, and he tried his best to lose himself in his work. When he got word that she was planning to spend a whole summer in Scotland, he shouted out with joy and immediately went out to rent a cottage. He found a lovely little place in the foothills overlooking Hunter's Quay, on the outskirts of Dunoon. Though the price was a little steep, he took it anyway, and as it turned out, Laurie fell in love with it at first sight.

What followed was the most glorious time of his entire life. He managed to secure several consecutive weeks of leave, and they spent it exploring the scenic, heather-filled countryside. Together they hiked the magnificent shores of Loch Lomond, took the train up to the Highlands, and even managed to visit the magical island of Iona, where Christianity first came to the British Isles. During a weekend stay in Edinburgh, they attended a musical festival at Usher Hall, and toured Edinburgh Castle, where they enjoyed a full-fledged military tattoo complete with massed pipers.

The rest of their summer together in Scotland sped by in a blur, and before he knew it, she was packing her bags for the flight back home. That final evening together, they made love long into the night. The dawn was too soon coming. And little did he ever realize that the last time that he would ever see his beloved again was from the deck of the Dunoon ferry as she sadly waved goodbye. Less than a month later, she was dead, the tragic victim of a traffic accident in downtown Washington D.C.

Thomas Moore's life had never been the same since. With Laurie's death, it was almost as if a vital part of his own self had been ripped from his body. This was especially apparent in the months following her funeral. His soulmate had been taken from him, and he would have to live out his remaining years with his only chance of love a distant memory.

It was later that year that he received his assignment at NIS, and was transferred back to Washington. He completely surrendered himself to his work. And his inner wound slowly healed. Even his nightmares ceased, only to emerge again from his subconscious when he least expected.

The monotonous chopping whine of the Seahawk's rotors called to him with a soothing song of a duty his entire life was now dedicated to. To serve his country with honor was all that mattered. All else was irrelevant.

Ever thankful for this renewed purpose, Thomas Moore redirected his gaze out the helicopter's plexiglass window. The sea was all but veiled by swirling tendrils of milky white fog, which extended all the way up to their current altitude, and it was like flying through a cloud bank that filled the entire sky.

"How about some hot coffee, sir?" asked the ATO.

"I'd like that," replied Moore, who found himself suddenly chilled.

The airman handed him a plastic cup, and filled it with steaming hot coffee that he poured from a silver thermos. The dark brown liquid was brewed navy strong, and Moore contentedly sipped it.

"I'm sorry that we don't have anything else to serve with the joe," said Knowlton.

"This coffee's more than enough for me," returned Moore.

The steady roaring pitch of the Seahawk's engines seemed to fluctuate, and the deck slightly tilted forward.

"Looks like we're going down," noted the ATO, as he proceeded over to Moore's side and peered out the window. "I sure wouldn't want to be flying this baby. That fog out there is as thick as my mom's pea soup."

The cabin began to vibrate wildly, causing Moore to spill a good portion of his coffee. Somehow he managed not to burn himself, and as he precariously balanced the cup in his shaking hand, the dim outline of a ship began to appear on the sea below. This vessel's sleek profile came into better view as they continued

53

losing altitude, prompting an excited response from the ATO.

"That's the USS *Hewitt*! We worked with her in the Philippine Sea last week."

The Seahawk swooped in low over the warship, passing over its streamlined superstructure, and Moore noted the lack of weapons visible on the Spruance class vessel's deck. It was outfitted with only a pair of 5-inch Mk45 lightweight gun mountings fore and aft, and an ASROC launcher forward of the bridge. Yet in reality, Moore knew that the *Hewitt*'s offensive capabilities were for the most part hidden within its hull. Here the ASROC launcher had no less than twenty-four Mk16 reloads, for its mission of attacking enemy submarines. For threats from the air, the destroyer carried a NATO Sea Sparrow launcher with sixteen reloads, and two Phalanx Gatling guns for close-in defense. It also was armed with eight Harpoon missiles, and six torpedo tubes capable of firing the Mk32.

One of the ship's other major capabilities became obvious when the Seahawk began hovering over its stern helipad. A large hangar lay forward of this sea-going landing strip, capable of handling two LAMPS helicopters, and it became apparent that this was where the Seahawk was headed.

They landed with a mild jolt, and as the engines were switched off and the rotors ground to a halt, the relief from the noise was instantaneous. The ATO slid open the hatch, and a khaki-clad lieutenant waited outside to greet them.

"Commander Moore?"

54

Moore gracefully peeled off his helmet and raised his hand. "That's me."

"Sir, I'm Lieutenant Kelso, the *Hewitt*'s weapons officer. If you'll just follow me, Captain Stanton is waiting for you out at sea."

Not really certain what he was referring to by this last remark, Moore followed the weapons officer forward, to a position beside the rail amidships, on the port side of the after funnel uptakes. Here a launch was being readied to be lowered into the water.

"Climb aboard, sir," instructed Kelso.

"But where's your captain?" asked Moore, totally confused by this whole turn of events.

"We'll be utilizing this launch to take you out to him, sir," revealed the weapons officer.

Moore could tell that Kelso was under orders not to say any more than he had to, and Moore resigned himself to this fact and climbed aboard the launch. A crew of three, including his tight-lipped escort accompanied him.

The launch was powered by an outboard engine, and they smoothly pulled away from the *Hewitt* and headed seawards. All too soon, the destroyer was swallowed by the fog, and a ghostly silence prevailed, broken only by the steady growl of the engine and the lapping of the water against the launch's rounded bow.

Lieutenant Kelso was their navigator. With the assistance of a hand-held compass, he guided them on a southwesterly course, through fog so thick that even the immediate sea around them was veiled.

Ten minutes passed, and Moore was just about to ask where they were headed, when Kelso signaled the helmsman to cut the engine. The weapons officer put a whistle to his lips and blew a series of three long blasts. This signal was answered by two short whistle blasts that emanated from a point nearby, though Moore could not determine the exact direction because of the fog. On Kelso's orders, the helmsman restarted the engine, and they inched forward at a bare crawl.

Seconds later, a dim, blinking red light cut through the murky twilight. Moore anxiously sat forward upon spotting an immense, black, rounded hull less than ten yards in front of them. He knew in an instant that it was a submarine, though he still couldn't determine its exact class. A duplicate version of their launch was positioned beside this submarine, beneath its massive sail. The launch was vacant, though several sailors were visible on the sub's deck, huddled aft of the sail. Two of them assisted Lieutenant Kelso as he threw them a nylon mooring line.

"Any sign of anyone yet?" asked the weapons officer as the two sailors pulled the launch forward and secured its mooring line to one of the submarine's deck cleats.

"Negative, Lieutenant. Captain Stanton's just about to pop the forward access trunk," replied one of the seamen, who lowered a rope ladder over the submarine's side. "Then we'll know what in the hell's goin' on here."

Lieutenant Kelso turned to address Moore. "Looks like we got you here just in the nick of time, sir. Be careful on your way up that ladder."

Moore left the launch, and climbed up onto the deck of the submarine without incident. He could tell now from the distinctive bulged casing that extended aft of the sail that this was an American, Benjamin Franklin class ballistic missile submarine. He was certainly no stranger to such a class of warship, since several were based out of Holy Loch. What bothered him though was the fact that the only American ballistic missile submarines supposedly assigned to the Pacific were the newer Trident class vessels, based out of Bangor, Washington.

Lieutenant Kelso joined him on deck and pointed towards the sub's bow. "That's where we'll find the skipper, sir."

Moore needed no more prompting to begin his way forward. As he passed by the sail, he halted for a moment upon spotting an accumulation of seaweed hanging from the vessel's hydroplanes.

"Lieutenant, what in the world happened to this submarine?" he questioned.

Kelso pointed towards the group of individuals gathered on the deck before them. "You'll have to ask the captain, sir. I have absolutely no idea."

Moore reached up and pocketed a sample of the seaweed before continuing forward. There were six individuals in all, kneeling around the closed access trunk. Two muscular chiefs were in the process of unsealing the hatch, with a pair of wrenchlike tools, especially designed for this task. A distinguished, grey-haired officer wearing a blue windbreaker stood beside them, supervising their efforts. He alertly looked up upon noting the approach of a newcomer.

"Ah, you must be Commander Moore. I'm Captain Edward Stanton, CO of the *Hewitt*."

Moore acknowledged this greeting with a nod. "Captain Stanton, I didn't think that we had any Benjamin Franklin class SSBN's in the Pacific."

"Neither did I, Commander Moore," replied Stanton. "Unfortunately, she has no hull markings, so we still don't know exactly which boat she is."

"What about her crew?" continued Moore.

"Would you believe that we've yet to hear a peep out of them," observed Stanton. "Therefore I'm afraid the outlook for them doesn't look good. Were you briefed at all before you arrived here, Commander?"

Moore shook his head that he hadn't been, and Stanton continued. "The vessel was originally discovered a little over nine hours ago, by a Japanese squidder. They notified the Japanese Maritime Self-Defense Force, and that's when we were called in to investigate."

"We've penetrated the first seal, Captain," interrupted one of the chiefs, who had been working on opening the access trunk.

This news caused Stanton to turn his attention back to his men. "Step back, Chief, while Doc lowers the dosimeter."

A tall, bespectacled officer stepped forward carrying a spool of wire with a small gauge attached on one end. As he lowered the wire into the partially open trunk, Stanton explained what was going on.

"Our medical officer jury-rigged a dosimeter to determine if we've got a radiation problem down there."

Moore thoughtfully nodded, and watched as the *Hewitt's* doctor unravelled a good twenty feet of wire before retrieving it. All eyes were on the medical officer as he bent over and carefully read the small gauge attached to the end of the wire. "It's in the safe range, Captain. I show absolutely no abnormal indication of radiation inside the inner hull."

"Can you test for chlorine?" asked Moore.

"I'm afraid not," answered the medical officer. "We're going to have to rely on our noses for that."

"I think that they had a fire down there," offered Stanton. "Most likely, all of them were asphyxiated before they could get off an SOS."

"Shall we go ahead and open up the trunk, Captain?" questioned the senior chief.

"Do it, sailor," ordered Stanton.

As the two chiefs went to work on the trunk with their tools, Stanton beckoned Thomas Moore to join him further up on the foredeck.

"Commander Moore, I understand that you're affiliated with the Naval Investigative Service. Because of your specialized training, Command wants you to lead the search party once we go down below. For discretion's sake, I believe that it's best if we keep this initial group to a minimum.

"I agree," concurred Moore. "Since we still don't know what we're dealing with down there, I think it's best if we leave everything just like we find it."

"You've got it," returned Stanton, who turned around when one of his men called out behind him.

"The trunk's open, Captain!"

"I guess the moment of truth's upon us," reflected Stanton. "Shall we see what all of this is about, Commander?"

Thomas Moore's gut tightened as he followed Stanton back to the access trunk.

"The initial search party will consist of Commander Moore, myself, Doc, Lieutenant Kelso, and Chief Daley," instructed Stanton. "Everyone else is to remain

59

topside, with absolutely no one going below except for an emergency."

"I hope someone brought along some flashlights," said Moore, who curiously peered down into the darkened recesses of the open trunk. "It's pitch black down there."

"Break out those lanterns and two-ways, Chief," instructed Stanton. "And for all those going below, don't touch a thing without my permission. If you come across anything suspicious, use your radios and let me know about it."

Moore soon had a battery-powered torch in hand, as well as a compact, two-way radio. With a minimum of ceremony, he stepped into the trunk and began his way downwards.

A steel ladder conveyed him directly into the sub's forward torpedo room. Cautiously, he sniffed the air, all the while scanning the compartment with his flashlight. There was no hint of chlorine, or even of smoke. As with all the submarines that he had ever visited in the past, the primary scent present was the characteristic smell of amine.

Neatly stacked on their pallets were a full complement of Mk48 torpedoes. These potent weapons would be launched from the vessel's four bow-mounted tubes. Curiously enough, there was no sign of the men who would supervise such a launch, and Moore stood by while his four associates joined him.

"Apparently it wasn't chlorine gas or smoke that got them," observed the *Hewitt*'s medical officer. "The air smells remarkably fresh."

"Let's continue aft," said Stanton.

Moore led the way through an open hatchway. The

passageway that lay beyond held several vacant berthing compartments, and it was Chief Daley who summed up the condition of these spaces.

"Most of the bunks appear to have been slept in recently. But where are the guys now?"

"If I remember correctly, the control room of a Benjamin Franklin class submarine lies on the other side of that bulkhead," said Moore, pointing further aft down the passageway. "Hopefully, we'll have some answers waiting for us there."

With his flashlight cutting a narrow swath of light before him, Moore proceeded in this direction. He found the far hatch sealed shut, and with Chief Daley's help, they undogged it, and Moore anxiously continued on. As anticipated, this next compartment indeed turned out to be the control room. It too was vacant of all personnel, and Moore had a distinct eerie feeling as he initiated his cursory inspection.

He began at the helm. Three padded chairs were bolted to the deck here. This was where the planesmen controlled the depth and course of the vessel, and Moore scanned the variety of instruments and gauges positioned on the forward bulkhead, immediately above the airplanelike steering yokes.

Beside the helm was the diving console, where the sub's all-important ballast functions were controlled and monitored. Unable to tell the status of the main vents because of the lack of electricity, Moore continued his rounds, and passed the vacant radar, sonar, and fire-control stations.

"Will you take a look at this!" a voice behind him broke the silence.

This was all Moore had to hear to join his co-workers beside the periscope well. The lights of their torches clearly illuminated the navigation table, where a detailed bathymetric chart lay exposed.

"This is sure one for the books," reflected the *Hewitt*'s astounded Captain. "Because this chart is of the Tongue of the Ocean in the Bahama basin! What in God's name is going on here?"

Moore examined this chart himself, noting that the last grease-pencil course update was off the north-eastern coast of Andros Island.

"Either someone's playing an incredibly sick joke on us, or we've got one hell of a strange mystery on our hands," observed Stanton. "What do you make of this, Commander Moore?"

"Right now, your guess is as good as mine," said Moore with a heavy sigh.

"Well, we've still got most of this vessel to search," continued Stanton. "And to cover it in the least amount of time, I think it's best if we separate at this point. Chief, why don't you head down below and check out the galley and officer's country. The rest of us will continue aft."

"I'm almost afraid of what we're gonna find in that missile magazine," said the *Hewitt*'s weapons officer. "This baby is designed to carry enough firepower to win World War III single-handedly."

"I want to get into that engine room, and make certain that the reactor is safely scrammed," added the medical officer.

"Then let's get on with it, gentlemen," said Stanton.

As Chief Daley turned for the accessway that would take him to the decks below, Moore led the way aft. Yet another hatch had to be undogged, before they entered a cavernous compartment dominated by sixteen missile-launch tubes. Painted dark green, the tubes were positioned in two rows of eight apiece, with a long passageway of latticed steel flooring between them.

"Back in Holy Loch, the boomer crews used to call this compartment Sherwood Forest," commented Moore.

"I can certainly see why," said Stanton, who followed his weapons officer over to the nearest tube.

Lieutenant Kelso hurriedly unscrewed the metal viewing plate set into the tube's base, and anxiously peered inside.

"The weapons load appears to be intact, sir," said Kelso, his relief most obvious.

"Thank God for that," returned Stanton.

It was while Moore peeked inside the missile tube to have a look himself, that the captain's two-way radio activated with a burst of static. This was followed by the excited voice of Chief Daley.

"I found one, Captain! I found one of the crew."

"Where are you, Chief?" asked Stanton into the radio's transmitter.

"In the galley, sir," replied Daley. "And you'd better bring along the doc, because he don't seem to be makin' much sense."

"We're on our way," returned the captain, who looked up and met the glances of his co-workers. "At long last," he triumphantly added. "We'll finally get some answers."

The sub's galley was located on the deck immediately below the control room. They got there by way of the officer's wardroom. This tastefully decorated compartment was filled with a large conference table. Two place settings of china sat on this table, still partially filled with food.

"Looks like someone never got to finish their breakfast," observed the weapons officer. "Those hotcakes still look fresh."

It was Thomas Moore who spotted the picture hung on the wardroom's forward bulkhead. This rendering showed two frontiersmen standing on an elevated river bluff, looking out to a vast wilderness valley.

"I believe I know what boat this is," he suggested. "From the looks of this picture, she's the *Lewis and Clark*.

"That answers one of our questions," said Stanton. "Now let's answer the rest of them."

A short passageway led them directly into the galley. Three pots were secured to the stove here, including one filled with hardened oatmeal. The deck was covered with several inches of water, and as they continued on aft, they heard Chief Daley's voice sound out softly in the distance.

"Come on, sailor, chill out. I'm not gonna hurt you."

They found the chief perched beside the flooded space containing the trash disposal unit. A single, red-headed sailor, dressed in wet dungarees, sat on the deck before him. This lanky, wild-eyed individual was shivering from the dank chill that pervaded this portion of the ship. He had some sort of leather-bound notebook held tightly in his grasp, and reacted to the arrival of the newcomers with instant horror.

Quick to note his mentally imbalanced condition, the *Hewitt*'s medical officer cautiously stepped forward.

64

"Hello, sailor," he said, displaying his best bedside manner. "I'm doc Weatherford, and these are my friends. We're here to help you. So you can relax now. Everything is going to be just fine."

"I'll try to find him a blanket and some dry clothes," volunteered Lieutenant Kelso.

"Has he spoken at all?" asked Stanton.

"When I first discovered him here, he was mumbling to himself," answered the chief. "I couldn't make much sense out of him, though I believe his name's Homer."

"How are you doing, Homer?" greeted the *Hewitt*'s CO with a forced smile, as he positioned himself beside his medical officer. "I'm Captain Stanton. What the doc here says is true. We're your friends, and we've come to help you. But before we can do that, you've got to relax and trust us. Is there anything we can get you?"

This question generated silence, and the medical officer intervened.

"Homer, I want you to take a couple of deep breaths, and then tell me what's bothering you so. Does it have anything to do with the location of your shipmates?"

Homer Morgan's eyes opened wide, and he began babbling. "I didn't mean to do it. I swear! All I did was shoot the trash!"

"Where are your shipmates, Homer?" asked Stanton. "You've got to tell us!"

Homer's expression was one of pure bewilderment as he stared out at the forward bulkhead and cried out. "I killed them all!"

Lieutenant Kelso picked this emotional moment to return with a blanket. The medical officer wasted no time wrapping it around Homer's shoulders, and took this opportunity to wrench the book from Homer's grasp. Thomas Moore was the first to examine it, while the doc turned his attention back to his sobbing patient.

"It's the ship's log!" exclaimed Moore, who excitedly turned to the last entry.

What he saw there caused him to gasp, and he struggled to find words.

"I know that this is going to sound utterly illogical," he managed while skimming the page. "But the *Lewis and Clark*'s last log entry was dated only yesterday, when the sub was transiting the waters between Andros Island and Nassau."

"But that's on the other side of the world!" objected Chief Daley.

"Tell that to the person who wrote this entry," retorted the perplexed investigator, whom fate had picked to solve this strangest of nautical mysteries.

Four

The Mir habitat program was an immediate by-product of a United Nations effort to encourage the peaceful exploration and development of the sea floor. For the first time, scientists, marine architects, and engineers from around the world, collaborated to create a self-sustaining, underwater community, capable of sheltering a group of humans for an extended period of time.

One of the primary objectives of the program was to tap the virtually unexploited resources of the continental shelf, the richest and most accessible region of the ocean. This portion of the sea floor hugged the earth's major landmasses, and extended to a depth of six hundred feet before dropping off to the black depths. It was home to abundant oil, natural gas, and various minerals such as manganese, gold and even diamonds. It also provided the ideal location for undersea fish farms and other aquaculture ventures.

By having a stable base on the sea floor, divers would no longer have to decompress each time they surfaced at the end of a day's work. Decompression was time-consuming and dangerous, and was a necessary evil that divers never looked forward to. A liveable, undersea habitat would free them of this often-painful ordeal.

After searching the world's oceans to find a suitable place to locate the Mir habitat, it was decided that the waters of the Bahamas offered the best advantages. They were readily accessible, of the proper depth, and filled with an abundance of marine life. An ideal location was then found off the northeastern coast of Andros Island.

The habitat itself consisted of four major structures, the largest of which was called Starfish House. This comfortable, underwater villa had five rooms radiating from a central core. One arm was reserved for a complete marine laboratory, while the others held the crew's sleeping quarters, kitchen, and diver's ready room.

In addition to Starfish House, there was a domed structure called Habitat One. This all-important building was where the air tanks were stored, and it was here that electricity and water were produced. The team's minisub was stored in an onion-shaped hangar, that had a supply warehouse and several fish pens attached to it.

Designed and constructed by a worldwide consortium, the various pieces of the habitat were shipped to Nassau from the far corners of the planet. Here they were put together and towed to the sparkling blue waters off Andros.

It took over two hundred tons of lead ballast to anchor the habitat to a coral shelf, sixty feet beneath the sea's surface. Once this was accomplished, the world looked on as five brave divers donned their scuba tanks and descended towards the sea floor, to become Starfish House's first full-time inhabitants.

This multinational group of aquanauts had lived in this watery environment for over three weeks now, and they hoped to extend their stay to over two months if possible. Leading the team was Pierre Lenclud, a fifty-four-year-old, retired French naval officer, who was known simply as *Commandant* to his co-workers. The bald-headed, debonair Frenchman was a former submariner, whose current interest was in the field of marine biology.

Dr. Ivana Petrov was the team's geologist. A graduate of the Soviet Union's famed Black Sea Institute, the tall, attractive redhead was also an archaeologist, who gained world renown when she discovered the long-lost remnants of an ancient Greek city, buried beneath the Mediterranean seabed off the Peloponnesian coast in the late 1980s.

From Osaka, Japan came thirty-three-year-old Tomoyaki Nakata, one of the world's foremost authorities in the field of aquaculture. Tomo as he was called, had already designed several profitable fish farms in the Sea of Japan. While stationed aboard the Mir habitat, he was monitoring the growth rate of several species of edible sea plants, and conducting experiments on the farming of the local sea conch.

The team was also extremely fortunate to have the expert services of a talented, resourceful marine engineer, who at twenty-four years of age was also the group's youngest member. Karl Ivar Bjornsen had been born in far-off Haugesund, Norway, where he worked as a North Sea oil-rig diver. The likable blond could fix almost anything, and was a self-avowed workaholic.

Rounding out the group was Lisa Tanner, a pert, twenty-five-year-old kiwi from Auckland, New Zealand. Lisa was a premed student, who had been recruited to be both the habitat's cook and its nurse. She did both jobs extremely well, and was also responsible for making Starfish House a real home, by providing atmosphere in the form of posters of her beautiful homeland. She managed to tack them to almost every available vacant wall space.

Regardless of what was on the menu, mealtime was an event inside Starfish House. It was a time for the group's members to relax and interact, and this evening's dinner proved no exception.

The dining table had been set up in the central module, beside a large picture window. Currently seated around the red-checkered tablecloth were all the members of the team, except for their young engineer. Tomo had picked this evening's music, and in the background sounded the haunting, new-age strains of Kitaro's "Silk Road."

"I'm sorry that the only vegetable that I had to serve this evening is cabbage," apologized their cook. "But all the canned veggies that they sent down on the last shipment seemed to be spoiled."

Ivana Petrov cut into a piece of raw, salted herring and bitterly voiced herself. "That's what we get for having a Russian supply ship."

"I should be able to provide us with a good quantity of fresh sea grasses, in another week's time," offered Tomo. "When steamed, this particular variety is most palatable, with a taste much like spinach."

"I congratulate you on this conch meat, Tomo," said Pierre Lenclud, who sat at the head of the table sipping a glass of white wine. "Why I could swear that it was chicken."

Tomo looked over to Lisa Tanner and sincerely complimented her. "We can all thank our cook for preparing it so excellently. But be forewarned, the local natives consider the meat of the queen conch to be an aphrodisiac."

Lenclud smiled. "Ah, just what a Frenchman has to hear to ask for seconds!"

The room filled with laughter, which generated a shrieking response from the habitat's mascot, a large, green-feathered Amazonian parrot with the name of Ulge.

"What's so funny? What's so funny?" mimicked Ulge in his best parrot voice.

Ulge had two roles to play inside Starfish House. Not only was he the only pet allowed aboard, but he also served a more practical purpose. Just as miners took canaries into the pits to warn of high concentrations of poisonous gases, so they had Ulge as an early warning system, to detect unhealthy accumulations of carbon monoxide.

"Quiet down, *mon ami,* and come have a drink," said Lenclud, who raised his wine glass towards the parrot.

Ulge shot across the room and obligingly landed on the Frenchman's forearm. Lenclud held up his glass, and the parrot gulped down several healthy sips.

"Easy does it, *mon petit,*" warned Lenclud, as he pulled back the glass. "Or you'll earn yourself another nasty hangover."

71

"I wonder if Karl Ivar will be joining us?" asked Lisa as she finished off her borscht.

Ivana Petrov shook her head. "I seriously doubt it, Comrade. At least not until he completes his repairs to *Misha,* so that we can continue on with tonight's excursion."

"How deep do you plan on going?" asked Tomo.

"At least nine hundred and seventy-six feet," answered the Russian. "That's where I made my initial discovery."

"Isn't that awfully deep for the remnants of a stone roadway?" questioned Lisa.

"Not really," replied Ivana. "You see, because of this region's geological instability, it could easily have been pulled into the depths during an earthquake, or other seismic disturbance. And besides, we still don't know for certain that it is indeed a man-made formation."

"If it is, it could be the first real evidence of the lost continent of Atlantis!" suggested the excited kiwi.

Lenclud discreetly expressed his own opinion while trading a guarded glance with their archaeologist. "Let's not jump to any wild conclusions just yet, Lisa. Don't forget, as Ivana pointed out when she first reported her find two days ago, that it could be ordinary beachrock or lava that's been broken away at right angles. I'll hold back any further opinion on my part, until I see it with my own eyes."

Ivana looked at her wristwatch and added. "If Karl Ivar's efforts are successful, you'll be viewing the formation before the next sunrise, Commandant. Shall we proceed to the hangar and get on with it?"

"By all means," replied Lenclud, who drained his wine glass, then stood and passed Ulge over to Tomo.

Lenclud and Petrov put on their wet suits and scuba gear in the habitat's ready room. An open hatch was cut into the floor here. Because the habitat's interior atmospheric pressure was equal to that of the surrounding ocean, this opening to the sea did not need to be sealed.

Before leaving Starfish House, both divers signed a chart and recorded the exact time of their departure. Then Lenclud led the way down through the hatch.

A ladder protected by a sharkproof grill guided him to the sea floor. The water was comfortably warm and pitch black. He switched on his flashlight, and was momentarily startled by a large pair of glowing yellow eyes, that swam by only inches from his masked face. With his light, he illuminated this creature's narrow, six-foot long body.

Lisa had named the barracuda Uncle Albert. It lived in the nearby reef, and was a frequent nighttime visitor. Uncle Albert took a special delight in the scraps of food that Lisa often fed him. And he could even recognize her when she was outfitted in her own wet suit and mask, and he would take food from her hands only.

Ivana's torch cut through the blackness beside him, and both divers headed towards the glowing yellow dome, positioned on the sea floor less than twenty yards distant. Yet another open hatch was cut into the floor of the hangar, and Lenclud swam between the structure's adjustable telescopic legs, and directed his flashlight upwards.

Feeling like he was diving upside down into an inverted swimming pool, he swam up through the circular hatch, whose diameter was just wide enough to admit *Misha,* the name they had given to their diving

73

saucer. His mask broke the surface, and he immediately spotted the blond-haired Norwegian working on *Misha*'s battery charger.

"Hello, Karl Ivar," greeted Lenclud as he pulled himself out of the water and pulled off his mask.

Misha hung above him, suspended on an iron cable from a ceiling mounted winch. Originally designed in the Soviet Union, the bright yellow, saucer-shaped minisub could carry two prone crew members. Its batteries powered a series of pumps that shot seawater out of a set of dual jet nozzles. The pilot could steer by turning these jets, and adjust the craft's ballast by taking on or jettisoning yet more seawater.

"Karl Ivar, will we be able to sail tonight?" asked Lenclud, who waited beside the hatch for Ivana to show herself.

"No problem, Commandant," answered the Norwegian. "Although I can't really say how long the new alternator that they sent down will last us. This Russian equipment is inventive, yet pure garbage all the same."

Ivana's head broke through the open hatch, and Lenclud reached down and pulled her up onto the latticed steel platform that encircled the hangar. She pulled off her mask and questioned Bjornsen while removing her diving gear.

"Did they send the proper parts, Karl Ivar?"

"That they did, Doctor," answered Bjornsen.

The young mechanic made a final adjustment to the component that he had been working on, then snapped shut the cover panel, and screwed it back in place.

"It's a miracle that they had the spare parts in the first place," observed Ivana. "And then to actually

74

send down the ones that you wanted. Russian bureaucracy never worked so well!"

Bjornsen displayed a dimpled smile as he reacted to this comment. "Mind you, I can make no guarantee that the new alternator won't fail once you're underway. As far as I can tell, it's no better than the others that they sent me."

"As long as *Misha* can hold enough charge to get us to our destination and back, that's all that I ask," returned Ivana.

Bjornsen reached up and depressed a switch located on the side of the hangar. In response, the winch activated, and the diving saucer slowly dropped down into the water. He then removed the iron cable from which it had been suspended, undogged the hatch, and beckoned inside.

"Your underwater chariot awaits you," he added with a grin.

Ivana was the first to crawl inside. Lenclud followed, and before transiting the narrow access trunk, he took a moment to address Bjornsen.

"Your hard work is most appreciated, *mon ami*. This entire project would have been impossible without you. Now, go get something to eat and drink. And we'll be back by the time you've finished dessert."

Bjornsen saluted, and Lenclud returned this gesture before continuing on into the minisub's interior. He dogged shut the hatch, then lay down flat on his stomach, on top of the vacant vinyl mattress to Ivana's right. The archaeologist was in a similar prone position, with her own individual viewing port situated only a few inches from her face.

With practiced ease, she addressed the control panel

75

and started up the oxygen recirculation system. With the assistance of her shipmate, she completed the pre-dive checklist, and then switched on the echo-sounder.

"Here we go, Comrade," she said as she tightly grasped the joystick.

The ballast pumps activated with a muted whine, and *Misha* sank straight downwards. With a flick of her wrist, Ivana pushed forward on the joystick, and the saucer shot out through the hangar's telescopic legs.

Lenclud switched on the powerful, mercury-vapor spotlights and carefully monitored the echo-sounder. The monitor screen filled with the gently sloping outline of the trench below, and down they plunged into the blackened depths.

A manta ray gracefully swam by the porthole, followed by an immense hammerhead shark, with eyes the color of burning, red hot coals. At a depth of two hundred feet, they passed through a milky layer of seawater some thirty feet wide, and it was the Frenchman who identified it.

"We're penetrating the first deep submergence layer."

"It wasn't here during my last dive into the trench," commented Ivana.

Lenclud was quick with his reply. "That's because your dive didn't take place at night. That's when the myriad of micro-organisms that comprise the DSL ascend from the great depths, where they live during the daylight hours."

"What's the reason for this movement?" asked Ivana.

"Would you believe that marine biologists still don't

76

have a definite answer to that question? My personal belief is that it has something to do with feeding patterns."

"Well, there's one brute who's certainly doing his fair share of feeding," observed Ivana, in reference to the monstrous whale shark that lazily swam by the porthole.

One of the largest fishes in the sea, the whale shark lived off the microscopic plankton, which it strained from the sea through its gill rakes. To do this, it had to keep its massive jaws wide open, therefore appearing much more vicious than it was in reality.

"I once rode on the back of one of those monsters," revealed Lenclud. *"Mon amie,* that was a ride that I'll never forget!"

A moment of reflective silence followed, and *Misha* continued its descent, only to come to an unexpected halt at a depth of four hundred and three feet. Again, it was Lenclud who offered an explanation as to what was occurring outside.

"I bet it's the thermocline that's stopped us. This means we've reached the spot where the warm surface waters meet the cooler depths, and *Misha* is now floating on top of this denser, cold layer. Take on some ballast. That should get us moving once more."

Ivana activated the ballast pump, and several hundred gallons of additional seawater poured into the diving saucer's ballast tanks. Then all that was needed was a quick flick of the joystick for them to continue their dive.

With each additional foot of depth, the temperature inside the minisub continued to drop, going from ninety degrees to seventy in a matter of seconds. Fortunately, for the comfort of the vessel's two operatives, this was the extent of the temperature drop. And it was several minutes later when they finally hit bottom, at a depth of nine hundred and seventy-six feet.

The spotlights were angled downwards slightly, to illuminate the sea floor. Twelve-inch-long nimertine worms were burrowed into the mud, their tapering bodies rippling in the gentle current. Also clearly visible were large brown sea urchins, colorful sea stars, and a gigantic grouper, that was easily as big as the entire minisub.

"I've heard stories about groupers like that swallowing unlucky divers whole," reflected Lenclud. "Some even say that it was a grouper that swallowed Jonah, and not a whale as reported in the Bible."

"Are those lobsters out there in the distance?" asked the Russian, who made a minor course change to bring them closer to an outstretched line of shuffling, clawless crustaceans, that extended as far as the eye could see.

"Mon Dieu, what a wondrous sight!" exclaimed Lenclud. "Those are the local variety of spiny lobster all right. This must be some sort of mating ritual. Let's record it on the video camera."

Ivana reached up to activate the camera that was mounted on the rounded nose of the minisub, between the two forward portholes. They followed the lobsters for over a quarter of a mile before losing them in a jagged, rock-strewn ravine.

Almost reluctantly, they were forced to turn the diving saucer due south at this point, back to the relatively flat, sloping gradient of the trench.

"Wait until Tomo sees these video pictures," commented Lenclud. "Surely we should be able to farm such a vast collection of lobsters. What a delectable way to satisfy the planet's insatiable hunger for protein!"

Ivana was in the process of unfolding a detailed bathymetric chart, displaying the contour of the sea floor beneath them. With a red grease-pencil, she circled the approximate location of their current position. This put them well into the northern extremity of the geological feature known as the Andros Trench. This mile-wide channel-like gorge continued in a southerly direction, where it steadily deepened, until merging with the vast three-thousand-foot-plus depths of the Tongue of the Ocean.

"We should be close to the place where I first discovered the formation," reported Ivana, who gently pulled back on the joystick causing *Misha* to slow to a bare crawl.

Sand covered the sea floor here, and they continued due south, to a spot where the current had swept bare a wide swath of sediment. Ivana anxiously switched off the engine, and the minisub hovered only inches from the bottom and an interconnected network of flat, rectangular stones. Ivana made a minor adjustment to the saucer's spotlights, and Lenclud peered out the porthole and expressed himself.

"So this is it, *mon amie*. You know, it does look like a cobblestone roadway."

"Every time I lay my eyes on it, I think the very same thing, Comrade."

"Could it indeed be naturally fractured bedrock that's responsible for this phenomenon?" asked the Frenchman.

"It's certainly possible," answered Ivana. "But if it is, nature has sure done an amazing construction job. Wait until you see how far it extends."

They proceeded to follow the stone roadway for a good mile. Though much of the thoroughfare was covered by sediment, other sections were clearly visible, and displayed the same exact workmanship. As wide as a two-lane highway, the smooth stone pavement was uniformly composed of rectangular sections, each of them two feet in length, and one foot wide. It appeared to be laid out on a precise north-south axis, with an ultimate destination somewhere in the Tongue of the Ocean.

Yet long before they could determine this fact for certain, an electronic warning tone began sounding from inside the cramped confines of the diving saucer. Ivana hurriedly scanned her monitor screen, and in a matter of seconds determined this alarm's source.

"So much for Russian engineering. I'm showing a partial failure in the new alternator that Karl Ivar just installed. Our battery charge has just gone critical."

"Will we be able to get back to the hangar?" questioned the concerned Frenchman.

Ivana answered while reaching out to lighten the sub by releasing a substantial portion of its seawater ballast. "Don't worry, Comrade. Our emergency battery pack has more than enough power to get us back home. Although I'm afraid we'll be forced to postpone any further exploration of this mystery until a later date."

Ivana yanked back on her joystick, and the diving saucer angled sharply upwards. Their new course put them on a northwesterly heading, as they steadily climbed the steep walls of the Andros Trench, to reach the relatively shallow coral clearing where the Mir habitat was situated.

Five

It took them a full hour to complete their search of the submarine. Much to their dismay, the red-headed sailor that they found in the galley, proved to be the only crew member aboard the vessel. With Thomas Moore's blessings, it was decided to convey the seaman back to the USS *Hewitt,* where the destroyer's medical officer would try to get additional information out of him through hypnosis.

Lieutenant Kelso and Chief Daley were instructed to remain on the submarine, while the rest of the group returned to the *Hewitt,* where they would inform Command of their find, and await further orders.

The short voyage back by launch seemed to take place at a snail's pace. Since their departure from the *Hewitt,* the fog had thickened, and with the setting sun, the air was chilled.

Moore sat in the launch amidships, doing his best to ward off the damp cold by pulling his thin khaki jacket tighter around him. Lieutenant Weatherford and his patient, who remained wrapped in a blanket, sat near the bow, with Captain Stanton seated close at Moore's side. The *Hewitt*'s CO held the sub's log in his lap, and was doing his best to skim its contents by the light of a flashlight.

"Whoever recorded this log had to have made a mistake with these dates," whispered Stanton, so that only Moore could hear him.

"I can't wait to find out what Command has to say about all this," returned Thomas Moore. "Most likely, that log's from a previous cruise, though for the life of me, I still can't figure out what happened to the rest of the *Lewis and Clark*'s crew."

Stanton thoughtfully grunted. "My best guess is that there was some sort of serious accident aboard the sub, and that caused the crew to abandon ship."

"But surely they'd have the time to get off an SOS," countered Moore. "And you saw yourself the condition of that vessel. Except for that minor flood in the galley, it was in perfect shape."

"I hear you loud and clear, Commander. And I guess we're just going to have to wait for the results of Doc's hypnosis session to get some real answers."

Stanton slammed shut the log, when a blinking white light cut through the swirling mist. The sharp grey outline of the *Hewitt*'s foredeck suddenly loomed above them, and an alert sailor at the destroyer's rail threw down a weighted nylon mooring line.

Five minutes later, Thomas Moore was entering the ship's wardroom, with a hot mug of coffee in hand. A trio of officers were in the midst of their evening meals, and Moore sat himself down on a leather lounge chair, positioned on the opposite corner of the fairly spacious compartment. He pulled out a small notebook from his breast pocket, and jotted down all that he remembered about his visit to the *Lewis and Clark,* while the facts were still fresh in his mind. These initial impressions would comprise an integral part of his official report, and would provide a firm groundwork for his full investigation of the perplexing incident.

He was in the process of documenting the moment when he had first laid eyes on the sub's only apparent surviving crew member, when an intercom page directed him to the captain's stateroom. A bright-eyed seaman escorted Moore to the proper cabin, and he knocked on the closed door before entering.

Inside was an office much like that of a successful junior executive, though a bit more cramped for space and without a view. The ship's CO sat behind a compact, wooden desk, with a telephone nestled up to his ear. He beckoned Moore to have a seat in one of the two high-backed upholstered chairs in front of the desk, and then continued with his telephone conversation, all the while taking notes on a legal pad.

"I understand, Chief. Inform CINCPAC that we'll do so at once."

Stanton hung up the telephone handset and looked his newly arrived guest straight in the eye.

"As I expected, CINCPAC wants us to take the *Lewis and Clark* in tow. We'll be conveying it to a top-secret anchorage on the northern coast of Okinawa."

"Any word on the sub's operational orders?" asked Moore.

"I'm afraid not, Commander. Though I did receive a message from CINCPAC that I was to pass on to you. It seems that Command merely wants you to stand by for further orders."

"The story of my life," said Moore with a sigh.

Stanton's phone rang with a growl and he picked up the handset and gruffly spoke into the transmitter. "Captain . . . I hear you, Doc. We're on our way."

He hung up the telephone and addressed Moore while scooting back his chair and standing. "Follow me to sick bay, Commander. Doc's ready to put our redheaded friend under hypnosis."

They arrived at sick bay by way of the ship's high-tech bridge, where Stanton stopped briefly to discuss details of the *Hewitt*'s new towing assignment. Satisfied that his XO could handle this task, that was complicated by the ever-present fog, he then led Moore back down into the destroyer's bowels.

Thomas Moore had never seen an individual hypnotized before. He was genuinely surprised how very easy it all seemed.

The patient had the benefit of a relaxing hot shower beforehand, and was dressed in a fresh set of dungarees. He also managed to wolf down a couple of ham and cheese sandwiches, before being led into one of the examination rooms. Homer hadn't spoken since his frantic outburst in the submarine's galley, and Doc Weatherford made certain that he was comfortably seated, before bringing out a shoe-box-sized object with a strobe light mounted inside. Homer was then instructed to keep his eyes on this box, while the medical officer flicked off the room's lights and activated the strobe.

Shielding his eyes from the intense, flashing light, Moore listened as Doc's smooth voice induced Homer into a relaxed, sleeplike state of trance. It took him less than thirty seconds to succeed, and his first suggestion was for Homer to close his eyes and totally make himself at ease.

The strobe was deactivated, and the room light switched back on. Homer appeared to be calmly sleeping, his previously tense facial muscles at long last slackened, his breathing deep and regular.

From their vantage point on the other side of the room, both Moore and Stanton looked on as the medical officer carefully began his interrogation.

"Son, this is Doc Weatherford once again. Please give me your full name and rank."

Homer readily replied. "Seaman Second Class Homer Earl Morgan, sir."

"How old are you, Seaman Morgan, and where were you born?" asked the physician.

"I'm twenty-two years old, sir, from Eureka Springs, Arkansas."

Lieutenant Weatherford glanced over to meet the gazes of his rapt audience before continuing. "Seaman Morgan, I'm going to ask you some questions now about your current duty. Some of them might be a bit painful to think about. But I want you to take your time answering them and be as truthful as possible. What ship are you presently assigned to, son?"

Homer's voice slightly quivered. "The USS *Lewis and Clark*, sir."

"And what do you do aboard the *Lewis and Clark*, Seaman Morgan?"

"Sir, I'm assigned to the ship's galley."

"How do you like this duty?"

Homer hesitated a moment. "It's okay, sir, especially now that the chief's designated me assistant wardroom server."

A moment of doubt briefly clouded Homer's previously tranquil expression, and he appeared temporarily puzzled. Lieutenant Weatherford noted this character change and pursued it.

"It's very important that you tell me just what you're feeling right now, Homer."

"It's the chief!" shouted Homer, his tone strained and bordering on panic. "I'll never see him again, because I'm responsible for killing him and the others!"

"What do you mean by the others, Homer? The rest of the crew?"

Homer looked confused and dumbfounded as he nodded yes, and brushed a tear off his cheek.

"You're not going to sit there and tell me that you killed all one-hundred and forty members of the *Lewis and Clark*'s crew, are you, son?"

"But I did!" admitted Homer bluntly.

"I think that you're lying to me, Seaman Morgan. No one could kill that many men at one time."

"Well, I did, by opening the TDU!"

Homer appeared flustered, and his inquisitor allowed him a moment to calm down and catch his breath before continuing.

"Now this is going to be the real hard part for you, Homer. Because I want you to describe in detail just how you managed to kill all of your shipmates, and then survive yourself. Why don't you start off by telling me all about the TDU."

Homer sat forward and thoughtfully replied with ever-increasing intensity. "I guess you could say it all started when I went and shot the trash. I could have sworn that Chief Cunnetto gave me the authority to do it. But he said that I messed up, and that I caused the sea to come pourin' in. As sure as rain in spring, we all would have drowned. And when the XO asked for volunteers to try to seal the TDU, I was the first in line.

"I went under a good five feet of water just like he instructed, and even managed to locate the hand crank and close up the sprung ball valve. Yet when I went to surface, all that weird shakin' began. And when I popped my head out of the water, and saw what was happenin' to the chief and the rest of the guys, I knew then that I was too late. I tell you, I killed every single one of them!"

Homer's eyes were wide with horror, like they were when he was first discovered back on the submarine, and the strained tone of his voice indicated that he was rapidly approaching his breaking point. Regardless of this fact, Lieutenant Weatherford knew that it was now or never.

"Don't stop now, Homer. No matter how painful it

is for you, you've got to tell me just what it was that you saw when you surfaced. What happened to the rest of your shipmates?"

"They just went and disappeared, that's what happened!" screamed Homer with tears cascading down his flushed cheeks. "I don't know what the hell I did, but there was the chief fading away before my very eyes. I'll never get his cries of pain out of my ears. It was like a pack of dogs was tearin' him apart, and then the others started in. And before I could get myself out of the water to help them, they were gone, all of them vanished, right into thin air! Oh Lord, what did I do? What did I do?"

Homer began sobbing uncontrollably and Lieutenant Weatherford was forced to break him from his trance and administer a strong intravenous sedative. This signaled the end of the session, and both Moore and Stanton left the examination room even more confused than when the session first started.

"It sounds to me like that young man is totally insane," offered the captain as he led the way back to the ship's bridge. "What do you think, Commander?"

Moore offered his own opinion while following his escort down a long passageway. "You could very well be right, Captain. Though one thing that you can be sure of, is that he certainly believes his story. I could see it in his eyes."

"But what about all that crap about his shipmates disappearing into thin air?" countered Stanton as he stepped through a hatch and began his way up a steep stairwell. "To me, that sounds like the wild ramblings of a crazy man."

Moore held back his reply until both of them had completed transiting the stairs, and were crossing yet another passageway. "Right now, the only scenario that makes any real sense is your theory that the crew abandoned ship during an emergency, and Seaman Morgan was somehow left behind. Who knows, perhaps it was all precipitated when Homer shot the trash, and the TDU began flooding."

"But why no distress call on the part of the crew?" returned Stanton. "And better yet, why haven't they shown up yet?"

Unable to answer any of these questions, Moore soon found himself entering the destroyer's bridge. The compartment was abuzz with activity. While the captain joined his XO beside the helm, Moore walked over to the wraparound observation window. Though fog veiled any view of the ocean, he could readily see several lookouts on the exterior catwalk, with their binocular-amplified gazes focused out into the swirling mist.

"I've got a visual on the sub!" cried one of these lookouts, his outstretched hand pointed out to sea. "It's off our port bow, range twenty yards."

The XO alertly ordered the ship's gas turbine engines cut to a crawl, and the *Hewitt* crept forward to make good its rendezvous. Behind him, a pair of ensigns were discussing how the tow line was to be attached, while the radar operator continually called out the range to their floating target.

"Commander Moore," said the captain from the

helm. "It looks like you finally got some orders."

Moore turned, and joined Stanton beside the digital annunciator.

"This just came in for you," added the captain, as he handed Moore a folded dispatch.

The brief directive was from his superiors in the NIS. Without any mention of his current assignment, he was merely ordered back to Washington with all due haste.

"As soon as you can manage it, Captain, I'm going to need a lift to Sasebo," requested Moore.

"So you're leaving us just when all the fun is about to start," said Stanton, who looked at his watch. "I can have a Seahawk ready on the helipad in fifteen minutes."

Moore checked his own watch, and as he folded his orders and put them in his pocket, his hand made contact with a stringy, alien substance that had been stored there. He was genuinely surprised when he pulled out the seaweed sample that he had previously taken from the *Lewis and Clark's* sail.

"Captain, before I leave you, I'd like to try to identify this seaweed sample that I found tangled in the sub's hydroplane. Is there a set of encyclopedias on board?"

Stanton's attention was diverted by the latest range update from the *Hewitt's* radar operator, and when he answered Moore, he appeared a bit distracted. "Check Doc's office, Commander. It's on the way to the helipad. And good luck to you."

Taking this as the extent of the captain's good-bye, Thomas Moore hurriedly left the bridge and headed aft. A series of stairwells conveyed him below deck, and with the invaluable assistance of several members of the crew, he found his way back to the sick bay.

Lieutenant Weatherford was seated at his desk, when Moore entered the office. Pushing away his paperwork, the medical officer smiled and warmly welcomed this newcomer.

"Do have a seat, Commander. Can I get you some coffee?"

"No thanks, Doc," returned Moore, who remained standing. "I'm afraid that I'm in a bit of a rush. You see, I'm going to be catching a flight for the mainland in another couple of minutes, and I stopped by to see if you had an encyclopedia that I could take a quick look at."

"May I ask what you need it for?" asked the curious physician.

Moore pulled out the seaweed sample and handed it to him, adding. "I found this hanging from the *Lewis and Clark's* sail, and I'd like to know just exactly what it is."

"That should be easy enough," returned Weatherford, who took a moment to study the greenish-brown specimen under his halogen desk lamp.

"It looks like a type of brown algae," he said. "These hollow, berry-like objects that branch out from the central stem, appear to be air bladders of some sort. I know I've seen this type of sea plant before. Let's check the computer data bank, and see if we can't get you an exact genus."

Moore looked to his watch, while the *Hewitt's*

medical officer reached over to address his keyboard. It took a full minute for the monitor screen to blink alive, and Moore wondered if he shouldn't wait to continue this portion of the investigation back in Washington.

Sensing his impatience, Lieutenant Weatherford did his best to calm Moore's anxieties, all the while efficiently addressing the keyboard. "Hang in there, Commander. I've just got to access the right source, and we'll get you that answer. While we're waiting for it to key up, I'm sure you'll be glad to hear that our patient is doing just fine. His pulse rate's back to normal, and as of ten minutes ago, he was still out cold."

"What do you think it was that caused him to have those strange delusions?" asked Moore, whose eyes never left the blank, green-tinted screen.

Weatherford thought a moment before answering. "I don't know, maybe Seaman Morgan's experiencing post-traumatic shock syndrome. It's also very apparent that he's feeling his fair share of guilt for being the only one of his shipmates left behind."

The computer beeped a single time, and Weatherford turned his attention back to the monitor. "Ah, here we go."

The screen filled with what appeared to be a page from a botany textbook. A number of detailed specimen sketches were included in this text, and Weatherford scanned several pages of the document until he found what he was looking for.

"I believe that this is our baby. What do you think, Commander?"

Moore peered over his shoulder and viewed an almost exact duplicate of the sample that he had been attempting to identify. "That's it, all right. What is it, Doc?"

The physician hastily read the text that accompanied the sketch and wondrously observed. "So that's why it looked so familiar. It's nothing but common sargassum, otherwise known as gulfweed."

"But that can't be," countered Thomas Moore. "I thought sargassum was only found in the Atlantic Ocean."

The medical officer looked back to his monitor screen like he was seeing a ghost. "The text concurs with you, Commander. Sargassum is indigenous to the Atlantic—which means that unless someone is playing one hell of a sick practical joke on us, we've got us one strange mother of a mystery on our hands!"

Six

After the day's work had been completed, it was the custom of the occupants of Starfish House to convert the dining area of the habitat into a motion-picture theater. Lisa would prepare the popcorn, and the aquanauts would sit back to enjoy a movie selected from their video cassette library. Afterwards, with the room still blackened, they would often turn on the exterior spotlights, and watch a fascinating show of a vastly different sort take place right outside the habitat's observation window. Attracted by the unnatural light, the stars of this live performance were hundreds of species of colorful reef fish. And most of the time, their spellbound audience would watch them glide by until the wee hours of the morning.

Instead of a Hollywood spectacle, Ivana Petrov chose for this evening's entertainment a film that both she and Pierre Lenclud had directly participated in making. Its characters were thousands of shuffling lobsters that covered the sandy sea floor in a single, orderly file.

"Exactly where did you say this event occurred?" asked Tomo, his popcorn all but forgotten.

"We first turned on *Misha's* video camera at a depth of nine hundred and seventy-six feet," answered the Russian. "That put us well onto the southern slope of the Andros Trench, near the northern terminus of the Tongue of the Ocean."

Lisa Tanner shook her head in wonder. "At the very least you could have brought back a dozen or so of those beauties to Starfish House. Why my mouth's watering just lookin' at all those meaty tails!"

"I've read about such phenomena occurring before," admitted Tomo. "But this is the first time that I've ever seen it with my own eyes."

"Is it a mating ritual?" questioned Lenclud, between sips of his sherry.

"That it is, Commandant," replied Tomo. "The behavior in this instance is much like that of the spawning salmon, though to my knowledge the actual breeding ground of the spiny lobster has yet to be found."

"And here we were so close to discovering it," reflected Ivana, a hint of disappointment flavoring her tone.

"I'm anxious to see the first pictures of your other discovery, Dr. Petrov," said Karl Ivar, who had been seated at the back of the room, casually dressed in a pair of cut-off jeans and a *Save the Whales* T-shirt.

"They'll be coming up very shortly," returned Ivana.

"And I guarantee you that you won't be disappointed with them," added Lenclud. "I must admit that I was a skeptic at first. But after personally seeing the formation, my instincts tell me that it's got to be man-made. But I'll let each one of you come to your own conclusions, once you see the film we brought back."

Bored by the seemingly endless procession of lobsters that continued to fill the video screen, Lisa Tanner let her thoughts wander to a much more exotic subject. "I sure wish that *Misha* hadn't broken down. Who knows, that road could have led you right to the front gates of Atlantis."

"If that's the case, the fabled lost continent lies somewhere in the Tongue of the Ocean," offered Ivana lightly. "Because that appeared to be right where the road was headed when we were forced to turn back."

"Speaking of *Misha*, what's your exact prognosis on its condition, Karl Ivar?" questioned Tomo.

The Norwegian solemnly shook his head. "Right now, it doesn't look all that good. Without a proper alternator, I can't get *Misha* to hold a battery charge. We've already gone through three spares, and even if they send down another, it won't make much difference, unless it's of a totally new design."

"Couldn't we borrow one of the other diving saucers?" asked Lisa. "It's a shame to have to stop our exploration right when it's getting so interesting."

"Since the *Academician Petrovsky* carries two of

these vessels, I asked for the services of one of them in my dispatch," informed Ivana. "And now we'll just have to wait and see if fate is on our side."

Lenclud excitedly pointed towards the screen. "Look, there are the first video pictures of Dr. Petrov's latest discovery, the Andros road!"

All eyes went to the screen, as it began filling with a wide-angle shot of a section of the flat, rocky pavement that had originally sent them down into the depths. Though it was partially covered with sandy sediment, the tightly interlocking, square-cut stones were clearly visible, prompting an instant response from the habitat's head cook.

"It's simply incredible! Its origin has to be Atlantean. Who else could have built it? I tell you, mates, this goes to prove that Plato was right after all."

A bell suddenly chimed three times in the distance, and Ulge came flying into the room with feathers madly flapping. The parrot picked the top of the video projector for its landing pad, all the while loudly squawking.

"Dolly's home! Yes siree, Dolly's home! Hello, Dolly!"

"I bet she's got an answer to my request," said Ivana.

"Or maybe she's brought the spare part that I need to fix *Misha*," offered Karl Ivar.

Without further hesitation, both stood and darted off to the adjoining ready room. With his curiosity also aroused, Lenclud joined them.

He found his associates gathered around the open hatch, facing the head and upper body of a full grown bottlenose dolphin. Known to all as Dolly, the dolphin was their link to the support ship that always remained on station above them. Dolly was responsible for delivering the mail, various foodstuffs, and other items such as the spare parts that Karl Ivar was waiting for. She carried these objects in a watertight pressure cooker, with a specially designed strap, which fit over the dolphin's blunt snout. One of these pressure cookers lay beside the hatch, next to the bell that Dolly was trained to ring to announce her arrival. Remembering well the day that Ulge arrived in just such a manner, Lenclud walked over to greet their newly arrived guest.

"Bon soir, ma chérie. What did you bring us from above?"

Lenclud kneeled down to scratch the underside of Dolly's neck, and the dolphin responded with a burst of animated clicks and whistles.

"You don't say," deadpanned the Frenchman, who reached into a nearby bucket, and fed Dolly a mullet.

Meanwhile, Karl Ivar anxiously unscrewed the lid of the newly delivered pressure cooker. Much to his disappointment, it held only a single white envelope, which he pulled out and handed to Ivana. She opened it, and read its contents out loud.

"Dear Dr. Petrov, I regretfully inform you that I am unable to grant your request at this time. Because of mechanical difficulties, both of our diving saucers have been indefinitely taken out of service. We are currently waiting for newly designed spare parts to be flown in from the *rodina*. Will advise upon their receipt. Yours truly, Admiral Igor Valerian, Commanding Officer, *Academician Petrovsky*."

Disgustedly flinging this dispatch to the deck, Ivana sarcastically added, "So, they're going to have newly designed spare parts flown out to us from Mother Russia. Now that's a joke if I ever heard one. Such a thing could take months to happen. And in the meantime, all of us will be long gone from this habitat. Why did the U.N. have to go and provide us with a Russian support ship? Now I'll never be able to learn the extent of my new find."

"I wouldn't go that far, Doctor," advised the Norwegian. "Why don't I go and take another look at *Misha*. There's got to be something that I can do to get that charge to hold."

With practiced ease, Karl Ivar slipped on a wet suit and shouldered a scuba tank. He then signed the diving log, spit into his face mask, pulled it over his head, and joined Dolly in the water.

"Come on, Dolly," he said before putting the regulator hose in his mouth. "We've got some work to do."

He left with a thumbs-up, and seconds later, disappeared beneath the water with the dolphin close at his side.

"Don't look so glum, *mon amie*," said Lenclud to his sulking co-worker. "If anyone can fix

100

Misha, it will be Karl Ivar. So let's return to the others, and finish our film, before the popcorn goes cold."

Admiral Igor Valerian stared down at the black waters from the *Academician Petrovsky's* prow, visualizing the unique collection of structures lying on the sea floor sixty feet below. The sixty-seven-year-old Russian naval officer had to admit that when he first saw the original plans to the Mir habitat, he didn't think that the project would go beyond the planning stage. But reality had proved him wrong, and the underwater habitat had been home to a group of five aquanauts for three weeks now.

The mere thought of men and women actually living beneath the seas amazed the white-haired old-timer. He had certainly seen his share of astounding scientific advances. And the Mir habitat was only another example of the rapid pace at which modern technology was moving.

In many ways, the vessel that he currently commanded was yet another example of this new, high-tech generation. The *Academician Petrovsky* was officially classified an oceanographic research ship. Launched in 1990 from Leningrad's United Admiralty complex, the three-hundred foot long, steam-turbine-powered vessel was built with no expense spared. Its operational systems thus incorporated state-of-the-art Soviet marine design.

A crew of ninety manned the ship. They were a mix of civilians, scientists, and naval technicians.

They also carried along three representatives of the United Nations, whose flag they currently sailed under. Such a dual loyalty was new to Valerian, who was used to sailing beneath the red banner of the Russian fleet. But these were new, so-called enlightened times, and as a veteran survivor of the Great Patriotic War and Stalin's bloody purges, he had long ago learned to swim with the tide of change, and to not fight a current which one couldn't alter even if one wanted to.

They had left their home port on the Baltic four and a half weeks ago. After stops in Sweden, Norway, and the United Kingdom, they crossed the Atlantic, making port in New York City. This was Valerian's first visit to the place known as the Big Apple, and he'd never forget his first view of the Statue of Liberty, and the amazing island of Manhattan. Never before had he seen such incredible buildings. And there seemed to be people everywhere. It was in New York that they picked up the observers from the United Nations, and then set sail for the Bahamas, where they had been since.

Unlike many of his fellow sailors, Igor Valerian had never liked duty in the tropics. He was a native of Siberia, and his solid, six-foot-four-inch frame was stifled by constant heat and humidity. His body thrived on fresh, cool air, and it was in a vain search for this rare commodity that he left his cabin below deck, and climbed up to the *Academician Petrovsky*'s prow.

The night was but a carbon copy of all the others. The air was thick and heavy, smelling richly of the sea. An occasional breeze blew in from the east, though its oppressive heat was far from refreshing.

Doing his best to make himself comfortable, Valerian wore a lightweight pair of white cotton slacks and a short-sleeved shirt. Yet sweat constantly poured off his forehead, and it was an effort merely to breathe.

To ease his discomfort, he brought along a bottle of his finest potato vodka. Without bothering to use a glass, he brought the bottle to his lips and swallowed a long, satisfying mouthful. The vodka had been distilled alongside the shores of Lake Baikal. Its sharp, distinctive taste coursed down his throat like a red-hot flame and hit his belly with a jolt, making him feel truly alive again.

Oblivious to the gently rocking deck beneath him, and the distant, muted cry of a lonely gull, he let his thoughts go back to his beloved homeland. Soon he'd be forced to retire, and a life spent sailing the planet's oceans in defense of the *rodina* would be over.

It was at the tender age of seventeen that Valerian first put on the uniform of the Soviet Navy. With his childhood prematurely shortened by the invasion of the Nazi horde, he became a man beneath the frozen Arctic sea, when he was assigned to a submarine that was based in the besieged city of Murmansk. An exploding German depth charge all but deafened him, and to this day he still heard a ringing in his ears, to remind him of his shipmates who never survived this same blast.

Yet another physical legacy of the Great Patriotic War was the patch that he wore over his left eye. This was the by-product of a Nazi artillery barrage. He was assigned to Naval headquarters in Leningrad at the time of this near-fatal injury, and he came to the attention of his superiors when he all but refused treatment so that he could continue on duty.

Hard work and the ever-present hand of fate guided his career, and by the time the war was over, he was a full-fledged captain. The postwar years were a time of unparalleled growth for the Soviet Navy. From a mere coastal defense force, the fleet grew into a legitimate blue water navy, capable of reaching the farthest corner of the planet.

In the years between Stalin's death and Khrushchev's rise to power, he worked as an aide to Admiral of the Fleet Sergei Gorshkov. Appointed to this post at the unprecedented age of forty-five, Gorshkov was a great visionary, and it was under his expert tutelage that Valerian was able to realize his full potential.

Igor was there the day the first Soviet Zulu V class submarine test launched the first sub-carried ballistic missile, a good two years before the U.S. Navy was to begin construction of a vessel with similar capabilities. He was also privileged to work on the new Krupny class destroyers, the first surface combatant ever to be outfitted with surface-to-surface missiles, designed to counter threats from Western aircraft carriers.

In 1967, he was made executive officer of the

Moskva, the world's first helicopter carrier. Five years later, he received full command of a Krivak class destroyer, a post that led to over a dozen other distinguished commands on a wide variety of surface combatants and submarines.

It was strangely ironic that he should end his long, distinguished career in command of an oceanographic research ship. Yet Valerian knew that this could very well be his most important assignment of all. And if it was successful, it would be a most fitting way to announce his retirement.

The mere thought of returning to civilian life — with nothing to do but write his memoirs — scared him, and he once more raised the vodka bottle to his lips to ease his anxieties. There was a sound of voices behind him, and he turned and spotted two young sailors gathered at the rail in the midst of a smoke. One of these individuals was a woman, her high-pitched laugh most discernible. He could tell from their light-hearted conversation that they didn't seem to have a care in the world, and in this manner they represented their entire generation.

With the spicy taste of the vodka still flavoring his tongue, he contemplated the vast changes that had all but stripped the soul from his homeland. Today a new generation had come of age — they had already forgotten the painful lessons that Valerian and his contemporaries had learned during the conflict with Germany and the Cold War that followed. These spoiled, pampered youngsters didn't know the true meaning of sacrifice, and all they seemed to do was complain and whine. Because of them, the greatest social revolution that the world had ever known was threatened, doomed to failure by this generation's indifference.

Of course, the force that led these youngsters astray was capitalism. Like a malignant cancer, the selfish, wasteful ways of the West gnawed into one's soul. And today Soviet youth was blinded by the petty desires of consumerism. What began innocently enough with blue jeans and rock-and-roll music, led to the destruction of the Russian family, and the values that had guided generations past.

The first real sign that the disease was reaching fatal proportions was when East Germany abandoned its communist path. Eastern Europe soon followed, with the Soviet Union the next inevitable victim.

Like the scared old men that they were, the *rodina's* leaders allowed the sickness to spread into the republics, threatening the cohesive structure of the motherland. The decision to abandon state control and adopt a free-market system was a *fait accompli,* and showed how deep the cancer had spread.

When faced with a potentially terminal illness, the patient has an ever-shrinking list of strategies for survival. One of the most desperate choices is the severing of a limb, in the hope of strengthening the rest of the body. This was just the course of action that the Soviet Union's leaders decided upon, when they turned their backs on the socialist principles of Lenin, and chose to make massive cuts in the military.

Vessels such as the *Academician Petrovsky* didn't come cheap, and in today's Russia they could never be produced at all. What really bothered Valerian was the fact that his countrymen had forgotten that it was because of a strong military that no outside enemy had crossed their borders in the last four and a half decades. This was a bloodless victory, whose only expense was in rubles, not human lives.

But would they be so fortunate in the near future? With all their talk of disarmament and peace, the United States of America continued to build up its arsenal of both nuclear and conventional weapons. To realize this frightening fact, one had only to look at such advanced systems as the Stealth aircraft, Star Wars, and the new generation *Seawolf* submarine.

Because submarines were the true capital ships of today's navies, Valerian especially feared America's *Seawolf* program. *Seawolf* would be the first new class of submarine to enter the U.S. fleet since the 688 class was introduced in the 1970s. Reported to be ten times quieter than its predecessors, with three times the sensor range and a greatly expanded weapons capability, *Seawolf* represented the most advanced underwater warship ever to sail beneath the seas. It alone would shift the balance of power to a point where the Russian Navy would be completely defenseless.

Since the leaders of the Soviet Union had decided in their blind folly to abandon any further spending in the all-important area of research and development, the red banner fleet could never hope to field a submarine as advanced as *Seawolf.* That meant that the only way for them to get ahold of such vital technology was to steal it. And this was just what Admiral Igor Valerian hoped to do during this last and most important mission of his lifetime.

With no less an issue than the very future existence of his beloved homeland at stake, the one-eyed veteran mariner anxiously looked up to scan the northwestern horizon. From his current vantage point, he could just make out the distant flickering lights of Nicolls Town, on the northern tip of Andros Island. In two more weeks, from this general direction, the first *Seawolf* submarine would come for test trials, beneath the deep waters of the Tongue of the Ocean. And if all went as planned, this prototype vessel would never make it to the nearby U.S. Navy underwater test range, and instead become the invaluable property of the Red Banner fleet.

Thrilled by this exciting prospect, Valerian lifted his bottle up before him, and silently toasted for success to the warm, tropical trade wind. He then sealed this toast with a mouthful of vodka that stung his throat and left him red-faced and gasping for breath.

At this inopportune moment the ship's *michman*—warrant officer—climbed up onto the prow. Viewing his commanding officer in apparent distress caused a look of sincere concern to cross the senior enlisted man's bearded face.

"Are you feeling all right, Admiral?" he worriedly greeted.

"Of course I'm all right, Comrade," managed Valerian. "And you can feel this good as well, if you'll just join me in a sip of vodka."

"I'm afraid that I'm on duty, sir," replied the embarrassed *michman*.

"Since when has that ever stopped a red-blooded Russian sailor?" returned Valerian as he held out the bottle and winked.

Looking like a thief in the night, the *michman* hurriedly put the bottle to his lips and downed a healthy swig.

"My, that is tasty," he observed while handing the bottle back to its owner. "What brand of vodka is that?"

Valerian readily answered. "It's Irkutsk potato vodka, Comrade, distilled on the distant shores of Lake Baikal. Have you ever seen Lake Baikal, my friend?"

The *michman* shook his head that he hadn't, and Valerian passionately continued. "Well, I grew up on its northern shores, in the tiny village of Kosa. And I can personally attest to the fact that there is no more beautiful spot on this entire planet. The water is cool, sweet, and crystal clear, and even the air smells like nectar."

"Sounds wonderful, sir," shyly returned the *michman,* who abruptly changed the course of this unexpected conversation. "Admiral, Senior Lieutenant Alexandrov instructed me to inform you that Lieutenant Antonov and his team are on their way up, and will be returning to the ship shortly."

"Do we have the results of Antonov's mission as yet?" questioned Valerian, suddenly all business.

"Not that I know of, sir. The senior lieutenant is waiting beside the moonpool, where the team is to be debriefed."

"Then by all means, let's join them, Comrade," said Valerian, who drained off the rest of the vodka and threw the empty bottle overboard.

One design feature unique to the *Academician Petrovsky* was a large, rectangular opening cut into the bottom of its hull. Known as the moonpool, it offered the ship's technicians a relatively safe, convenient access to the sea below.

To get to the moonpool, Valerian had to travel below deck, and proceed aft — towards the ship's stern. A steep stairwell conveyed him down to the spotlight-illumined waterline, where a steel-latticed catwalk completely surrounded the moonpool itself. A tall, distinguished officer, with a two-way radio clipped to his belt, waited for him here.

"Viktor Ilyich, I thought that the team was on its way up," impatiently chided the one-eyed veteran.

"That they are, sir," replied Valerian's second-in-command, Senior Lieutenant Viktor Ilyich Alexandrov. "If you look towards the center of the moonpool, you can just see their air bubbles now."

By the time Valerian spotted this disturbance, the first of two diving saucers broke the waters surface. The bright yellow minisubs were exact duplicates of the one used by the occupants of the Mir habitat,

110

with the one exception being a properly designed alternator. As the lead saucer crept over to the edge of the catwalk where the two officers stood, its hatch sprung upwards and out popped a devilishly handsome, blond-haired sailor, dressed in dark blue coveralls. His appearance caused a broad smile to turn the corners of Valerian's face, and the new-comer returned this greeting with a grin of his own.

"So Neptune has sent you back to us after all, Comrade," welcomed Valerian.

Lieutenant Yuri Antonov answered while climbing up onto the catwalk. "Even Neptune knows better than to fool with the *spetsnaz*, Admiral."

This comment caused Valerian to break out in a hearty laugh, and he reached out to give the ruddy-cheeked commando a firm handshake.

"Now tell me, Lieutenant Antonov," said Valerian in all seriousness. "How did the inspection go? Did you find the malfunction?"

"I can't really say," replied Antonov, while watching his copilot climb out of the saucer. "Per your instructions, we followed the power cable from the moonpool all the way down to the floor of the trench, a thousand feet beneath us, and we didn't see a hint of damage. When we arrived at the device itself, our first test was of the magnetic reso-nator. As far as I can tell, the degaussing pattern was strong and true."

"How about the electromagnetic generators?" asked Valerian. "Were they pulsating on the proper frequency?"

"That they were, Admiral. We only recorded the slightest of variances, and most likely that was but a fault in our testing equipment."

"If the malfunction is not in the resonator, then I still say that we're projecting the improper energy field," offered the senior lieutenant. "And the only way to tell for certain is to bring up the entire device and recalibrate it."

"But that could take an entire week," protested Valerian. "And even if we do get it back in place by the time *Seawolf* passes through the trench, we still won't know for certain whether it's operational or not."

"Maybe the problem's with the equipment in Vladivostok," offered the commando.

"I've considered that possibility," admitted Valerian.

"Well, at least our first test here was a partial success," said Yuri Antonov optimistically.

Valerian heavily sighed. "Unfortunately, a partial success is not good enough to guarantee us *Seawolf*. No, Comrades, it appears that I have no choice but to play our trump card. Though I promised Moscow that we could succeed without him, it's time to call in the only individual who can find the malfunction and repair it in time to insure our success."

The footpath led away from the dacha, deep into the surrounding birch forest. Dr. Andrei Petrov knew its every turn, for he had been walking it almost every day for the past five years. This was quite an amazing feat considering that he had just turned seventy years old, and that the doctors at the cancer institute had doubted that he'd ever see sixty-five.

Ever thankful that he had listened to his wife Anna, and worn his winter coat, he pulled the woolen collar up over his neck when a chilling gust of wind swept in from the north. The slender birch trunks swayed to and fro like a single entity, and Andrei looked up to scan the sky. A wall of low, dark grey clouds met his eyes, and he sensed that the first real snow of the season would soon be falling.

Though the official start of fall was still several days away, the lazy days of summer had long since passed. Here in the heart of central Russia, the snows came early, with the winters lasting well into the spring. This was fine with Andrei, who loved nothing better than to sit before a blazing fireplace, with the wood he chopped himself crackling away, as he watched the snow fall outside through the dacha's central picture window.

Winter was the time to read books, and to listen to classical music on the phonograph. Occasionally, friends and colleagues would drop by, often staying overnight when the weather made travel difficult. These unscheduled slumber parties always turned out well, with plenty of lively conversation, and excellent food and drink to share. Andrei most anticipated these visits when the guests were former co-workers of his at the institute. Then he had a chance to get caught up on the latest gossip, and to learn more about the projects currently under development.

A raven loudly cried out overhead, and Andrei directed his attention back to the path. With increasing strides, he continued further into the forest, to the spot where a bubbling brook split the path in two. All too soon these crystal clear waters would freeze, and Andrei cautiously approached the pebble-strewn stream bank.

Only yesterday, he had seen a fat speckled trout swimming in the waters here. In the spring, he hoped to try his luck with a fly rod, in an attempt to catch this fish. For now he was content merely to catch a glimpse of it.

As he kneeled down behind a fallen birch trunk to await the trout, a rustling in the underbrush on the other side of the creek caught his attention. Something large was moving through the berry bushes there, and he was somewhat surprised when a full-grown male elk broke through the thick cover and sauntered up to the creek to drink. It was a powerful-looking creature, with a tremendous rack of pointed antlers and a shaggy brown coat. Such elk freely roamed the woods here, and were coveted by the local hunters for their meat.

Andrei was not the type who could ever shoot such a magnificent animal. In fact, he didn't own a rifle, and he had learned to fire one only for self-defense during the war. Quite happy to coexist with nature in peace, he decided to quietly return to the footpath and get on with his hike. As he turned around to do so, yet another elk crashed out of the woods directly in front of him. This one was obviously a female, and appeared already to have gotten his scent.

Andrei now found himself in the unenviable position of being sandwiched between the two creatures. Fall was rutting time for the elk, when the males were particularly aggressive. This was especially the case if another animal happened to get between the buck and its mate. Only last November, a local woodsman had been found fatally gored to death by an enraged male elk. Not wishing to share the man's fate, Andrei did his best to continue on his way as quietly as possible.

He almost succeeded in making good his escape, when he inadvertently stepped on a fallen branch, making it snap in half with a loud, cracking crunch. This was all the buck needed, to spot the retreating human between him and his current beloved. Instinct instantly took over, and the creature lowered its massive rack and charged.

Andrei could think of no better defense than to turn tail and run for it. He hadn't moved so fast in years, as he frantically crashed through the forest, with the persistent elk ever close on his heels.

He broke out of the underbrush like an Olympic sprinter. This put him back on the relatively clear footpath, and the retired septuagenarian did his best to lengthen his weary stride.

As he passed back into the birch wood, he realized that his pursuer had finally given up the chase. Andrei immediately halted at this point, and his first priority was to catch his breath. Sweat matted his forehead, and a familiar pain suddenly shot up his left arm and once more left him dizzy and breathless.

Yanking off his mittens, he fumbled in his pants pocket for his pill case. His hands were wildly shaking, yet he still managed to snap open the compact metal container and slip one of its tiny, yellow pills under his tongue. The medication took a full minute to take effect, and even then a dull pain continued to course through the entire left side of his upper torso.

An icy gust of wind swept through the tree limbs, further adding to his discomfort, and Andrei realized that it was beginning to snow. And then he heard the distinctive, muffled chopping whine of a helicopter in the distance. He could tell merely from this sound's deep pitch that it was a military vehicle. And this observation proved true when a dark green, Mil Mi-8 utility helicopter, with the red star fuselage markings of the Russian Army, roared almost directly overhead, only inches from the swaying tree tops.

Because there were no military bases nearby, Andrei wondered what this vehicle was doing here. It seemed to be headed straight for his dacha, and this could only mean that it had come for him. Andrei had expected this day to come, and he did his best to gather his physical composure and continue homeward.

Sure enough, as he broke into the clearing where his dacha was situated, the helicopter could be seen parked beside the wood pile. A lone soldier stood beside its elongated fuselage, with a lit cigarette between his lips. A column of thick white smoke poured from the dacha's stone chimney, and Andrei prepared himself for the worst as he walked up to the front door and stepped inside.

Waiting for him beside the crackling fireplace, was a short, bespectacled, middle-aged man, dressed in an ill-fitting brown suit. This steely-eyed visitor needed no introduction. Dr. Stanislaus Bolimin had been the head of the Kirov Polytechnic Institute on the day that Andrei was forced into retirement. It was Bolimin who coldly notified him that after five decades of loyal, unselfish service, he would no longer be needed. That very afternoon he was escorted out of his laboratory, never again to be allowed to set foot inside it.

"Good morning, Comrade," greeted Bolimin, his nasal tone sharp and irritating. "Your fireplace is a most welcome sight after my long, cold flight up from Kirov."

Andrei was saved from having to reply by his wife's entrance into the room. Anna held a steaming hot mug of tea, which she proceeded to give to their guest.

"Thank goodness that you got back before the snow really began falling, Andrei Sergeyevich," said Anna as she walked over to help her husband remove his coat. "Are those thorns all over the back of your jacket, husband? I thought that you promised me that you would always remain on the trail."

"So you're still straying from the path, even in

117

retirement," observed Bolimin with a sardonic grin. "Some things never change."

"I guess they don't, Doctor," returned Andrei disgustedly. "I hope that I'm not being too blunt, but to what do we owe the pleasure of your company?"

Bolimin took a sip of his tea and directly responded to this question. "Your bluntness is most appreciated, Comrade. For you see, a matter of great urgency brings me here, and I have no time for pleasantries. Though I must say that this tea is certainly delicious."

"I'm glad that you're enjoying it," said Anna, who turned towards the kitchen and added. "Andrei Sergeyevich, warm yourself by the fire before you catch pneumonia, and I'll bring you some tea and honey."

Quick to follow her orders, Andrei joined his guest beside the brick hearth. There was a look of defiant anger in his blue eyes as he opened the fireplace screen and attacked the burning embers with a poker. The kindling crackled and spat, and Andrei threw in another log before closing the screen and readdressing Bolimin.

"So what exactly is this urgent matter that brings you here, Doctor? I thought that the state no longer had need for a senile old man like myself."

"You underestimate yourself, Comrade," returned Bolimin in a condescending tone. "In the five years that you've been gone from the Institute, not a day goes by without your name being mentioned. Your textbooks still grace our classrooms, your many theories are still the subject of intense debate."

118

"Don't stand here in my own house and patronize me, Bolimin!" spat Andrei. "Or have you already forgotten that you're the one who sent me packing from the Institute without so much as an explanation."

"That's not true," countered Bolimin. "You know well why you were asked to leave. The choice was yours, Comrade. And when you continued your antistate remarks to the Western press, we had no choice but to let you go."

"Antistate remarks," repeated Andrei bitterly. "No one loves this country more than I. And what you mistook for dissent was only my way of sharing with the world what I considered to be the greatest threat to humanity since the development of the atomic bomb!"

Bolimin took a deep breath and replied as calmly as possible. "I haven't come here to argue with you, Comrade. Rather to ask your help in a matter of grave importance to this state that you say you love so."

Before he could further explain, Anna returned with her husband's tea.

"Is there anything else that I can get for you?" she politely asked. "Perhaps you'd like some herring?"

Finding no takers for this offer, she shrugged her shoulders and returned to the kitchen. Only when she was completely out of earshot did Bolimin continue.

"What I'm about to share with you is to be held in the strictest confidence, Comrade. Five years ago, on the very day that you were asked to leave the Institute, the Ministry of Defense gave us the go-ahead to begin construction of a full-scale magnetic resonator. We utilized the original plans that you yourself created, and had a working degausser ready to test, twelve months later."

"You're not going to tell me that you went and actually built the antimatter device after all I warned you about?" retorted Andrei, his face red with disbelief.

"That we did, Comrade. And as Lenin is my witness, except for a few unexpected side effects, it worked just as you said it would."

With gathering enthusiasm, Bolimin added. "If I hadn't seen the incredible results with my own eyes, I would have never believed them. This went for the representatives of the Defense Ministry as well, whose daily reports to Moscow generated nothing but doubt and skepticism at first. That was until the Minister himself paid us a visit. Needless to say, he left us a full believer, and even went as far as to suggest nominating you for a Star of Lenin."

Not at all impressed by this revelation, Andrei solemnly interjected, "Spare me the accolades, Doctor. Against my innermost wishes, you went and converted my theories into reality. And now humanity is going to have to pay the price. I guess you know that you've succeeded in opening a Pandora's box and you could reap the most disastrous of consequences."

Bolimin thoughtfully nodded. "Though I don't see it in exactly those terms, Comrade, I must admit that those side effects that I mentioned are a bit puzzling. We seem to be having particular problems with the transferal process."

Looking somber and totally defeated, Andrei dared question. "And where is this working prototype now?"

Bolimin sensed that his white-haired colleague had taken the bait, and he readily answered. "In the Bahama Islands, Comrade, beneath the waters of the Andros Trench."

This revelation caused Andrei's eyes suddenly to open wide with horror. "You bastard! That's where my daughter Ivana's working!"

"Believe me, Comrade, the device is in no way related to the Mir habitat program," urged Bolimin. "All that they do is share the same support ship."

"I don't care whose authority you need, but you must find a way to take me there at once!" demanded Andrei forcefully.

Bolimin had to keep himself from smiling as he responded to this request. "What do you think that helicopter is doing outside, Comrade? It's been provided for your personal use, to convey you to Kirov, where an Ilyushin IL-76 transport awaits to fly you to Havana. And from there, you'll be less than an hour's flight away from the waters of the Andros Trench.

121

Seven

The C-5A transport plane carrying Thomas Moore landed at Andrews Air Force base a little after five in the morning. Feeling tired and disoriented after his almost nonstop flight around half the earth, he decided to make a quick stop at his condo to freshen up before continuing on to the office.

A shuttle van conveyed him onto the Capital Beltway, over the Potomac River via the Woodrow Wilson Memorial Bridge, and into the heart of historic Alexandria, Virginia. It was a chilly, cloudless morning, and the first colors of dawn were on the eastern horizon as he climbed out of the van and ambled down the narrow brick walkway leading to his home. He ignored the collection of community papers that were scattered before the door, and after disarming the security system, reached into his pocket for the key. Much to his surprise, it wasn't there, and only after searching the rest of his pockets and his wallet's secret compartment, did he conclude that he had most likely lost it in the plane's restroom. It was Laurie who came up with the idea of hiding an extra key outside. Fortunately, he found it hidden beneath one of the loose porch bricks, still wrapped in aluminum foil and plastic wrap. It was a bit rusted, and Thomas mumbled a quick, silent prayer of thanks to his wife as he put it into the lock and felt the cylinder turn over.

What little he had in the way of luggage, he tossed onto the couch as he headed straight into the kitchen to brew some coffee. Because he hadn't cleaned the coffeemaker after its last use, he was forced to do so now. He emptied the used filter and stale coffee grounds into the garbage, and discovered from the horrible smell when he lifted up the garbage can lid that he had also forgotten to empty the trash. He had to remove a thick stack of dirty plates from the sink to be able to position the coffeepot under the faucet. He filled it up to the six-cup line, and after emptying it into the brewer's receptacle, went to get the coffee, which he found in the nearly empty refrigerator, alongside a box holding a moldy, half-eaten anchovy pizza. To add to his distress, a search of the drawer where he kept the filters resulted in only an empty plastic wrapper, and he had to resort to removing the used filter from the trash to complete the final preparation.

While the coffee was brewing, he showered, shaved, and brushed his teeth. Because his extra uniforms were still at the local dry cleaner, he had to slip back into the same set of wrinkled khakis that had accompanied him on his long flight from Japan.

Never known for his organizational skills when it came to everyday household matters, he really missed Laurie at times like these. Even while holding down a full-time position as a teacher, she still managed to keep the place spotless, the refrigerator stocked, and his closet filled with clean clothes. These were things that he had always taken for granted, until she was abruptly taken from him, and he realized how very much he had depended upon her.

The inviting scent of fresh coffee called him back to the kitchen. Though he would have loved nothing better than to get a couple hours of sleep, he knew that once he hit the mattress, he'd never get up in time to make it to the office today. Once more, caffeine would have to see him through yet another long day, until he'd have the time for a real rest.

He filled his white, ceramic Naval Institute mug up to the rim, flicked on the radio, and sat down at the kitchen table. The black, Colombian coffee was strong, and as he contentedly sipped it, he listened to the morning news. There was the usual depressing economic news, and a report of a series of fatal shootings only two blocks from the White House. Yet the story that really got his attention was the brief mention that an American ballistic missile submarine, the USS *Lewis and Clark,* was overdue in contacting command, and that a search for this boat was currently being initiated off the eastern coast of Florida.

Suddenly, thoughts of his own fatigue were far from his mind, as he struggled to figure out the true significance of this shocking news report. The one thing that was most evident, was that whoever released this story was deliberately misleading the American people. Because the *Lewis and Clark* was not missing at all, but was currently being towed to Okinawa by the USS *Hewitt*.

Yet why spread such disinformation to the public? Could it be that the Navy actually couldn't explain how the *Lewis and Clark* ended up in the Pacific, and that they had to release this report as a red herring? All but forgetting his coffee, Thomas Moore knew that there was only one place where he could get the answers to these disturbing questions.

He hurried to the adjoining garage, stopping only to reset the condo's security alarm. His only automobile was a 1969 Corvette convertible, which he hoped to restore to mint condition one day. Hurriedly, he yanked off the canvas car cover, and regardless of the fact that the top was down, jumped inside. A remote-control switch allowed him to open the garage, and he found the key waiting for him in the ignition. He carefully pressed the accelerator to the floor three times, shifted the gear into neutral, and then turned the key, causing the engine to start with a throaty roar. Without waiting for it to warm up, he shifted into reverse, and backed out onto the cobblestone street.

The sun had already risen, yet Moore found the air to be crisp and cool, especially with the top down as it was. Sorry that he hadn't taken the time to put on a jacket, he guided his vehicle down St. Asaph Street. Rush hour had yet to begin on the picturesque roadways of Alexandria, and he sped through the town's historic section, where two-hundred-year-old town houses were surrounded by majestic oak and elm trees, that once shaded the likes of George Washington and Robert E. Lee. The leaves of these ancient trees were just beginning to be at their peak of fall color, and Moore wished that he had more time to enjoy them.

Autumn had been Laurie's favorite time of the year. She actually charted when the local trees would be their most colorful, and made certain that they'd ride their bicycles to Mt. Vernon at this time. Thomas Moore missed the carefree fall excursions, which had kept him in shape and had given him a better appreciation of nature.

The traffic began to pick up as he crossed the Potomac and turned north onto the Anacostia freeway. Across the river, a plane could be seen taking off from National Airport, while in the distance, he could just make out the towering, white spire of the Washington monument.

Ten minutes later, he was passing through the guarded gates of the Washington Navy Yard. One of the oldest naval bases in the country, the yard was home to a variety of commands including the Naval Investigative Service. The NIS had several missions including general law enforcement, security, and counterintelligence. Having been assigned to this post for two years now, Moore knew just where to find a parking space located nearest his office.

"Good morning, Commander Moore," welcomed Gus Tomlin, the bright-eyed, black guard at the security desk. "We sure haven't seen you around here in a while. How's the 'Vette running?"

"Smooth as silk, Gus," replied Thomas with a distracted smile. "Is the old man in yet?"

"He sure is. I think he spent the night, because his car was out there when I arrived for duty two hours ago. He left word for you to meet him in data processing as soon as you arrived."

"Thanks, Gus," said Moore, his thoughts already refocusing on the many questions he had for his superior officer.

An elevator conveyed him down into the sub-basement level. Before the door to the lift would open, he had to access his security code I.D. number into a keypad located beside the floor selector. Once this was accomplished, an electronic chime rang out overhead, and the door slid open with a low hiss.

A linoleum-tiled hallway led him into a cavernous room, completely filled with mainframe computers and scurrying workers, most of whom were in uniform. It was most unusual to see so much activity this early in the morning, and Moore sensed that a crisis atmosphere prevailed here as he spotted a familiar, silver-haired figure perched above a bank of glowing monitor screens.

Rear Admiral Daniel Proctor was the current commander of the NIS. A thirty-year Navy veteran, the distinguished, easy-going flag officer was a popular father figure to the men and women who served under him. Not afraid to pitch in and work right alongside his troops, Proctor anxiously peered over the shoulder of a seated chief, to read the contents of her monitor screen. As usual, he wore a green woolen sweater with leather elbow patches—a British SAS colonel had given it to him—and he held an unlit briar pipe at his side. Displaying the sixth sense that most successful intelligence officers possessed, he looked up and spotted Moore while the unannounced newcomer was still a good twenty yards distant.

"Well, just look what the wind blew in," he said with an outstretched hand. "How's our favorite globe-trotter doing?"

Moore answered while accepting his superior's firm handshake. "I'm holding up pretty good considering that yesterday at this time, I was floating in the Pacific, halfway around the world from here."

"So I understand," said Proctor as he guided Moore over to a vacant console. "You did a hell of a fine job on the *Iwo Jima,* Thomas. Undercover drug busts are never fun, and I want to tell you in person that it was a job well done."

"Thank you, sir. You know, so much has happened to me since leaving the *Iwo Jima,* that I almost forgot about my assignment there. Admiral, about the *Lewis and Clark.*"

Proctor alertly cut Moore off before he could continue any further. "I'd rather not discuss this subject out here, Thomas. Let's grab the conference room."

It was obvious that his mention of the sub had hit a raw nerve, and Moore readily followed Proctor into an adjoining room. Again the veteran showed uncanny intuition as he spoke out while seating himself at the head of the room's rectangular table.

"I bet you heard this morning's newscast."

"You're damn right I did," replied Moore impatiently. "Admiral, what the hell's going on out there in the Pacific?"

Proctor looked the young investigator directly in the eye and replied. "I know that you're going to find this hard to believe, Thomas, but I can't really say myself. Right now, all I know for certain is that

128

we've currently got a nuclear-powered, ballistic-missile submarine on its way to Okinawa, after disappearing in the Bahamas, only two days ago!"

"Surely this has to be a disinformation ploy of some sort," countered Moore. "Or maybe OP-02 concocted this whole thing just to put us to the test."

Proctor solemnly shook his head. "You have it right from me that OP-02 is just as perplexed by this entire incident as any of us are. And the only disinformation that's being deliberately released is that story about *Lewis and Clark* being overdue off the coast of Florida. And from what I understand, the decision to make this cock-'n-bull story public came right from the White House."

"But why lie to the American people?" retorted Moore. "Sooner or later, the stories are bound to get out, and then what are we going to do?"

"Come off it, Thomas. We can't just sit back and tell the world that we've got a nuclear-powered submarine that's unexplainably traveled halfway around the world overnight, and has proceeded to lose every member of its crew except one along the way. We'd have a panic on our hands that could create disastrous consequences."

"I guess you're right," reflected Moore.

"You're damn right I am. And until we can figure out what happened out there, all of us can only pray that we can keep the lid on this thing."

Inwardly, Moore had been hoping that Command was going to have some sort of rational answer for him. But now he realized the truth in his CO's response, and that Rear Admiral Proctor was relying on him for the answers.

"In my entire thirty years of service, this one takes the cake for weirdness, Thomas. Because whatever happened to the *Lewis and Clark,* that wasn't the only strange thing that came down that day. At about the same time that the sub was reported overdue, an American Airlines 747 flying from San Francisco to Tokyo arrived in Japan four hours early, and that was into a headwind!"

"Could these incidents be related?" asked Moore, clearly disturbed by the strange direction in which the investigation was now heading.

"Before I attempt to answer that, Thomas, let me share with you yet another enigma, that we learned about only this morning. Shortly before that 747 touched down at Narita, the world's largest radio telescope, at Arecibo, Puerto Rico, monitored what seemed to be a powerful burst of undecipherable radio activity originating from somewhere in the Bahamas. This electromagnetic disturbance lasted less than thirty seconds, and was directed into deep space, towards the distant star cluster Cygnus X-1, where the nearest black hole to earth supposedly lies."

Moore was now completely confused. "I'm sorry if I sound dense, but what does all of this mean?"

Proctor sat forward, his tone firm. "Apologies on your part aren't necessary, Thomas. This thing has stumped all of us, and only the computer has offered a semirational explanation so far. Do you know much about black holes in space?"

"I'm afraid my knowledge of the cosmos is limited to basic celestial navigation," answered Moore.

"Well, no matter, because all you need to know is

130

that a black hole is a sort of cosmic bottomless pit which appears to swallow up any unfortunate object that comes along, distorting the space-time continuum along the way. The only substantial theory that the computer has to offer so far, is that a black hole somehow struck the earth, in the general area of the Bahamas, and in the process, altered the *Lewis and Clark*'s electromagnetic composition, subsequently pulling it through the core of the earth, and depositing it in the Pacific. The 747's early arrival was one of the aftereffects of this bizarre stellar collision, though there's still no explanation of what happened to the submarine's crew."

"That's a wild one, Admiral," observed Moore. "And I expect any minute now that you'll be telling me that it's a UFO that could be responsible, or even the Bermuda Triangle for that matter."

"I understand your skepticism, Thomas. And I've got to admit that the Black Hole theory is even a little too much for me to swallow. And in an effort to bring this whole thing back to earth, I've been working all morning on my very own hypothesis, that I believe is substantially more plausible. If you'll just bear with me, I'd like to show you a portion of a presentation that I'm preparing for a National Security Council meeting to be held later this afternoon."

Proctor utilized a remote-control switch to dim the lights and lower a white screen on the wall facing them. From a wall-mounted slide projector, the screen filled with a picture of a sleek, ocean-going ship, with a streamlined prow and a single funnel located amidships. It was Proctor who provided the commentary.

"This ship is the Soviet oceanographic vessel, *Academician Petrovsky*. It was originally launched in 1990, to provide the fleet with acoustic and hydrographic information. To accomplish this task, it's been outfitted with a first-class suite of sensors, and even has an interior moonpool capable of launching a variety of small manned minisubs and ROV's. Four and a half weeks ago, it left its home port on the Baltic sea, and after brief stops in Scandinavia and the U.K., set sail for New York, where it picked up a team of United Nations observers for its current mission as primary support ship for the Mir underwater habitat program."

Proctor readdressed the remote control switch, and the screen filled with an artist's rendering of the Mir habitat.

"I'm certain that you've read all the press accounts of the habitat program, Thomas. You're also aware that it was placed in its current location, off the northeastern coast of Andros island regardless of our most strenuous objections. As far as the U.S. Navy was concerned, it was just too close to our Tongue of the Ocean underwater test facility, where *Lewis and Clark* was bound to when we originally lost contact with her."

The next slide showed a tall, square-shouldered Soviet naval officer, with a distinctive patch covering his left eye. Again it was Proctor who identified him.

"This is Admiral Igor Valerian, CO of the *Academician Petrovsky*. At sixty-seven years of age, Valerian is a decorated veteran of World War II. He's also an outspoken hardliner, with strong Party ties. Of course, my suspicions were immediately aroused when I learned that the Soviets had made Valerian the ship's commanding officer. Having skippered everything from a helicopter cruiser to a nuclear submarine, a mere oceanographic vessel seemed a bit out of his league."

The next picture on the screen showed a white-haired old man. He was dressed in the clothes of a civilian, and was captured from a distance chopping wood.

"This is a rare shot of Dr. Andrei Petrov, the famed Soviet physicist, who five years ago was fired from his position at the Kirov Polytechnic Institute, and forcefully sent into exile in the Ural foothills. Petrov is known as a brilliant theoretician, in the vein of Albert Einstein. Like Einstein's, his main body of work concerned the basic properties of matter. Most of Petrov's early experiments revolved around the relation of electromagnetism to gravity. And he was said to be working on a device that could influence the basic composition of matter through magnetic resonance. In other words, make material objects invisible."

"Hold on a minute, Admiral," interrupted Moore. "This is starting to sound like science fiction once again."

Proctor was anticipating such a remark and quickly responded to it. "Don't forget that less than forty years ago, the mere idea of putting a man on the moon, or having him live on the sea floor would have been greeted with equal skepticism. So just hang in there, Thomas, and try to keep an open mind—because, as you're about to learn, the U.S. Navy has conducted its own experiments in the so-called field of antimatter, that began over five decades ago."

The next slide showed Albert Einstein seated in his study, with two uniformed U.S. Navy officers close beside him. Proctor cleared his throat and continued.

"In 1940 Einstein and Rudolph Ladenberg first proposed using strong electromagnetic fields to counter mines and torpedoes. The Navy officially put Einstein to work on May 31, 1943. He was employed as a scientific consultant for the Bureau of Ordnance and the Navy office of Scientific Research and Development.

"Given the exclusive use of a destroyer to conduct his initial experiments on, Einstein was attempting to utilize pulsating energy fields to produce electromagnetic camouflage. Yet the famed scientist was to get much more than he bargained for."

The slide of Einstein was replaced by one showing a single, World War II era destroyer, and Proctor went on: "This is the USS *Eldridge*. While at port in the Philadelphia naval yard, Einstein and his team installed a series of pulsating and nonpulsating magnetic generators aboard the ship. Much like modern-day degaussers, which we use to neutralize a ship's magnetic signature, these generators were pulsed at specific resonant frequencies to create a powerful magnetic field around the *Eldridge*. And much to everyone's surprise, the destroyer seemed momentarily to vanish in a light green mist. A later experiment with a more powerful magnetic field produced even more drastic results. And it was rumored, though never officially verified, that the *Eldridge* disappeared from its berth in Philadelphia, and was instantaneously transferred to Norfolk, where a sister device had been positioned."

"I've heard of the so-called Philadelphia Experiment, Admiral," revealed Moore. "But I always considered it the product of someone's overactive imagination. Are you saying that the *Eldridge* was actually rendered invisible, and then teleported to Norfolk?"

"That I am, Thomas," returned Proctor curtly.

"But what does this have to do with the *Lewis and Clark?*" asked Moore, his patience all but exhausted.

Proctor readdressed the remote control switch, and the screen once more filled with the photo of Dr. Andrei Petrov.

"I believe that the answer to your question lies with this man, Thomas. Since Einstein's death, he's become the world's foremost expert in the fields of electromagnetism and gravity. Much like Einstein, he feared that his revolutionary work would be misused by mankind, and he dared to speak out to warn the public. The Soviet government responded by forcing Petrov and his wife into exile.

"They have been living in forced seclusion for over five years now, with extremely restricted contact with the outside world. That was, until yesterday, when we learned that Andrei Petrov had been flown by helicopter to Kirov. There, a Soviet transport plane was waiting to fly him to Havana, where he was subsequently transferred via helicopter, to the deck of the *Academician Petrovsky*."

This surprising revelation hit home, and Moore alertly sat forward, as Proctor added:

"So now not only do we have a hard-line Russian fleet admiral as the CO of one of their most capable oceanographic research vessels, but one of their most brilliant physicists as well, all aboard the same ship. And to make matters even more interesting, is the fact that Petrov's daughter, Ivana, is currently living in the Mir underwater habitat, on the upper slopes of the Andros Trench. I don't have to remind you that this is almost precisely where the *Lewis and Clark* was supposed to be when we lost her, Thomas. Which leads me to believe that the Russians are somehow responsible for this whole confusing tragedy."

"Very interesting, Admiral," remarked Moore. "I've got to admit that it sure makes a hell of a lot more sense than that black-hole theory, even though I still find the idea of an antimatter device a bit hard to swallow. How do you propose that we continue with the investigation from this point?"

Most relieved that his hypothesis was not immediately shrugged off by Moore, Daniel Proctor answered him with a question.

"Ever embark on a 688 class attack sub before, Thomas?"

"I haven't had that pleasure, Admiral."

Proctor grinned. "Well, you're going to presently, son, because I'm ordering you to Norfolk. There COMSUBLANT will be providing you with your very own Los Angeles class attack sub to recreate the *Lewis and Clark*'s voyage up to the point where we lost them. To allow you unlimited surveillance of the Andros Trench, your 688 will be picking up the deep submergence rescue vehicle, *Avalon,* in Port Canaveral. My gut tells me that the Soviets are using the U.N. underwater habitat program as a cover, and I'm relying on you to verify my suspicions.

"To keep you busy on the flight down to Norfolk, I've got a file that I'd like you to take a look at. This top-secret report documents the only official U.S. Navy mention of Einstein's Philadelphia Experiment that I was able to put my hands on. It seems that when the Eldridge rematerialized in Norfolk, all hands below deck except one were inexplicably lost. An old friend in BUPERS was able to dig up a portion of the original medical report concerning this lone survivor."

"My God, that's just like what happened on the *Lewis and Clark!*" exclaimed the astounded junior investigator.

"You've got it," replied his superior, whose tone turned somber. "And by the way, Thomas, it's been decided to inform the families of *Lewis and Clark's* crew that the boat has been officially listed as missing at sea. We'll continue to stick to our story that the vessel was lost off the coast of Florida, with a press release from CHINFO to hit the wires later this afternoon."

Without waiting for a response to this, Proctor flicked off the slide projector and turned the room lights back on.

"Good luck with your sub ride," he said as he pushed his chair back and stood. "And for heaven's sake, don't go and disappear on me. This case is confusing enough as it is."

Eight

Mimi Slater had been waiting for them to arrive all day long. When the white U.S. Navy van finally pulled into the driveway, and the two uniformed officers solemnly climbed out, it was almost anticlimactic. She had inwardly known that her husband would never be coming home again from the first moment she heard the news report that the *Lewis and Clark* was missing, earlier that morning. And now true to custom, the U.S. Navy was taking the time to inform their own of the true extent of the tragedy that had befallen them.

Yet reality really hit home when they somberly informed her that Peter was officially listed as missing at sea. This meant that they had yet to find his body, or those of his shipmates for that matter. Being a submariner's wife, Mimi knew that if her husband was ever involved in a serious accident while on patrol, the chances were almost nil that his remains would ever be located. Such was the unforgiving nature of the elements he sailed beneath.

Though there was always the slimmest chance that the *Lewis and Clark* was not sunk, and that the crew

138

was still very much alive, Mimi didn't dare deceive herself. The arrival of the two officers at her door meant that all hope was forever lost, and to think otherwise was pure self-delusion.

She bravely accepted their sincere condolences, and stubbornly refused their offer of assistance. When they finally left, and she locked the door behind them, she found herself so numbed by shock that not even tears would fall. But all of this quickly changed when she returned to the living room, and spotted the familygram that she had received only yesterday.

The tears began welling up in her eyes when she reached for this single-page dispatch, which she had lovingly placed on top of the glass coffee table. Sent by her husband in honor of her thirty-seventh birthday, it had been initially received with the greatest of joy. Little did she ever realize at the time, that this would be her last communiqué from the man that she adoringly called Dutch.

She cried, reread the familygram, and wept once more. And thus went the coldest, loneliest day of her life.

Later that evening, she managed to drink some tea, and to call Tina Bressler, the wife of Peter's XO. Earlier in the summer, Tina had told Mimi that she was expecting their third child. And now this baby would have to grow up without its birth father.

As it turned out, Tina was too distraught to come to the phone, and after expressing her sympathy to Tina's mother, Mimi returned to the couch to continue her lonely vigil. It was well after midnight when she pulled out a photo album and began leafing through it. Since they had never been fortunate enough to have children, these pictures were all that remained of a glorious, twenty-year relationship.

She began in the back of the album, where the most recent photos had been placed. This series chronicled their summer trip to Catalina Island. One of Peter's submarine buddies, who was based out of San Diego, had lent them his twenty-eight-foot sailboat, and it was on this vessel that they crossed over to the island. The voyage itself was a great adventure, and she scanned the various shots of herself and Peter at the boat's helm, beside its mast, and inside the rather cramped cabin.

She fondly viewed a photo showing Catalina's Avalon harbor. They had arrived at dusk, and there was just enough light left for them to photograph the famed Casino, the Wrigley mansion, and the colorful collection of boats anchored before the quaint seaside village.

The next series of shots had been taken the following day, when they initiated their exploration of the island. They began with a hike up to the Wrigley Memorial, where William Wrigley Jr. of chewing-gum fame had been buried. A botanical garden had been planted beside the art-deco memorial tower, and Peter made certain to get pictures of the many unusual indigenous plants and cacti there.

Per the suggestion of a group of locals, they hiked up into the hills behind the memorial. Peter had taken several shots of Mimi as they climbed a trail high up onto a surrounding ridge. From this lofty vantage point, they could clearly see Avalon and the smog-enshrouded coast of Southern California, twenty-eight miles in the distance.

Yet it was in the opposite direction that a truly magnificent view of nearby San Clemente island was encountered. Peter tried to capture this vista with several photographs showing the sparkling channel of water separating the two islands. One of these pictures showed a sleek U.S. Navy cruiser. Of course, Peter was thrilled by this sighting, and explained in detail how the Navy used San Clemente as a weapons test-range.

It was as they prepared to return to Avalon, that she took a very special picture of her husband that she enlarged, framed, and placed on the mantel. She had caught him thoughtfully staring out to the sparkling blue waters of the Pacific. The sun had been directly behind her, and perfectly illuminated his ruggedly handsome face. His determined stare, blondish-brown hair, and sharply dimpled chin gave him additional character, and he could have easily passed for a middle-aged version of the actor Kirk Douglas. For the rest of her life, this would be how she would always picture Peter, so handsome, so curious, with the eyes of a poet and the heart of a silent warrior.

Finding herself close to breaking out into tears once more, she turned to the front of the album. The first photo had been taken on the night they met, almost twenty years ago. It was snapped inside the Naval Academy auditorium, and showed Mimi decked out as Minnie Mouse, and Peter dressed as a little Dutch boy. Somehow he had managed to see beyond her huge artificial mouse ears and erect whiskers, and as he always said, fell in love with her at first sight. Mimi was but an impressionable teenager at the time, and she found herself enchanted by the tall, dashing midshipman, who bravely limped around all evening in hand-carved

141

wooden shoes, that were much too narrow for his wide feet.

Quickly flipping through the pages of the album now, Mimi caught brief glances of spirited Navy football games, hay rides, sailing trips on the Chesapeake Bay, and other glimpses of their whirlwind romance, that abruptly ended when the two officers knocked on her door. And now to be left with only these snapshots, and memories of a love that could never be duplicated in this lifetime.

Mimi's grief found temporary solace when sleep finally overcame her. Without bothering even to undress, she stumbled into the bedroom and crawled beneath the comforter. She slept soundly at first, drained by sorrow and longing. Then dreams took her on another trip through her past, and she watched as Peter was commissioned, waved goodbye to him for the first time from the pier in Groton, and even enjoyed a canoe float trip with her parents, on the Buffalo river in her home state of Arkansas.

She awoke to the cold before the dawn, and stared out at the empty place on the bed beside her. Being a submariner's wife, she was used to sleeping alone for half the months of a year. But this was different — her beloved called on a patrol from which he'd never return.

Long drained of tears, she could only lie there and moan in silence. And again it was sleep that came and rescued her from her forlorn sorrow.

The sun was well into the morning sky when the ringing telephone awoke Mimi from her slumber. She didn't respond at first. But the ringing persisted, and to silence the incessant racket she reached out towards her nightstand and pulled the handset to her ear.

"Hello," she mumbled.

"Mrs. Slater?" said a scratchy, high-pitched female voice with a definite Brooklyn accent. "Is this Mrs. Peter Slater?"

"Who is this?" quizzed Mimi, still groggy from sleep.

"You don't know me, Mrs. Slater. I'm Dr. Elizabeth, and I have a message for you from Dutch."

This last word caught Mimi's full attention, and she bolted upright, with the phone nestled tightly to her ear. "Did you say, Dutch? Who is this?"

"Like I said, Mrs. Slater. I'm Dr. Elizabeth, and Dutch was the name of the fellow who asked me to contact you."

"Look, lady," spat Mimi. "I don't know what the hell your problem is, but I don't find this whole thing the least bit funny."

"Neither do I, Mouse," replied the caller, who sincerely added, "I don't blame you for being suspicious, hon. I'd feel the same way if I was in your place. And all I can ask of you is to at least hear me out. After all, this is long distance."

"How did you know to call me Mouse?" asked Mimi, her curiosity fully aroused. "And who told you about Dutch?"

"Why your husband, of course. Although we didn't communicate with each other as long as I would have liked, I believe he passed on enough information for me to convince you that I'm legit."

"And when did you speak to him?" questioned Mimi breathlessly.

"Although the initial contact took place several days

143

ago, our actual link wasn't finalized until just this morning."

"You spoke with Peter this morning!" exclaimed Mimi, her doubts all but forgotten.

"Easy does it, hon. Take a couple of deep breaths and listen closely to what I have to say. You see, I'm what you call a psychic healer. I'm a New Yorker, who just set up shop near Charleston, in my niece's place on the Isle of Palms. If you care to check my references, just give Geraldo, Oprah, or Sally Jesse a ring. They all know Dr. Elizabeth, as well as their millions of viewers. But that's another story, and this is costin' me sixty cents a minute as it is. Anyway, like I was sayin', your husband came to me while I was in trance, and asked me to let you know that he hopes all your champagne wishes and caviar dreams come true. Do the letters *CYK* mean anything to you, hon?"

Mimi's only reaction was startled silence, which prompted her caller to speak out quickly. "If you're still there, hon, I want you to know that I'm only passin' this info on as a public service. I ain't no charity, and I work solely on donations. Hon, are you there?"

"I'm . . . sorry," stuttered Mimi, who finally summoned the words to express herself. "But I can't help but think that this is all a sick joke of some sort."

"I understand, hon. It's only natural to feel that way. All I can tell you is to listen to your heart. And if you want to talk more, just call me for an appointment."

Not about to let this mysterious caller hang up without getting some additional information, and with nothing to lose, Mimi allowed her instincts to guide her reply. "Dr. Elizabeth, you've got to tell me more about Peter. Isle of Palms is less than an hour's drive from here. Can I see you this afternoon?"

"Hon, I seriously doubt that I could keep you away even if I had a full schedule, which I don't. So here's my address and telephone number. And if you can get your kiester into gear, I'll even throw in lunch with your reading, all for the same fifty-dollar donation."

Mimi's hand was excitedly shaking as she copied down the caller's address and phone number. When she finally hung up the telephone, she had the distinct impression that the woman that she had just talked to hadn't been real at all, but merely a figment of her imagination. And then doubt clouded her consciousness.

Surely this Dr. Elizabeth was only a slick opportunist, who had heard about the *Lewis and Clark* on the news, and was playing on Mimi's grief to make a quick buck. But if that was the case, how did she know about their familygram passwords? No one knew this code but Peter and herself. And besides, the dispatches themselves were sent via the same discreet, top-secret Navy channels over which operational orders were delivered. Overhearing such a broadcast would be all but impossible. That meant that she either somehow got a copy of the message from the censor's office, or was indeed a psychic like she said.

Though Mimi's rational mind cautioned her that Dr. Elizabeth was nothing but a fraud, her intuition urged her to check the woman out. On the recommendations of friends, Mimi had visited various psychics in the Charleston area several times before. In one instance, she even dragged Peter along. Though she never became an occult fanatic, she did read her horoscope everyday, and enjoyed having her tarot

145

cards, palm, and aura read from time to time.

Much of the advice that she got from these psychics was nothing but good old-fashioned common sense, delivered with a degree of poetic imagery. Yet sometimes they hit upon personal things that were revelations, and it was in these rare moments that Mimi was a true believer.

Until Dr. Elizabeth awoke her, she had never even considered contacting one of her local psychics to learn Peter's fate. And now that she had this opportunity practically thrown in her lap, she didn't dare walk away from it.

With a new sense of purpose guiding her onwards, she rolled out of bed and headed straight for the shower. She then dressed herself simply in jeans and a sweater, and with a bare minimum of make-up on her face, bravely headed into the outside world.

She had long since missed morning rush hour, and the drive to Isle of Palms was completed more quickly than she had anticipated. The weather was gorgeous, with a bright blue sky that seemed to darken as she came closer to the sea.

The address that Dr. Elizabeth had given her belonged to a quaint, English-style cottage, whose backyard merged into a wide sandy beach, with the crashing Atlantic the nearest neighbor. Strangely enough, she felt completely at ease here, experiencing none of the normal anxieties that would usually be generated when meeting a stranger in this manner. With her doubts all but forgotten, she anxiously walked up to the heavy oaken front door and knocked three times.

"Who's there?" asked a familiar, high-pitched voice from inside the house.

"It's Mimi Slater."

There was the dull clicking sound of a deadbolt being unlocked and a door swung open to reveal a short, overweight, white woman in her fifties. Her eyes were hidden by sunglasses, and she wore an abundance of pinkish red rouge on her cheeks, and matching lipstick that seemed to blend with the bright colors of her loose-fitting Hawaiian muumuu. On first appearance, she certainly seemed pleasant enough, though a bit of an eccentric all the same.

"Do come in, hon," she said with a warm smile. "My, you sure made good time getting over here. It seems like we just got off the phone."

The house was tastefully decorated, with a predominance of white wicker furniture and plenty of green plants. There was a good deal of antique marine paraphernalia hung on the walls, and it fit in perfectly with the wonderful ocean view from the adjoining screened-in porch.

"You can credit my niece for all the furnishings," said Dr. Elizabeth. "I always said that she would have made a great interior decorator."

"What does she do for a living?" questioned Mimi, who watched a large, black Persian cat emerge from the kitchen to check her out.

"She's a magazine travel writer of all things," answered Dr. Elizabeth. "That one should have been born with wings instead of legs. Right now, she's touring Asia, and won't be back until winter. So when she asked me to house-sit, how could I refuse? I'll tell ya, hon, this sure beats fightin' the crowds on the Upper West Side."

There was a hint of incense in the air, and Mimi could just hear the crashing surf in the distance.

"Please join me on the porch for some herb tea, hon. That's where I feel most comfortable doing my readings."

Mimi noted how her host pronounced the *h* in *herb* as in the man's name, and she couldn't help comparing her to the character of Minnie Castevets, in the movie version of Ira Levin's *Rosemary's Baby*. She vibrated a trusting innocence, that made Mimi feel as if she were visiting a long-lost aunt. With this impression in mind, she followed her to the porch, and sat down in one of two comfortable wicker rockers.

While Dr. Elizabeth went to get the tea, Mimi gazed out the room's massive, screened-in windows. The crashing sound of the surf was a bit more noticeable here, as well as the distinctive cries of the local sea birds. There wasn't a soul on the beach, where white sand was rippled into ridges tufted with green grass.

The cat made its presence known by gently rubbing up against Mimi's leg. It was one of the largest Persians that she had ever seen, and as Mimi bent over to scratch its head, she saw that it had strikingly clear blue eyes, that appeared almost ethereal.

"My, now that's certainly most unusual," observed Dr. Elizabeth as she arrived pushing a tea cart. "Usually Isis keeps well away from strangers."

"So your name's Isis," said Mimi, while continuing to stroke the Persian's silky fur mane. "That sure is an unusual name."

"Isis was a most revered Egyptian goddess," revealed Dr. Elizabeth. "She was the wife of

Osiris, the sun god."

Satisfied that the newly arrived human was a friend, Isis sauntered over to the screen to peer out at the circling gulls. This left Mimi's hands free to accept a delicate bone-china cup, filled with a steaming hot, light green liquid.

"I hope you enjoy this tea, hon. It's a combination of chamomile flowers, spearmint leaves, orange blossoms, and rosebuds. I blend it myself."

"Sounds wonderful," said Mimi, who took a sip from her cup and pleasingly nodded.

"You know, hon, I hated to have to call you out of the blue like I did, but I didn't have much of a choice in the matter. I've seen the news, and can just imagine what you're goin' through right now. But that's just another reason why I had to go and bother you."

"Please tell me about Peter, Dr. Elizabeth," pleaded Mimi. "Is he still alive? And if so, where is he?"

As the psychic settled down into the rocker beside her guest, she reached out and softly grasped Mimi's hand. "Hon, your husband contacted me from a place that he'll never be able to return from. But I can't really say that he's deceased. You see, he's been sent on a cosmic voyage, along with the rest of his crew, to a universe far from this solar system. And it was during this initial transfer that the entity contacted me and made me aware of their plight."

"I'm afraid that I don't understand," replied Mimi, with her slim hopes quickly fading. "You say Peter's not dead, but that he'll never be able to come back home. Then exactly where is he, and what in the world occurred to send him there?"

"My dear, your husband has been conveyed to a distant star, in the constellation Cygnus, the swan. The entity who guides me also comes from this far-off place, and it's from his lips that I learned of the capstone's activation."

"Capstone?" questioned Mimi, her tea completely forgotten.

"Hon, I can tell right off that you're no stranger to the psychic world. You've lived on this earth before, in many previous lives, all of which have contributed to the present high evolutionary state of your soul. In one of these reincarnations, you lived on the continent of Atlantis, so what I'm about to share with you will only be like a trip homeward.

"The great land of Atlantis once occupied a major portion of this earth, lying primarily in the area where today there lies nothing but ocean. Except for the accounts of Plato, details of the Atlantean civilization have been all but wiped from modern man's consciousness. And what a shame that is, because there's so much we could learn from Atlantis and apply today.

"Their advances in the arts and sciences easily outdistanced our current level of technology. This was primarily due to the fact that the Atlanteans were energy independent, having learned to harness the very forces that energize the universe. To tap this dynamic force, they built a pyramid with a specially designed crystal capstone, known as the Tuaoi Stone. Acting as a self-sustaining energy relay station, this pyramid was located in an area that's today known as the Tongue of the Ocean, between the Bahamian island of Andros and Nassau's New Providence Island.

"In brief, Atlantis fell apart because of a conflict between the forces of peace and those of war. This eternal struggle between good and evil reached its climax when a combination of natural and man-made disasters tore apart the Atlantean continent, with much of its landmass being sucked beneath the sea.

"This was the fate of the crystal capstone. Preprogrammed to activate when the heavens were properly aligned, the Tuaoi Stone continues to draw down the powers of the universe from its current position on the sea floor. Your husband's warship had the misfortune of passing over the remains of the pyramid at the exact moment that it was energizing. And it was in this manner that he and his crew were teleported to Cygnus, where they dwell in peace in the land of the Tuaoi entity."

Dr. Elizabeth appeared emotionally drained upon finishing this strange discourse. And as she sat back in her chair, she let go of Mimi's hand and momentarily closed her eyes. Beside her, Mimi's tear-filled gaze centered itself on the crashing surf. With all her hopes of ever again seeing her husband alive completely dashed, she contemplated the mystifying tale that she had just heard.

Once again, she found herself torn in two. Her rational side remained totally skeptical of mystical lost continents and crystal capstones that could magically convey one to the ends of the universe. But how could she account for the psychic's knowledge of the family-gram? This puzzling question, and her genuine trust and fondness for her host, overrode her inherent skepticism, and shaped the course of Mimi's response.

"Dr. Elizabeth, is it possible for you to recontact my husband?"

The psychic's voice seemed lacking its usual high-energy edge as she answered. "Now that he's settled in his new home, that would be very difficult, my dear. Our best chance for success would be to time this effort to coincide with the capstone's next activation."

"And when's that?" asked Mimi as she turned away from the sea to meet her host's warm smile.

"Hon, you really are a trouper, aren't you? I like that kind of spirit in a person, and I sure don't want to disappoint you. So, I'll tell ya what we can do, to guarantee success in contacting your Dutch. As fate would have it, our next window of opportunity is less than a week away, during the upcoming autumnal equinox. And to insure that my call to the entity gets through, I think it's best that we go right to the source. If you don't mind pickin' up the tab, a little trip to the Bahamas is just what the ole doc here needs so as to insure that our efforts aren't wasted."

Nine

To get the day started off properly, Lisa Tanner made certain to prepare a hearty breakfast. Back in New Zealand, this was a custom that her mother had passed on to her, and Lisa took it most seriously. Today's menu was no exception. She started off with thick Cream of Wheat. Then she served grapefruit sections and prunes, followed by blueberry waffles, bacon, and piping hot Irish breakfast tea, flavored with milk and honey.

Though space inside Starfish House was at a minimum, the designers had wisely paid special attention to the kitchen. Lisa had lived on her share of boats in the past, and her current galley was more than adequate. And how many kitchens could offer the spectacular view that she currently enjoyed?

As she stood by the sink, scrubbing clean the morning's pots and pans, she was able to gaze from a strategically placed porthole and catch sight of the many fascinating creatures that made the surrounding reef their home. Earlier in the morning, she spotted a family of brightly colored angel fish, several red-skinned snappers, a squirrel fish, and even a passing moray eel. Presently, her visitor was a familiar, six-foot-plus, narrow-bodied creature with large eyes, and a huge gaping jaw, that displayed a mouthful of razor-sharp teeth.

The barracuda, called Uncle Albert, seemed to know precisely when mealtime was over and the table scraps were to be gathered. The alert fish had initiated its unrelenting patrol just as Lisa began her cleanup. And back and forth it continuously swam, only inches from the kitchen porthole.

"That was a delicious breakfast, *mon amie,*" commented Pierre Lenclud behind her, in his deep voice.

As the Frenchman placed his plate in the sink, his gaze was also drawn to the porthole and their waterborne visitor. "You'd better do something about your friend out there, Lisa, before it goes and takes its frustrations out on one of us."

"Uncle Albert can sure be a real pest sometimes," she observed while gathering the remaining table scraps into a bowl. "But I guess that's the price we've got to pay to have our very own living garbage disposal."

"Back home in Rouen, where I grew up, we once had a pig that squealed its head off every evening after dinner. The only way my father could shut it up was to throw it the leftovers. *Mon amie,* it's funny how that technique never failed to do the trick."

As Lisa picked up the bowl of scraps and turned for the ready room, Ulge came flying into the kitchen and landed squarely on Lenclud's shoulder. The parrot peered down at Lisa, and in its best squawking voice, vented its curiosity.

"Awk, where ya goin'? Where ya goin'?"

"Come on, *mon petit,*" said Lenclud to Ulge. "Lisa's got her work to do, as we have ours. For we have a date in the library to begin the supply requisition. You wouldn't want me to forget to order your birdseed, would you, my fine feathered friend?"

Ulge didn't dare utter a word of protest, and Lenclud grinned and left Lisa with a warning. "Don't forget to watch those fingers out there, *mon amie.* This mission wouldn't be the same without your culinary magic."

Taking this as the compliment that it was meant to be, Lisa headed for the adjoining arm of Starfish House, where the diver's ready room was located. Ivana Petrov and Tomo were in the process of strapping on their scuba gear here, and Lisa barely paid them any attention as she put down the bowl of scraps and proceeded to zip off her coveralls. This revealed a lean, well-built body, covered by the briefest of bikinis. She reached out for a mask, rubbed some spit into its inner glass plate, then dumped the contents of the bowl into a mesh net, and walked over to the open hatch.

"Thanks for feeding Uncle Albert before we started to look appetizing to him," remarked the Russian, who was making final adjustments to her weight belt. "It's too bad you're the only one he'll accept food from, or we'd save you from getting wet."

"Actually, I sort of look forward to my morning dip," said Lisa. "Where are you two off to?"

"Tomo and I are headed for Habitat One to inventory supplies and do maintenance. Then while Tomo checks his aquafarm, I'm going to see how Karl Ivar is doing with *Misha.*"

Lisa responded to this while climbing down the ladder. "Please try to drag our hard-working Norwegian friend back for lunch, Dr. Petrov. He was up and out of here at the crack of dawn, long before I could even put the kettle on."

Lisa took a deep breath, and initiated the short climb down into the warm, soothing water below. With the net full of scraps firm in her grasp, she pulled herself up to the sharkproof grill that protected the hatch, and struck one of the tubular steel bars several times with the net's metal handle. This improvised chow call had immediate results. Uncle Albert came shooting over to the side of the grill, and Lisa wasted no time carefully emptying the contents of the net into the water before him. In a matter of seconds, the leftovers were history, and Lisa climbed back up through the hatch, barely winded.

"Can you imagine that ungrateful brute?" she said as she pulled herself out of the water and grabbed a towel. "He didn't even say thank you."

This remark caused the two divers to laugh, and it was Ivana Petrov who led the way into the water. "See you for lunch with Karl Ivar in tow, Comrade."

Once Ivana was through the hatch, the barracuda was nowhere to be seen, and she felt a bit more relaxed as she floated beside the habitat and made some final adjustments to her equipment. Tomo soon joined her, and together they slowly made their way to the onion-shaped dome positioned beside the similarly shaped, but larger hangar.

A collection of cables snaked out from the bottom hatch of this all-important structure. These life-support cables serviced both Starfish House and the hangar, and conveyed air, water, and power — all the vital elements that allowed the Mir habitat to be self-sufficient.

Ivana startled a group of spiny-finned wrasse that had been nibbling on the algae that was growing on one of Habitat One's telescopic legs. Tomo was a good distance behind her, inspecting one of the cables, and she took a moment to survey the coral clearing before climbing up into the dome's hatch.

Like yellow welcoming beacons, lights shined from Starfish House's portholes. A funnel-shaped column of exhaust bubbles shot out of the roof and rose to the surface, where the distinctive hull of the *Academician Petrovsky* could be seen bobbing in the distance. It was somewhat reassuring to know that this well-equipped support ship was near should they need help. But in another way, the gently rolling hull seemed to belong to an alien world that she was no longer part of.

A stingray gracefully swam by, followed by a school of fast-moving mullet. These were the rightful inhabitants of Ivana's present world, where humans were outsiders.

She suddenly felt small and insignificant, and wondered what her father would think of this amazing underwater world. It was because of him that she had become a scientist, and he had always been a source of support and inspiration.

How powerless she had felt when she learned that he had cancer. And then only months later, the state further tore apart his life, by forcing him to retire and sending him into exile, merely for expressing his opinion.

Whereas the human world could be cruel and unfair,

157

the sea seemed a far cleaner, more understanding place. Its laws were those of nature, where species killed not for political or economic gain, but for survival.

Her father had been a visionary in many ways. Just as he foresaw the very composition of matter, he also anticipated the demise of the party that had subjugated their homeland for too many years. Unfortunately, he spoke out before the transfer of power was completed, and lost the chance to participate in Russia's second revolution in a single century.

As soon as she completed her work with the habitat project, she promised herself that she would take the time to visit her parents. She had so much to share with them. And as she gazed out at the magical underwater world around her, she prayed that she could find the proper words to express herself.

It was Tomo's presence beside her that redirected her thoughts back to their current duty. Turning her gaze away from the clearing, she followed her co-worker up the ladder that led into Habitat One's interior.

The same compressed air that kept the water out of the dome's open hatch, allowed them to remove their air hoses and their scuba tanks. The muted hum of machinery greeted them, and Tomo switched on the main bank of overhead lights, illuminating the equipment from which this constant noise emanated.

"I'm going to check the gauges," informed Tomo. "Then I'll help you with the inventory, before we get on with the routine equipment maintenance."

"That's fine with me, Comrade," replied Ivana, as she followed a narrow latticed-steel catwalk past the electric generator. The energy produced by this powerful unit also ran the nearby hydrolysis unit, as well as the air compressor, which constantly pumped out a carefully monitored mixture of oxygen and helium.

She stopped beside the equipment locker, where the materials needed to maintain their life-support systems were stored. Because of space limitations, many of the substances kept there had to be continually restocked from above. Fuel to run the generator, oxygen, helium, and a variety of spare parts and fresh foodstuffs, had to be sent down from the *Academician Petrovsky* on a regular resupply schedule. Thus there was a limit to the extent of their self-sufficiency.

They envisioned a future underwater city that could run totally on its own resources. The Mir habitat was but a forerunner of such a futuristic ecosphere, that would grow its own food, synthesize its air from water, and tap the forces that determine the tides, in order to create the energy needed to sustain such an active community. This was the reality that Ivana was working for, and her hard work was a necessary precursor of things to come.

A clipboard with a pen attached to it hung from a nail, and Ivana picked it up and entered the date and time on the inventory sheet. She then stepped into the locker and began counting the various supplies that were stored here. She was well into this process, when Tomo joined her.

"Sorry that I took so long, Doctor. The pressure gauge on the air pump was registering in the red. The compressor itself was in the normal range, so my first guess was a stuck needle."

"Were you able to repair it?" asked Ivana, who had been in the midst of counting how many tanks of helium that they had left.

"That I was, Doctor, without even having to go to the tool box. It's amazing what a sharp, well-placed blow with your knuckles can fix these days."

The Russian chuckled. "Even with all this high-tech gear, the old-fashioned ways can often be the best."

"How's the supply situation, Doctor?"

Ivana recorded the results of her latest count before replying. "It looks like we're finally going to need machine oil, and a couple of extra tanks of helium. We might as well order some air filters while we're at it, and another water-purification test kit."

"Doctor," said Tomo. "If you'd like, I could finish the inventory and do the rest of the maintenance. I know that you're anxious to find out how Karl Ivar is getting along."

"I'd appreciate that, Comrade," returned Ivana, who wasted no time handing her co-worker the clipboard. "I guess my preoccupation with *Misha* shows."

"I know how much getting the minisub operational means to you, Doctor. I could just imagine what it would be like, if something happened, and I wouldn't be able to visit my aquafarm anymore. I'd be heartbroken."

"Thanks again, Comrade," she said as she turned for the catwalk. "As they say in America, I owe you one."

Less than five minutes later, she was entering the water once again, with her air tanks strapped securely to her back. With a quick flutter of her flippered feet, she began her way over to the hangar. Halfway to her goal, as she was passing over a massive, brain-shaped clump of coral, she spotted an unwelcome trio of eight-foot-long visitors swimming directly towards her from above. It only took a single look at the splash of white that colored their triangular dorsal fins to identify them as white-tipped sharks.

The white-tip was an aggressive species, that along with its cousin the great white shark, posed the greatest outward threat to man. It could not be taken for granted, and because it was obvious that the sharks had already classified her as potential food, she had to proceed with the utmost caution.

Armed with only a diver's utility knife, strapped to her calf in a plastic sheath, Ivana swam straight down to the clump of coral. She used the coral to protect her back, and looked on worriedly as the sharks continued to close in.

They were huge, evil-looking creatures, with dull gray skin that held several hitchhiking remoras. With instinctive cunning, they began circling the clump of coral in ever-tightening bands until Ivana could almost reach out and touch them. She felt a bit foolish as she reached down to pull out her knife. Doubting that she'd even be able to pierce their rawhide-tough skin, she knew that her only chance to scare them off would be a well-placed blow to the nose, eyes, or underbelly.

Commandant Lenclud had warned them about going out alone. But she had been impatient to find out how Karl Ivar was coming along so she failed to heed his advice, and now she was about to pay the ultimate price for her mistake.

The sharks seemed to sense that their prey was helpless. The largest of the threesome actually bumped Ivana with its tail, and then made a wide, sweeping turn, that signaled a final attack was imminent. With only seconds left to live, she wondered if she should try to make one valiant last effort to reach the hangar. Though it was less than fifteen yards away from her, there was no chance of her getting to it safely. She decided to make her final stand right where she was.

The largest of the sharks had completed its broad turn, and was now coming straight at her, meaning business. Ivana regrasped the knife in response, and was all set to use it, when a swift-moving, torpedo-shaped object came spiralling out of the depths and smacked into the shark's exposed underbelly. The stunned white-tip lay momentarily motionless in the water, and Ivana saw that her unlikely savior was none other than Dolly, the bottlenose dolphin.

Dolly used her snout to get the message across to the remaining sharks, and soon all of them were in the midst of a hasty retreat to safer waters. Ivana couldn't believe her good fortune. She held out her hands to hug Dolly, before following her protector to the shelter of the hangar.

She swam through the hatch and surfaced, with Dolly close at her side. Barely taking the time to yank the air hose from her mouth, she once more reached over to give the dolphin another hug. Dolly responded with an animated burst of whistles and clicks. This racket quickly gained the attention of Karl Ivar, who was seated beside the hatch, with a collection of loose parts surrounding him.

"Hey, what's all that noise about, Dolly?" complained the grinning Norwegian.

"Karl Ivar, you'll never believe what just happened out there," managed Ivana between breaths. "Dolly just saved me from a group of white-tips!"

"You don't say," he thoughtfully replied as he stood, helped Ivana out of the water, and directed his next remark to Dolly. "So my friend, you are good for something else than delivering the mail and eating mullet."

"I'll say she is," said Ivana, who accepted a plastic bucket from Karl Ivar. Several hand-sized mullets floated inside this container, and she pulled one out by its tail and gratefully fed it to Dolly.

"Dolly's been keeping me company all morning," revealed Karl Ivar. "Luckily for you, she decided to go out for a stroll. Otherwise, you might never have been here to witness *Misha's* rebirth."

This matter-of-fact comment caused an expectant smile to turn the corners of Ivana's mouth. "Does that mean that you've finally figured out a way to repair the diving saucer, Comrade?"

Karl Ivar returned her warm smile with one of his own. "I guess it does, though we won't know for certain until the adapter that I'm currently working on is completed."

"That's wonderful news, Comrade! Because like *Misha,* I too feel reborn, with this second chance to return to the depths of the Andros trench, and find out just where our mysterious roadway leads to."

Ivana Petrov would have had extra cause to celebrate, if she had known that her father was a mere sixty feet above her, in the wardroom of the *Academician Petrovsky*, studying a bathymetric chart of the same trench that she soon hoped to return to. With Admiral Igor Valerian anxiously peering over his shoulder, Andrei traced the rugged walls of the trench,

163

following it southward until it eventually merged into the black depths of the Tongue of the Ocean.

"The spot you picked seems suitable enough," said Andrei with a heavy sigh. "Though I still find it incredible that you had the audacity to try the device on an unsuspecting target. At the very least, you could have waited until the prototype was perfected."

"There was no time for such a luxury, Doctor," replied Valerian.

"You military types are always in such a mad rush," observed Andrei disgustedly. "And now look what it got you, absolutely nothing for all your efforts."

"I wouldn't exactly go that far, Doctor," said Valerian, his good eye gleaming.

Not certain what the silver-haired naval officer was referring to, Andrei looked up from the chart and watched as Valerian pulled a photograph from the file folder that he held. He then handed this snapshot to Andrei, who identified the subject matter as a single, surfaced submarine.

"She's the *Lewis and Clark,*" revealed Valerian. "Launched in 1964, this American Benjamin Franklin class vessel was recently retrofitted to carry sixteen Trident C-4 missiles. As you very well know, the Trident is accurate enough to have hard-kill capability. When one considers that each of these missiles can carry up to eight 100-kiloton MIRVed warheads, all of which are able to hit targets almost anywhere in the *rodina,* what you have pictured before you is a potent first-strike weapons platform of the most dangerous sort."

"So this is the unfortunate vessel that was your guinea pig," reflected the physicist.

"Unfortunate vessel?" repeated Valerian as if he

couldn't believe what he was hearing. "Open your eyes, Doctor! This warship has only one purpose, to strike our homeland a crippling preemptive blow, should the imperialists so desire."

"I hardly think that such a first strike would be in America's best interest anymore," offered Andrei, who handed the photograph back to Valerian. "But that's the subject of an entirely different argument. Right now, my only concern is that innocent submarine that you attacked without provocation. Does anyone know what happened to it?"

"All that we can say for certain, Doctor, is that it didn't end up in Vladivostok as we planned. The Americans have recently released a news story saying that the ship was lost with all hands off the coast of Florida, while on routine patrol. But we know that this is an utter fabrication. The U.S. Navy knew precisely where that sub was located when they lost contact with it, and so far, they haven't even bothered to send out a single rescue ship to scan the waters of the Andros trench."

"Then I wonder where in the world it could have ended up?" reflected Andrei, while searching his own mind for an answer to this question.

"As long as we have one less Yankee guided-missile submarine on patrol, that's all I really care about," said Valerian, who pulled yet another picture out of the file folder and handed it to his guest.

Andrei looked down at an artist's rendering of a submerged submarine with a torpedo shooting out of its bow tube. The vessel had a sleek, teardrop-shaped hull, with its hydroplanes protruding from the hull itself, and not out of the sail, as was customary

165

with the majority of American submarines.

"I don't believe that I've ever seen a vessel quite like this one before," admitted Andrei.

"Join the crowd," said Valerian with ever-rising passion. "For this is an artist's conception of SSN-21, or as it's better known, *Seawolf.* The first entirely new class of attack submarine in the U.S. fleet in over twenty years, *Seawolf's* sensors are reported to be over ten times as effective as those on its predecessor, the ever-capable 688 class. It also carries an incredible weapons load, and is outfitted with a newly designed reactor, and the state-of-the-art in computerized fire-control systems. When it sets sail on its maiden voyage, sometime in the next couple of weeks, *Seawolf* will be the most formidable undersea warship that the world has ever known.

"Our country's own naval architects hoped to field a submarine in the near future to compete with *Seawolf.* But the breakup of the Union and our grim economic situation make such an expensive R&D project virtually impossible. Thus the only way for us to get our hands on *Seawolf's* advanced technology is to borrow it. And to carry out this important task, the *rodina* is relying upon you, Andrei Segeyevich. For the sake of the continued safety of the homeland, you've got to help us fine-tune the device that your own genius invented over five decades ago. To do otherwise will guarantee the Americans complete domination of the seas for generations to come, an extremely dangerous situation that can't be allowed!"

Not appearing the least bit affected by Valerian's passionate plea, Andrei put down the picture on the wardroom table, immediately beside the open chart.

"So you want me to help you steal *Seawolf.* What makes you think that I could have any more success controlling the device than your own technicians?"

"Come now, Doctor. They are only flunkies. You're the mastermind behind the project, whose visionary genius will allow us to pull this thing off."

"And if I decide not to help you?" dared Andrei defiantly.

Valerian squared back his shoulders and answered directly. "Then not only would you be a traitor to your own people, but you'd be endangering the lives of the brave men and women who are currently living on the sea floor beneath us."

This comment caused a pained expression to cross the physicist's wrinkled face. "Are you trying to blackmail me, Admiral, by threatening to harm my daughter?"

"Why of course not, Doctor," replied Valerian, with the sincerity of a snake. "I was just thinking of what could happen to those aquanauts, if we tried to repair the device without you, and it were to malfunction once more. There's no telling what it could do to them."

The physicist suddenly looked very old, and very tired. "Extortion is the way of the criminal, Admiral. It's also a clear indicator of how very desperate you and your co-conspirators must truly be. If I were any younger, I'd fight to expose you with every means at my disposal. But I'm old and sick, and only want to live out what little remaining time I have left, with my loved ones beside me. Guarantee the safety of my Ivana, and I promise you that I'll do what I can to get the device functioning properly."

167

Taken aback by the ease with which Petrov capitulated, Valerian felt both relief and joy. "This is a decision that you will never regret, Comrade. Once our mission is successfully completed, you will be hailed not only as the savior of the Motherland, but also as the greatest scientific genius to walk this planet since Albert Einstein. Your place in history will be assured!"

Ten

Before leaving for Norfolk, Thomas Moore gratefully took Admiral Proctor's advice and returned home to get some badly needed rest. He slept soundly for a solid eight hours, and was even able to do a load of laundry before repacking his seabag and hiking across town to the nearest Metro stop. He arrived at National Airport ten minutes later, in plenty of time to catch the noon commuter flight.

The Boeing Canada Dash 7 dual turboprop was crowded with businessmen and military personnel, and Moore took a lone seat in the small plane's tail. Their scheduled flight time was an hour, and he waited until after takeoff before pulling out the large, flat envelope that his superior had given him to read.

The envelope had a Priority One security stamp on it, and had been pulled from the files of BUPERS. He was somewhat surprised when he broke its seal and pulled out an original copy of a seven-page report dated September 1, 1943. The paper was brittle and yellow with age, and appeared to have originated at the

Norfolk Naval Hospital, from the typewriter of Dr. Charles Kromer, the facility's chief of staff.

After declining the steward's offer of a drink, Moore sat back and carefully read the document, which consisted primarily of a patient interview conducted in the hospital's psychiatric ward. The patient was Petty Officer First Class Lewis Marvin, a machinist assigned to the destroyer USS *Eldridge*. Marvin had been admitted a week earlier, suffering from paranoid delusions, sleeplessness, and fits of abnormal behavior ranging from depression to uncontrollable rage.

Throughout the interview, he continually made veiled references to an experimental device that had been placed inside the *Eldridge*. When activated, this device made a loud humming noise. It also produced a greenish haze around the ship's waterline, for the supposed purpose of camouflaging the warship from the enemy.

Marvin swore that the device had a variety of harmful side effects. It made the crew edgy and nervous, and no one seemed to have an appetite when it was operational.

Yet things really got out of hand when the scientists running the experiment ordered Marvin and his men to prepare the device to accept a vastly increased power surge. A series of large electromagnetic generators were then moved onto the pier, until they all but surrounded the *Eldridge* on three sides. Marvin was ordered below deck at this point, and his memories of the confusing sequence of events that followed were hazy at best.

He remembered returning from the engine room

after his watch was completed, deciding to skip chow and head straight for his rack. Yet first he went to the head to shower, and that's when all hell broke loose. While he was rinsing the soap off his body, the ship began to vibrate wildly, until he had to make an effort merely to remain standing. Thinking that the *Eldridge* was about to explode, Marvin managed to exit the shower stall and that's when he saw one of his shipmates scream out in pained horror while being engulfed in a swirling, green, funnel-shaped cloud. Strangely enough, when this cloud finally dissipated several seconds later, his shipmate was nowhere to be found, and Marvin headed topside to find out what was going on.

Much to his utter amazement, as he climbed up onto the foredeck, he found his ship anchored beside a new pier. Several white-coated scientists stood on the wharf, excitedly pointing at him. And it was as they instructed him to join them ashore that he learned the most incredible fact of all. Somehow the *Eldridge* had been conveyed from its original berth at the Philadelphia Naval Yard to Norfolk, Virginia, in the time it took Marvin to finish his shower.

The document went on to list a detailed description of Petty Officer Marvin's physical and psychological ailments, that were mainly attributed to psychotic delusions caused by dementia praecox. It was recommended that this dangerous schizophrenic condition be treated by a number of powerful drugs, with the patient to be discharged from the Navy and immediately committed to the hospital's psycho ward.

Though the report never indicated if this drastic

course of treatment had been put into effect, Thomas Moore had no doubt that it had been. His instincts also warned him that the entire incident had all the earmarks of a government cover-up. Yet this would mean that the so-called Philadelphia experiment actually occurred, and that Albert Einstein's efforts had succeeded. Inwardly, Moore remained a skeptic. As far as he was concerned, a device that could render matter invisible and then teleport it hundreds of miles in seconds belonged in the realm of science fiction. And Moore was all set to dismiss the report as meaningless, except for a single disturbing revelation.

Petty Officer Marvin had been in the shower when the device was supposedly activated. He described a wild vibration, and then hearing his shipmates scream out in pained horror before disappearing. While under hypnosis, Seaman Homer Morgan had described a similar sequence of events aboard the *Lewis and Clark,* except that instead of being in the shower, the submariner had been covered by seawater, beside the TDU. Had the cover of water somehow protected both sailors from sharing their shipmates' fate? This certainly appeared to be the case, and Moore made a mental note to share this thought with Admiral Proctor in his next report.

There was a sudden pressure on his eardrums, signaling the plane's descent to Norfolk. Absently peering out the window, he caught sight of the city below. They were coming in from the east, and as they passed over the James river, he viewed the gleaming glass and steel buildings of the Waterside financial district, and beyond, the dockside loading cranes belonging to the Naval base. A number of grey-hulled warships could be seen docked there, two of them aircraft carriers. This would be where Moore's next means of transport awaited him, and he somewhat anxiously pulled his seatbelt tightly over his lap, in preparation for landing.

A cover of grey clouds had accompanied them for most of the flight. Yet as they touched down on the runway, the sun broke through, illuminating the modern terminal building and a thick grove of trees nearby. These trees belonged to Norfolk's botanical garden. On a past trip to the area, Moore's flight had been delayed and he had spent time exploring this gorgeous park, whose several hundred acres were dotted with sprawling lakes, sculpture gardens, and an abundance of native flowers and plants.

The airport itself was not nearly as crowded as National, and they readily proceeded to their gate. Because they had been flying on a turboprop commuter plane, they unloaded right out onto the tarmac. It was a warm afternoon, and Moore spotted a khaki-uniformed chief waiting beside the terminal building.

"Chief Hunter?" he asked this sailor, after securing his seabag from the collection of luggage pulled from the plane's cargo hold.

"Ah, you must be Commander Moore," replied the relieved chief, who was assigned to the base's public affairs office. "Welcome to Norfolk."

"Thanks, Chief," said Moore, who followed his escort through the terminal and into a white sedan with U.S. Navy plates.

It took a good quarter of an hour to reach the front

gates of Norfolk Naval base. Quite content that this trip took place with a minimum of conversation, Moore accepted the salute of a tough-looking Marine sentry who carefully eyed each of the car's occupants before allowing them entry.

"The base has just gone on a stage-two alert," informed the driver as they headed towards the pier area. "Scuttlebutt has it that we might be deploying a carrier group to the Med in response to the latest terrorist threat there."

Such rumors continually circulated on almost every military base worldwide, and Moore merely grunted in response, his attention focused on the large auxiliary ship that they were headed towards. He identified this vessel as they pulled into a parking lot beside the pier. He took one look at the assortment of black-hulled submarines moored in pairs beside this ship, and recognized it as the sub tender, USS *Hunley*.

"Thanks for the lift, Chief," said Moore, who reached into the back seat and grabbed his seabag.

"Enjoy your visit, sir," returned the senior enlisted man.

Moore left the confines of the automobile, and before walking out onto the pier where the subs were moored, had to pass through another security check, protected by a steel barrier. This time he had to show his military I.D. in order to gain entrance to one of the most restricted areas on the entire base.

The dock was crowded with supplies and personnel. He found the vessel that he was looking for moored at the very end of the pier, beside a somewhat smaller 637 class vessel. Moore's stomach nervously tightened as he climbed onto the Sturgeon class vessel, then proceeded over an adjoining gangway, with a banner identifying the submarine as the USS *Hyman G. Rickover.*

An alert sailor holding an M-15 rifle stood at the end of the gangway, and Moore addressed the moustached sailor stationed at the adjoining watch stand.

"I'm Commander Thomas Moore."

"Welcome aboard the *Rickover,* sir. I'm Chief Ellwood, the boat's COB. If you'll just let me have a look at your orders, we'll get you checked in and headed below deck."

Moore pulled out his orders, and watched as the chief of the boat, or COB for short, read them, then checked his name off a clipboard-held roster.

"Do you know your way around a 688, sir?" asked the COB.

"I'm afraid not. This will be my first embark," answered Moore directly.

"No matter," returned the chief of the boat. "I'll have Petty Officer Lacey here escort you below deck and get you settled."

A tall, lanky, dark-haired sailor stepped forward, and grabbed Moore's seabag. He then led the way around the boat's sail, and over to the forward access trunk.

"Just follow me, sir, down into the wardroom," said the brown-eyed youngster.

"What's your specialty aboard the *Rickover,* son," asked Moore, who took one last look at the sky above.

"I'm a senior sonar tech, sir. When my team's on

watch, you're always welcome to join us in the house of pain."

"House of pain?" repeated Moore.

Lacey smiled. "That's what we call the sonar shack, sir. Come visit us and you'll see why."

"I'll do that," returned Moore, who followed his personable escort down a ladder, into the dark innards of the sub.

The distinctive odor of amine met his nostrils. This ammonia derivative was used in the ship's air scrubbers, and Moore remembered the familiar scent from his days spent servicing boomers in Holy Loch.

The ladder led him to a narrow interior corridor. Looking forward, Moore could just see several men gathered inside the control room. His guide led him in the opposite direction, down a stairway, and further aft into a long hallway. They passed a small copy machine, a paper shredder, and a bulletin board where the plan of the day was displayed. Chief Lacey beckoned to the left, towards the wardroom. The door to this compartment was open, and one person sat at its large, rectangular table.

"Doc, where should I stow Commander Moore's gear?" asked the senior sonar technician.

The boat's corpsman looked up from the report that he had been reading. "Bunk two in the nine-man berth," he answered, while taking a look at their newly arrived guest, and adding. "Hi, I'm HM1 Johnson, but you can just call me Doc, like everyone else on board. Please have a seat, sir, while I give you your TLD and a patch to keep you from getting seasick."

The TLD turned out to be a small, grey plastic do-

176

simeter that Moore was instructed to hook on his belt. This device would be checked at the conclusion of his cruise, and would determine if he had been exposed to any ionizing radiation.

Moore knew that it was extremely unlikely that he'd be exposed to any radiation while aboard the *Rickover*. America's nuclear submarines had been painstakingly designed, with the crew's safety a primary factor. The face of the man responsible for this costly effort, stared back at him from a plaque on the wardroom wall.

Admiral Hyman G. Rickover, the boat's namesake, was the father of America's nuclear navy. For sixty-three years, he served his country with distinction. Through his untiring efforts, *Nautilus* put to sea on January 17, 1955. For the next three decades, Rickover applied the lessons learned from the world's first nuclear-powered submarine, resulting in a radically new generation of undersea warships. His skillful technical direction, foresight, and unrelenting perseverance allowed the United States to attain a preeminence in the field of naval nuclear propulsion. Moore had never had the honor of meeting Rickover, whose legacy was visible in the form of one of the most technically advanced warships ever to sail beneath the seas.

With his TLD firmly hooked onto his belt and the circular medicated patch stuck behind his right ear, Moore was given a quick tour. Immediately outside the wardroom were the officers' quarters. He was shown the head that he would be using, and got a lesson on flushing the toilet and using the shower's water restrictor. His berth was off an adjoining corridor, on the way to the crew's mess. This cramped, dimly lit compartment held three tiers of three bunks apiece. His bunk was immediately inside the sliding doorway, on the middle level. A fluorescent light was situated above the sole pillow. Doubting that he'd be able to turn over in such a tight space, he stowed away his personal belongings in a small metal locker at the foot of the bed. He then lifted up the mattress, revealing the compressed space reserved for the rest of his clothes.

Just as he finished unpacking, a solidly built, blond-haired officer dressed in blue coveralls entered and introduced himself.

"Commander Moore, I'm Lieutenant Hopkins, the boat's supply officer. Please feel free to call me Hop."

"Pleased to meet you," replied Moore, who was instantly set at ease by the supply officer's warm smile.

"I understand that this is your first submarine embark, sir. I've taken the liberty of putting together a welcome-aboard packet for you. It contains a brief history of the *Rickover,* a schematic plan of its layout, our meal schedule, and a list of officers and petty officers."

"I appreciate that," replied Moore, as he took possession of a grey folder with the *Rickover*'s imprint on it's cover.

"The captain sends his regards, sir. And he has invited you to join him topside on the sail as soon as we're underway."

"And when will that be?" asked Moore.

Hop looked at his watch and answered, "We should be casting off any minute now. Why don't we proceed to the control room, so that I can introduce you to some of the other officers?"

Moore followed Hop to the deck above. The control room was abuzz with activity. No bigger than a small garage, the compartment was packed with equipment and men. He took a moment to familiarize himself with this important portion of the boat.

In the center of the room were the dual periscope wells. They were mounted into a slightly elevated platform, where the officer of the deck usually operated. From this vantage point, the OOD had an unobstructed view of the helm to his left. It was here that the two planesmen were seated, along with the diving officer and the chief of the watch.

On the other side of the compartment was the fire-control console, with a narrow doorway leading directly into sonar. While the navigation plot occupied the back portion of the room.

True to his word, Hop introduced Moore to several of the *Rickover*'s officers. The investigator met Lieutenant Roger Taylor, the boat's slightly built, bespectacled navigator, who looked more like a scholar than an undersea warrior. The current OOD was Lieutenant Douglas Clark, a short-haired, intense-looking redhead. Lieutenant John Carr was the weapons officer. Known as Weaps for short, Carr was a ruggedly handsome blond from Laguna Beach, California, where he practically grew up on a surfboard.

The atmosphere inside the control room seemed to intensify when the COB entered and took a seat between the helmsmen. With an almost theatrical flair, he took a fat cigar out of his pocket and lit it.

"COB always lights up a stogie before we set sail," informed Hop. "It guarantees us good luck."

"I'm all for that," said Moore, who had to reach up for a handhold when the deck lurched sideways.

"We're on our way," said Hop. "Why don't I go grab you a jacket before you go topside and join the captain. It can get awfully chilly up there."

Five minutes later, Moore was climbing up the sail's interior ladder. During this steep ascent, he passed by a sailor — with a sound-powered telephone around his neck — he was stationed inside the accessway in the event of an emergency. A rush of cool air whistled past as Moore somewhat awkwardly made his way to a narrow opening cut in the top portion of the sail. Two men wearing bright orange submergence suits were stationed there, focused on the view visible through a small, wraparound plexiglass windshield. Before the newcomer could introduce himself, a deep, bass voice boomed out from above.

"Commander Moore, why don't you join me up here?"

A firm hand guided him further upwards, until he was standing on top of the sail itself. A detachable tubular steel enclosure extended as far back as the raised periscopes. While holding onto this rail for balance, he joined the other three men stationed there. All were dressed in orange survival suits. One of them wore a sound-powered telephone, while his shipmate readied a pair of binoculars.

"Some view, isn't it?" said the deep-voiced, broad-shouldered sailor who stood between them.

Moore cautiously looked up and scanned the portion of the channel visible before them. The *Rickover* was already underway under its own power. With the water surging over its rounded bow, the sub was transiting Hampton Roads, on the way to the open ocean. The piers of the Navy base were passing on the right, and Moore spotted several warships, including an Aegis class cruiser and one of the new Arleigh Burke class guided-missile destroyers. They passed by a trio of Gator freighters, and the two aircraft carriers that Moore had spotted earlier from the air.

"I'm Captain John Walden," said the deep-voiced officer who had invited Moore to his current perch. "Welcome aboard my ship."

"Thank you, Captain," managed Moore as he gazed out at the massive square stern of the USS *America*. The crew of the carrier were topside, in the midst of an inspection, and Moore found himself speechless.

"That's a sight I'll never tire of," said the *Rickover*'s commanding officer.

Thomas Moore nodded, then redirected his line of sight back to the channel. A cool wind whipped at his face, and he was thankful for the jacket and gloves that the supply officer had provided.

"I hope that you were able to get settled into your new quarters all right," remarked Walden. "I know that they're not much, but space on this boat is at a premium right now. I even have a couple of junior officers hot-bunking."

"I'll be just fine, Captain," returned Moore.

A huge container ship passed them, on its way in from sea, and Moore watched as the *Rickover* carefully maneuvered itself into the center of the main channel. As the phone talker constantly called out the latest sounding, the Hampton Roads Bridge Tunnel gradually took form in the distance. The Captain waited until several small fishing trawlers were safely out of the way before ordering an increase in speed. When this directive was finally relayed, the three-hundred-and-sixty-foot-long vessel wasted no time gaining momentum. A white bubbling wake spewed out from the sub's single propeller, and all too soon the forward portion of the deck was awash as a result of this increased velocity.

"I understand that you're with the NIS," said Walden discreetly. "And that this is your first submarine embark."

"You've got it, Captain. And to tell you the truth, I'm still not certain just why I'm here."

"Join the crowd, Commander. My orders are just as sketchy. We're currently on our way to Port Canaveral, to pick up the DSRV *Avalon*. Then we'll be heading to the Tongue of the Ocean. My hunch says that this deployment has something to do with the loss of the *Lewis and Clark*."

Thomas Moore had full authority to share the exact purpose of his mission with the *Rickover*'s CO, yet he decided to wait for a more opportune moment before saying any more about it. Standing silently on the sail, he allowed his thoughts to wander to the passing scenery. The sea had a calming effect on him, and before he knew it, they were crossing over the Hampton Roads tunnel and turning due eastward to penetrate the Chesapeake Bay bridge.

A pair of air-cushioned landing craft sped by, on

their way to the nearby Little Creek naval amphibious base. In the distance, a Sea Stallion helicopter could be seen pulling a seaborne mine countermeasure sled. Because this proved to be the extent of the surface traffic, the *Rickover* was able to proceed at speed, and the sun was just beginning to be covered by an advancing bank of clouds as they crossed over the Chesapeake Bay tunnel.

The cold was all too noticeable as they prepared to round Cape Henry and enter the open Atlantic. Yet before Moore could excuse himself and return below deck, one of the lookouts pointed out an approaching submarine. It was extremely hard to see at first, its sleek profile almost indistinguishable from the watery horizon.

With the assistance of the captain's binoculars, Moore got a clear view of this vessel. It had a bulged casing on its stern, so he mistook it for a DSRV at first. The lookout identified the sub as the USS *John Marshall,* an Ethan Allen class boat, which was originally designed to carry ballistic missiles. Reconverted to hold special forces, the *John Marshall* was the ultimate in stealthy, clandestine operations delivery platforms, that could transport SEALs and their equipment to the far reaches of the planet.

"Prepare to give honors," instructed Walden.

As the *John Marshall* continued its approach, one of the *Rickover's* lookouts put a whistle to his lips. Moore joined his shipmates as they turned towards the passing sub and stiffened at attention. The sailors gathered on the *Marshall's* sail did likewise, and with the American flag blowing from both vessels' portable

183

mastheads, the whistle was sounded and both crews saluted.

This centuries-old Navy tradition had a strange effect on Thomas Moore, and his chest swelled with pride. In that inspirational moment, it was all so clear. One submarine was replacing the other, in defense of God and country, on a watch that never ended.

Only when the *John Marshall* had all but disappeared on the western horizon, did Moore excuse himself to return below deck. The control room crew was busy preparing the *Rickover* to submerge, and he took this opportunity to return to his bunk and lie down.

It took a bit of effort to climb up onto the thin mattress. As it turned out, there was just enough room for him to turn over on his back. He pulled the curtain shut, snapped off the overhead light, and found himself tucked inside a dark, cozy cocoon, the perfect environment in which to clear his mind and sort out his thoughts.

He was headed on a journey into the unknown, to investigate one of the most perplexing nautical mysteries of all times. What would they find beneath the waters of the Tongue of the Ocean? And would they ever be able to explain how the *Lewis and Clark* had been transported halfway around the world almost instantly? Was a man-made device indeed responsible for this amazing feat of teleportation? Or was it caused by a cosmic force beyond their comprehension? Having no idea what waited for them, Thomas Moore allowed the gentle rocking motion of the *Rickover*'s hull to lull him to sleep.

A gentle hand on his shoulder woke him from this

deep slumber. Momentarily disoriented, he looked out into the eyes of the supply officer.

"Sorry to bother you, sir," said Hop softly. "But we're just about at the one-hundred-fathom line, and I didn't think that you wanted to miss seeing your first dive."

"Thanks, Hop," returned Moore, who yawned, then looked down at his watch. "Do you mean to say that I've been out for over seven hours?" added the surprised investigator.

"That you have, sir," returned Hop. "You can blame it on that patch Doc gave you. Why I bet your mouth's as dry as cotton."

"As a matter of fact, Hop, it is," admitted Moore.

The supply officer wisely grinned. "We'll stop off in the wardroom and get you some joe. You slept right through the evening meal, but we'll be serving MIDRATS at 2300. And by the way, sir. I took the liberty of pulling you a poop suit. While on patrol, this is the uniform of the day. I believe that I got the size right."

Hop handed Moore a folded set of blue coveralls, that had a *Hyman G. Rickover* patch on the right shoulder, and an embroidered set of golden submarine dolphins above the left pocket.

"Those dolphins are compliments of the captain," added Hop.

Moore genuinely appreciated this gift, and wasted no time stripping off his khakis and pulling on the one-piece coveralls.

"The size is perfect, Hop."

"Now you're lookin' more like a submariner, except for just one more item."

Hop pulled out a dark blue *Rickover* ball cap. "Wear it in good health, sir."

Thus attired, Moore followed Hop into the nearby wardroom. Both of them filled up mugs of coffee before continuing on to the control room by way of the galley accessway.

The compartment was rigged for black, to protect the crew's night vision, and it took several minutes for Moore's eyes to adjust to the dim red light. His first stop was beside the navigation plot, where a brawny, moustached chief was bent over a detailed bathymetric chart, marking their current position with the help of ruler and pencil. It was Hop who led Moore around the plot, to a vacant space on the right-hand side of the compartment, beside the fire-control console. From this vantage point, Moore had an unobstructed view of the control-room crew in action.

There was a noticeable tenseness in the air as the crew prepared the boat to submerge. Orchestrating this effort, from the elevated platform beside the periscope well, was the sub's captain. Walden briefly acknowledged Moore's presence with a serious nod, before turning his attention back to the helm. The *Rickover*'s CO appeared to be in his late thirties. He was a handsome man of slight build, with jet black hair and dark eyes to match. With his hands stuffed inside the pockets of his coveralls, he anxiously paced to and fro, constantly alert to the updates being relayed to him by his junior officers and chiefs.

Most of the action seemed centered around the diving console, where the chief of the watch made the final adjustments to the boat's trim. The two planesmen sat to his right, with the COB acting as the current diving officer. True to form, Chief Ellwood had a fat cigar between his lips. With practiced ease, he scanned the assortment of red-lit dials and gauges before him.

Only after the test sounding was relayed, did the captain speak out with an authoritative tone. "Dive the boat. Make your depth sixty-five feet at two-thirds speed."

"Six-five feet at two-thirds speed, aye, sir," repeated the helmsman, who alertly pushed forward on his steering yoke.

There was a slight downward angle on the bow as the *Rickover* initiated its descent. Reaching up for a handhold to brace himself, Moore watched the two officers who currently manned the periscopes. Ever alert for any surface traffic, they continuously turned their scopes in quick circular sweeps.

"Fifty feet . . . Fifty-five feet," reported the diving officer between puffs of his cigar.

They attained their ordered depth seconds later, and the relaxed voice of the sonar officer boomed out from the intercom.

"Conn, sonar, we have a surface contact bearing two-three-five. Classify Sierra eleven, merchant."

Both of the officers manning the scopes immediately turned them in an effort to spot this vessel. Their efforts were unsuccessful, and the *Rickover*'s CO called out forcefully.

"Down scopes. Make your depth one hundred and fifty feet."

"One-five-zero feet, aye, sir," said the helmsman.

The bow angled further downwards, and once again Moore reached up to steady himself. The sub was in its intended medium now, no longer influenced by the sway of the waves above.

To test that all was properly stowed away, the captain initiated a maneuver called angles and dangles. Taking Hop's advice to brace himself, Moore widened his stance and regripped the ceiling-mounted, tubular steel bar that encircled the periscope well. As it turned out, he was glad he did so because they were soon in the midst of a steeply angled dive. There was the sound of crashing debris in an adjoining compartment, and Moore found himself abruptly pulled forward.

Barely allowing the sub to level out after reaching depth, the captain ordered them back up to one hundred and fifty feet. This time Moore's body was thrown backwards, and once again there was a crashing sound outside the control room.

While in the midst of this sharply angled ascent, a tall, moustached man with short brown hair managed to enter the compartment from the forward accessway. The boat's Executive Officer, Lieutenant Commander Rich Laycob, wasted no time reporting in.

"The stowage locker in your stateroom snapped open, Captain. Your textbooks are all over the place."

"I thought the chief was supposed to repair that locker," replied Walden, clearly upset.

The XO made a note in a small pad that he pulled from his breast pocket, as Walden turned back towards the helm. This time he ordered the engine room to answer to a wide variety of bells ranging from two-thirds speed, to standard, full, and flank. This last bell demonstrated the sub's top speed, that was attained regardless of noisy propeller cavitation.

An all-stop command caused the knot gauge to begin a sharp decrease, and Walden followed it up with yet another flank bell. This time, as the *Rickover* shot through the water, he ordered a series of tight, snap-roll turns. Like a jet fighter, the sub canted over hard on its side, completing turns ranging from fifteen to thirty degrees. This was the most impressive maneuver of all, and Moore had a new respect for the *Rickover's* capabilities as the drill was completed.

"Well, Commander Moore, what do ya think?" asked Hop, who had remained right alongside him during the entire sequence.

"The only word that comes to mind is awesome," replied Moore.

"I guess that says it all, sir," said Hop proudly. "Because nobody will be able to catch the *Rickover* once we get a bone in our teeth."

"I hope you're right," returned Moore, who inwardly wondered if they would have to soon put this boast to a real test.

Unbeknown to the crew of the USS *Hyman G. Rickover*, another submarine was silently hovering in the water, seven hundred and fifty feet beneath them. The *Pantera* was the lead ship of the newest class of Russian nuclear-powered attack vessels. Crammed within it's 360-foot-long double hull were a state-of-the-art liquid-metal-cooled reactor and the latest in sensors and weapons, all primarily designed for a single task — to hunt down other submarines.

For an entire week, *Pantera* had been tracking the USS *John Marshall* as it returned from an extended deployment in the Mediterranean. Relatively easy to follow because of the racket produced by its externally mounted swimmer delivery hangar, the special operations submarine led them practically right into the mouth of Hampton Roads, and the Norfolk Navy base. Forced to break off their pursuit at the hundred-fathom line, *Pantera* was awaiting new orders, when sonar reported a submerged contact approaching from the west.

Captain Alexander Litvinov was in the wardroom finishing his evening meal of beef stroganoff and pickled beets, when word arrived of this new contact. One of the youngest commanding officers in the Russian fleet, Litvinov reacted to this news with an expectant grin, and eagerly pushed away his plate and stood, to join his senior sonar technician in the attack center.

Seated to the young captain's left was the boat's *zampolit,* Boris Dubrinin. The portly, middle-aged political officer certainly didn't share Litvinov's enthusiastic zeal, especially at mealtime. Yet ever-true to his duty, he swallowed a last creamy mouthful of noodles and stood to follow the captain through the forward accessway.

The attack center was located amidships, directly beneath the boat's elongated sail. A hushed, tense atmosphere prevailed there, only to be further intensified by the arrival of the two senior officers, who headed straight for the sonar console.

"What have you got, Misha?" asked Litvinov to the

bearded sailor seated before the broad band CRT screen.

Senior Sonarman Mikhail Petrokov lifted up one of his headphones and excitedly answered. "I believe we've tagged an American attack sub, sir!"

"You don't say," returned the surprised CO.

The sonarman pointed towards the waterfall display visible on his monitor screen. "At first I thought it was nothing but a biological. But the closer it came, the more it appeared to be a transient."

The captain reached for an auxiliary set of headphones and listened for the sounds currently being conveyed by their passive sensors. First to meet his ears were the incessant chattering cries of the shrimp. Closing his eyes to focus his concentration, he could just make out a distant pulsating surge, which showed up on the CRT screen as a jagged white line broadcasting on a single-frequency band.

"I hear it, Misha!" revealed Litvinov as he opened his eyes wide. "I believe it is another submarine."

"So what's so surprising about that, Comrade?" asked the dour-faced *zampolit*. "Both of you sound as if you're astounded that our sonar is capable of doing its job."

"Locating another submerged submarine is never an easy task," responded the captain. "This is especially the case when it comes to tracking the American Trident and 688 class vessels."

"Captain," interrupted the senior sonar technician, "I believe I can get a screw count on them. Then if we can stay within range, I should be able to determine

191

precisely what sub it is that we've managed to chance upon."

"As you very well know, determining the exact signatures of America's submarine fleet is a number-one priority of ours," said Litvinov. "Therefore, we shall do our best to remain in this vessel's baffles for as long as possible."

The *zampolit* pulled out a wrinkled handkerchief from his pocket, and patted dry the thin sheen of sweat that had gathered on his forehead, before somberly expressing himself. "I still think that all of you are overrating the capabilities of the U.S. Navy's submarines. A decade ago I might have agreed with you that the Yankees were fielding the superior ships. But today we've more than caught up with them, as our sleek panther here so rightly proves. Thus it's not mere chance that precipitated this contact, but the effectiveness of a new generation of Russian-designed sensors."

Though he was prepared to contradict, Alexander Litvinov wisely held his tongue. He was certainly in no mood for arguments with the stubborn likes of their political officer. And besides, now he had more important things to do, like silently engaging their engines and plotting this new pursuit.

Eleven

Dr. Andrei Petrov felt tired and drained of all energy. Ever since arriving on the *Academician Petrovsky* he had been seasick, and his nausea persisted regardless of what medication the ship's physician tried. Adding to his discomfort was the intense tropical heat. The humidity never seemed to slacken, and the sweat poured out of his overheated body, making his clothing damp and uncomfortable. Sleep proved all but impossible, and his appetite was limited to quenching a thirst that he could never seem to satisfy.

To make matters even worse, Admiral Valerian was constantly badgering him. The one-eyed naval officer thought nothing of disturbing him in the middle of the night, to ask the most foolish questions. Because he still feared for his daughter's life, the physicist didn't dare incur Valerian's wrath. He thus answered Valerian the best he could, and prayed that the man would honor his side of their bargain.

Andrei spent his first full day of work studying a thick stack of blueprints. These mechanical drawings showed the manner in which the teleportation device had been designed and constructed. Though the theory appeared sound, he questioned the adequacy of the power source, and with Admiral Valerian close at his side, he was given authority to enter the ship's reactor compartment.

A small, water-cooled nuclear reactor had been placed in an auxiliary compartment beside the moonpool. It was of similar design to the reactors used in space, and much to his surprise, he found it producing sufficient power to run the series of submerged, electromagnetic generators that lined the trench below. Satisfied that this wasn't the cause of the malfunction, he returned to the control room, to begin an intensive check of the operational system's software. This was a time-consuming process, and Andrei often worked late into the night, with a computer keyboard and monitor screen his only companions.

He had just completed an exhausting twelve-hour-long analysis of the device's magnetic flux. Satisfied by what he uncovered, Andrei refilled his thermos with cold water, and walked out onto the boat's fantail in an effort to clear his mind and get some fresh air.

It was well after midnight, and the temperature was still in the mid-eighties. A dank, humid wind blew in from the east, and Andrei stretched his sore back and peered up into the star-filled heavens. It was while tracing Orion's belt that he heard a deep, resonant voice break from the shadows.

"For someone who has grown up knowing the fresh, cool pine-scented breezes of the taiga, this place is a godforsaken hellhole," bitterly reflected Admiral Igor Valerian.

A hand broke from the nearby darkness where these words originated, holding a liter bottle filled with a clear, white liquid.

"Here, try some of this," Valerian added. "It's guaranteed to quench a dry throat and fill your heart with fond pictures of the motherland."

Andrei took the bottle, and sniffed its contents. The familiar scent of clove-flavored vodka filled his nostrils. Well aware that this was his Anna's favorite drink, he put the bottle to his lips and swallowed a healthy mouthful. The spicy liquor coursed down his throat and filled his belly with a fiery warmth that momentarily calmed his queasiness.

"This nectar is our only contact with the *rodina*," said Valerian as he stepped from the shadows and took the bottle from Andrei. "It proves that the gulf that separates us is not so great after all."

Valerian's breath was heavy with alcohol, yet he displayed none of the outward signs of drunkenness as he walked over to Andrei's side and took a swig from the bottle. The physicist waved off his offer for another drink, prompting an emotional outburst on the part of Valerian.

"What's the matter, Doctor? When a fellow countryman offers you his bottle, he's sharing his life's blood!"

"I appreciate the offer," replied Andrei a bit sheepishly. "But I'm really not feeling all that good."

"Then vodka is just what the doctor ordered," returned the veteran, who softened his tone upon sensing the seriousness of his guest's physical discomfort.

"I understand from our medical officer that you're having trouble sleeping and are experiencing a serious loss of appetite," added Valerian with an almost brotherly concern. "You must get your rest, Comrade, and feed yourself to keep up your strength."

"I never was much of an eater," replied Andrei as he turned his gaze back to the sparkling heavens. "And as for sleep, an hour or two is all I really need to keep going."

"Your work habits are most impressive, Doctor. So tell me, how did today's analysis go?"

Andrei hesitated a moment before responding. "As far as I can tell, the software program appears to have been installed properly. That means the problem has to lie with the generators themselves."

"I feared that would be the case," returned Valerian. "Can they be repaired without conveying the equipment back to the surface?"

"That depends on the location of the fault. The only way to find out for certain is for me to go down there and personally inspect the equipment."

"Then let's get on with it, Doctor. I can have our diving saucers ready to descend within the hour. Have you ever travelled into the depths on a minisub, Comrade?"

Andrei shook his head that he hadn't, and Valerian continued. "Well then, you're in for a great adventure. As a scientist, I'm sure you'll find the experience most enlightening. It's just too bad that because of security

196

concerns, we can't allow you to drop in and visit your daughter."

The mere mention of Ivana caused Andrei's spirits to lighten. "You know, sometimes I almost forget that she's only sixty feet away from me. Though for that matter, she might as well be on the moon."

"All of us are proud of her achievements, Doctor. She is a shining example to the world of the type of brilliant scientist the *rodina* is capable of producing. Without her presence down below, this entire mission wouldn't be possible."

There was a bitterness in Andrei's tone as he responded to this comment. "If only Ivana knew that you were using the Mir habitat program as a cover for a military operation. Knowledge of such a thing would sicken her."

"Can you be so sure, Doctor?" retorted Valerian. "After all, she is a loyal citizen of the *rodina*. As such, she's most aware that it was because of military might that our country has been free from the sword of the invader for the past five decades. One has only to look at history to know that this hasn't always been the case. Thus for her own children to grow up in peace and prosperity, this mission is an absolute necessity."

"I just pray that something doesn't go wrong, and that the Americans do not learn of our duplicity," said Andrei. "Such a discovery would most likely lead to the very war that you're so worried about getting involved in."

"And that's why we decided to call you in, Doctor, so that such a horrible thing won't happen. So let's get moving. Time is of the essence, and there is yet much work to be completed if our efforts are to be successful."

With heavy step, Andrei returned to his stateroom to prepare for his underwater excursion. He took a cool shower, then changed into some dry clothing. On the way to the moonpool, he stopped in the galley for a sandwich and some tea. Anxious now to solve the problem that he had been called halfway around the world to attend to, he continued aft, to the rectangular pool of water lying within the ship's inner hull. Igor Valerian waited for him here, along with a young, blond-haired naval officer, wearing the blue-and-white striped tunic of the *spetsnaz*.

"Dr. Petrov," greeted Valerian. "I'd like to meet your driver, Lieutenant Yuri Antonov."

Andrei accepted the commando's firm handshake and looked down at the pair of diving saucers floating beside the catwalk. The vessels were painted bright yellow, and were outfitted with an articulated manipulator arm and a dual set of bow-mounted mercury-vapor spotlights.

"I understand that this will be your first trip in a submersible," said Antonov to his passenger. "Have no fear, Comrade. Though a bit cramped for space, our saucers are perfectly safe and in tip-top operational order."

"That's certainly reassuring to hear," replied Andrei, who was beginning to have second thoughts about this entire excursion.

Quick to sense the physicist's misgivings, Valerian

stepped to the moonpool's edge and pointed towards the lead saucer's open hatch. "Shall we get on with it, Comrades?"

With a light, deft step, Yuri Antonov stepped down onto the saucer's upper hull. Andrei followed, quick to grab the commando's hand when the minisub began bobbing beneath them.

"Take good care of our very special guest, Lieutenant," offered Valerian.

Responding to this lighthearted comment with a salute, Antonov carefully guided the white-haired scientist over to the hatch.

"Follow me," he instructed as he proceeded to climb down into the narrow opening.

Andrei did as he was directed, and before disappearing into the saucer's dimly lit interior, he took a last look at Admiral Valerian.

"May your journey be a successful one," offered the one-eyed mariner with a wave.

Andrei nodded and continued with his short climb downwards. Following his escort's lead, he lay down prone on an elevated mattress, occupying the right portion of the saucer. Antonov was positioned to his left, with a steel ballast tank between them.

The commando addressed the switches and dials of the control panel. As the oxygen recirculation system was started up, a jet of cool air blew down from the ceiling. The echo sounder began operating with a monotonous ping, and Andrei's gaze was drawn to his individual porthole when the spotlights activated with a loud click.

"Alpha Two, this is Alpha One, do you read me?" questioned Antonov into a miniature chin-mounted microphone.

"Alpha One, this is Alpha Two. We copy you loud and clear," a static-free male voice announced from an elevated intercom speaker.

"Very good, Alpha Two," replied Antonov. "I am rigged for dive and ready to descend."

"We'll be right behind you, Alpha One," returned the amplified voice.

Yuri Antonov took a deep breath and looked to his right. "Here we go, Doctor. Are you comfortable?"

"I'll be fine, young man," answered Andrei.

"Doctor, I'm going to need you to pull down that series of three levers situated to the right of your port-hole. Please begin with the one closest to me."

Andrei did as instructed, and the saucer filled with the gurgling sound of onrushing ballast. There was a sinking sensation, and as the minisub's water jet engines activated with a muted growl, the rounded bow angled downwards. A curtain of bubbles veiled the view from his porthole at first. But soon this disturbance cleared away, affording him an unobstructed view of the sea below.

They were racing into the depths now, with their mercury-vapor spotlights cutting a golden swath through the black waters. With his anxieties forgotten, Andrei peered out in wonder at the passing vista. They cut through a virtual wall of translucent jellyfish, their long ghostly tendrils billowing in the current. A curious sea turtle swam by, followed by a school of quick-moving mackerel. This was indeed a magical world, and the old-timer understood why his daughter had been drawn to making the seas her exclusive study.

Displaying an almost uncanny intuition, his blond-haired driver expressed himself while making a slight adjustment to the external hydraulic piston maneuvering jets. "The admiral tells me that your daughter is Dr. Ivana Petrov. I had the honor of meeting her last month, when the team of aquanauts arrived to transfer down to the Mir habitat. She seemed like quite an interesting lady."

"That she is," replied Andrei proudly. "Have you gotten a chance to visit the team since then?"

"No, I haven't, Doctor. One of the conditions of the U.N. charter is that we stay away from the habitat area except for emergencies. And I'm happy to say that so far, we haven't been needed."

"How have you managed to keep your operation from the team of United Nations observers aboard the *Academician Petrovsky?*" asked Andrei. "It would seem that one of them would be bound to stumble upon the machinery needed to control the teleportation device sooner or later."

"Actually, it's been quite simple to deceive them, Doctor. The reactor room, and all below-deck spaces aft of the galley have been placed off limits. So far, the observers have been content to go about their business, with absolutely no suspicions whatsoever."

A cloudy layer of swirling sediment suddenly veiled the view from the porthole, and it was Antonov who alertly identified it. "That's the deep scattering layer,

201

sir. It's over thirty feet thick, and is comprised of microorganisms that rise towards the surface with nightfall."

"I've heard of such a thing from my daughter. She described it as a vast pasture of plankton, and now I know why."

At a depth of four hundred and ten feet, Andrei was instructed once more to pull down one of the ballast levers. The added weight was needed to carry them through the denser, cooler waters making up the lower portion of the thermocline.

"Alpha Two, this is Alpha One, how do you read me, over?"

Antonov's hail generated a crystal clear response from the saucer that followed in their baffles. Content to sit back and enjoy this once-in-a-lifetime experience, Andrei focused his line of sight out the porthole. A trio of huge groupers swam by, as well as a graceful, fan-shaped manta ray.

They finally reached bottom at a depth of nine hundred and seventy-six feet. The other diving saucer made a rendezvous with them at this point, and side by side they proceeded due south, down the gently sloping floor of the Andros Trench.

Andrei spotted what appeared to be a fractured rock roadway embedded in the sediment of the sea floor. Of course, such a structure had to have been constructed by the hands of mother nature. Yet he carefully followed its meander all the same, as they continued their descent to a broad shelf of rock.

From the cover of this formation, Antonov angled

the spotlights downwards, illuminating two thick rubber cables that extended from the blackness above.

"The generators are positioned below this shelf," explained Antonov. "This is the narrowest portion of the trench, and any vessel wishing to transit into the Tongue of the Ocean has to pass this spot."

"You must have had quite a job transferring the equipment into these depths, Lieutenant."

"That we did, sir. We depended solely on the saucer's articulated manipulator arms to transfer and connect the components. Altogether, it took us over one hundred trips to complete."

"I congratulate you on your dedication," remarked Andrei. "And so that your tireless efforts will not be in vain, let's begin our inspection at the power cable coupling. Then we'll initiate a low-level test to determine if the magnetic field is properly resonating."

It was with the greatest of anticipation that Ivana followed Karl Ivar down into *Misha*'s hatch. They had spent most of the day reassembling the parts that the Norwegian had worked hard to redesign. Stopping only for a quick dinner, the team returned to the hangar to complete the job. It was well after midnight when the last part was snapped into place. A quick test showed that the batteries were holding their charge, prompting Ivana to accept Karl Ivar's invitation to accompany him on a test run.

After several days of frustrating inaction, it was good to be under way once again. Karl Ivar was at the helm as they left the hangar and streaked over the coral clearing where the habitat was situated. From her porthole, Ivana could see the yellow lights glowing from inside Starfish House, and the long tendril of bubbles rising from the domed roof of Habitat One.

A variety of colorful fish darted past their spotlights, as Karl Ivar guided *Misha* towards deeper water. Only when their echo sounder showed them directly over the Andros Trench, did the Norwegian initiate a series of steeply angled, high-speed turns. With his eyes never leaving the voltage meter, he opened the throttle wide, then closed it until they were travelling at a bare crawl.

"So far, so good," said the Norwegian in his usual curt manner.

"You're an absolute mechanical genius, Comrade," complimented Ivana. "I seriously doubted that I'd ever be able to reinitiate my exploration of that road network."

"If you'd like, why don't we continue this test run on the floor of the trench," offered Karl Ivar. "Our charge remains strong, and that's as good a place as any to monitor the success of our repairs."

"I'm willing if you are," replied Ivana, an expectant grin covering her face.

Without further ado, Karl Ivar pushed forward on the joystick, and *Misha*'s bow angled sharply downwards. A hushed silence prevailed as they sliced through the deep scattering layer and penetrated the thermocline. Confident in her pilot's abilities, Ivana worked the ballast levers as ordered, and spent the rest of her time gazing out the porthole. It seemed to take only seconds to complete their dive, and soon *Misha's* spotlights illuminated a familiar pattern of fractured stones lying on the trench's bottom.

"We're lucky that the sediment hasn't shifted," remarked Ivana. "Now the big question remains, how far south does this network extend?"

"Shall we find out?" returned the Norwegian, who briefly glanced over at his passenger and playfully winked.

The depth gauge dropped below nine hundred and eighty feet, as Karl Ivar guided *Misha* further down the sloping gradient. The jagged walls of the trench that lay on each side of them were veiled by the black void that persisted beyond the meager illumination of their spotlights. The side-scanning sonar unit allowed them to skim the sea floor at full throttle, without the fear of collision.

Amazingly enough, the stone roadway continued to lead them on an unerring course, due southward. Though several portions of the thoroughfare were covered by sand and mud, for the most part it was clear of debris.

Ivana couldn't believe their good fortune, and there was no doubt in her mind that this pathway had to have been laid by the hands of an ancient people. With the faint hope that it would lead them to an archaeological find of vast proportions, she looked on as Karl Ivar alertly pulled back on the throttle.

"Sonar shows an obstacle ahead," he explained as

the diving saucer slowed to a bare quarter knot of forward speed.

"I'll redirect the spotlight and see if I can illuminate it," volunteered Ivana.

Thirty seconds passed before her efforts paid off. Strewn on the sea floor before them were dozens of immense boulders. They nearly covered the portion of roadway on the sea floor below.

"This debris appears to have fallen from the walls of the trench," theorized Ivana. "It must have been deposited here during a seaquake."

Karl Ivar cautiously guided *Misha* through this jumbled maze of jagged rock. Once on the other side of the debris field, the road was again visible, and they continued following it, all the way to a broad rock shelf. The trench appeared to drop off abruptly, and Karl Ivar disengaged the throttle and inched *Misha* forward utilizing the saucer's thrusters.

It proved to be the Norwegian who first spotted the alien lights glowing from the depths on the far side of the rock shelf. Instinctively, he reached up to switch off their own spotlights, and then guided *Misha* gently to the smooth rock bottom.

"What ever is the matter, Karl Ivar?" questioned the confused Russian.

"We've got company!" he breathlessly revealed.

Following the direction of his pointed right index finger, Ivana scooted over to peer out his porthole. And it was then that she too saw the flickering pinpoints of light in the distance.

"But that's impossible!" she protested. *"Misha*

206

is the only vessel capable of exploring these depths."

"Think again," retorted the Norwegian, who watched as an exact duplicate of *Misha* was momentarily illuminated by the lights of yet another diving saucer.

Ivana also spotted the bright yellow minisub, which all too soon disappeared behind the distant walls of the trench.

"Those are the diving saucers from the *Academician Petrovsky!*" she exclaimed. "But I thought that they were supposed to be inoperable."

"Maybe those new parts arrived from Russia after all," offered Karl Ivar.

"Not a chance, Comrade. And even if they did, Admiral Valerian should at the very least have informed us of this fact. I wonder what they're doing down there."

"Shall we go and see?" asked the Norwegian.

With her suspicions aroused, Ivana guardedly responded. "Can you maneuver us in such a manner that we can check them out without being seen ourselves?"

"I believe that's well within the realm of possibility," returned Karl Ivar, who readdressed the joystick, while slightly adjusting their trim.

Without the assistance of its spotlights, *Misha* crept forward. The side-scanning sonar unit allowed them to proceed in this clandestine manner, until they were at the very edge of the drop-off itself. Approximately fifty feet below them, the two diving saucers could be seen hovering before a flat wall of rock. One of the minisubs was in the process of using its articulated manipulator arm to work on a large piece of machinery that was positioned on the rocky shelf. A pair of thick black cables was attached to this piece of equipment. The cables appeared to extend all the way up to the surface, and it was Ivana who voiced her concern for both of them.

"Something is not right here, Karl Ivar. The U.N. charter that we're currently operating under, guarantees us the exclusive use of these waters. The *Academician Petrovsky*'s diving saucers were only to be utilized in the event of an emergency aboard the habitat. Thus they have no business being here."

"Do you want me to try to get us closer, Doctor?"

"No, Karl Ivar, I've seen enough already. Let's return to the hangar and inform the others. I believe that this is one case when discretion is definitely the best policy."

The trip back to the habitat seemed to take an eternity. During the entire ascent, Ivana's thoughts remained focused on the sighting that they had just witnessed.

She knew enough about the man who was ultimately responsible for the deployment of the diving saucers to have reasons for her suspicions. Admiral Igor Valerian had been a strange choice to command the *Academician Petrovsky* from the very beginning. He was a veteran cold warrior, whose hard-line leanings were well known, and he was nothing but an anachronism. She wouldn't put it past him and his twisted cronies to try to use the habitat program as a cover for a clandestine military operation of some kind, though she didn't have the slightest idea what the operation could be.

Having lived under the shadow of such paranoid doubts and fears for most of her life, Ivana could only pray that there was a logical explanation. But until she learned otherwise, she would proceed with the utmost caution. This was a survival tactic that her father had taught her, after his own life was ruined by those cold-hearted Communist ideologies in the vein of Igor Valerian. Such dangerous men belonged to the Russia of the past. Responsible for the slaughter of untold millions of innocent persons, they were anathema to the spirit of humanity. Though she had hoped that their day was over, the evil had followed her even here, to the floor of the Atlantic. Yet this time, she would be ready for them.

They returned to the hangar without further incident, and after stowing away *Misha,* they hastily donned their air tanks for the short swim back to Starfish House. Even though it was well past midnight, all of their fellow teammates were waiting for them in the habitat's central dining room.

"Mon Dieu," worriedly greeted Pierre Lenclud as they stepped out of the ready room. "When you didn't return from your trial run, we thought that something horrible had happened to you."

"I'm sorry that we were the cause of any concern," replied Ivana. "But when we found *Misha* operating perfectly, we decided to return to the bottom of the trench and continue exploring the roadway."

"I was hoping that would be the case," returned the relieved Frenchman.

"Did you find the front gates to Atlantis?" asked Lisa Tanner in a lighthearted manner.

Ivana shook her head. "No, Comrade, we didn't find the fabled lost city, though we did make a discovery that has much more immediate significance."

Pausing for a moment, Ivana scanned the faces of her rapt audience before continuing. "While tracing the road network beyond our previous survey point, we came upon a precipitous drop-off, that appears to funnel directly into the Tongue of the Ocean. It was Karl Ivar who first spotted the lights belonging to another underwater submersible here. He wisely switched off our own spotlights before we were discovered, and it became apparent that a pair of vessels were working the walls of the trench before us."

"What kind of vessels, and where could they have come from?" interrupted Lenclud.

The Russian took a deep breath and directly answered him. "The two submersibles that we discovered were exact duplicates of *Misha,* meaning that they had to have originated from our support ship, the *Academician Petrovsky.*"

"But I thought that the saucer fleet was grounded until spare parts were flown in from Russia," interjected Lisa Tanner.

"That's indeed what we were led to believe," said Ivana. "But now we know differently."

"I wonder what such a thing could mean?" reflected Lenclud.

"I'd like to know exactly what they were doing down there in the first place?" offered Tomo.

Karl Ivar stepped forward and voiced himself. "It looked to me that they were working on some sort of heavy equipment that had been previously positioned alongside the walls of the trench."

"Heavy equipment, you say?" quizzed Lenclud.

"That's right, Commandant," answered Ivana. "We caught them working on this machinery with their articulated manipulator arms, and we even spotted what appeared to be a dual power cable extending to the surface."

"Now that is interesting," said Lenclud, who stood and began pacing. "The *Academician Petrovsky's* sole purpose is to act as our support ship. Because this machinery that you discovered is in no way related to the habitat program, what we have here is a flagrant violation of the U.N. agreement under which we operate."

"I feared just such a thing when I learned that Admiral Igor Valerian had been assigned to command the *Academician Petrovsky,*" remarked Ivana. "He's much too experienced for such a routine assignment."

"But what could they be doing down there?" asked Lisa Tanner.

"That's immaterial," replied Lenclud. "They have no authority to launch those diving saucers, unless the purpose is directly related to the mission of this habitat."

"And since it isn't," continued Ivana. "I'd say that Admiral Valerian is involved in a little extracurricular activity that most likely has military implications."

"Is there any way to stop them?" questioned Lisa.

Lenclud thoughtfully stroked his chin before answering her. "Since it would be much too dangerous to return to the site with *Misha,* our safest course is to inform Dr. Sorkin, the head of the United Nations observer team aboard the *Academician Petrovsky.* He will be in the best position to find out precisely what those saucers were doing down there."

"If you'd like, I'll draft the letter," volunteered Lisa. "Dr. Sorkin is a personal friend of my family. He's also from Auckland, and is not the type of chap who's easily deceived."

"Very well, *mon amie,*" replied Lenclud. "Begin this letter at once, and we'll have Dolly deliver it with the morning mail."

Senior Lieutenant Viktor Ilyich Alexandrov routinely began his morning watch with a comprehensive walk-through of the ship. His tour of inspection started in the *Academician Petrovsky's* engine room. The vessel's diesel-electric drive, single-shaft engine had seen little use since arriving in the Bahamas. While at anchor, the 3,600 shaft-horsepower engine was used solely to operate the ship's thrusters, and power its electrical and life-support systems.

So that the engine-room crew would have something other than routine maintenance to do, Alexandrov had ordered them to clean and paint their compartment. This unpopular directive was initially received with the usual moans of complaint, but as loyal Russian sailors, his men eventually buckled down and got on with their duty.

212

The results were noticeable as the senior lieutenant entered the engine room and scanned its interior. The bulkheads shone like new, with a coat of fresh white paint, and even the engine was wiped clean of grease and grime. Making a mental note to pass on a job-well-done to the *michman,* Alexandrov headed forward, to the adjoining reactor room.

To gain access to this restricted portion of the ship, he had to input his security code into a bulkhead-mounted keypad. Once this series was properly keyed in, the door slid open. He quickly entered, and the portal was sealed shut behind him.

A single white-smocked technician currently sat behind the central control panel. Before him was a complicated assortment of dials, gauges, digital readout counters, and switches. Alexandrov could see from the temperature gauge that the reactor wasn't critical. To bring it on line, all the operator would have to do was trigger one of the compact pistol switches that were directly connected to the control rods. As the rods were slowly removed, the uranium-235 fuel elements would begin interacting, causing the coolant to be heated. The resulting steam would then power the turbine, creating an abundance of power to operate the series of magnetic generators placed on the sea floor beneath them.

"How are you doing this morning, Comrade?" asked Alexandrov.

"Fine, sir," returned the reactor operator as he recorded the assortment of data visible on the console in a log book.

213

"I understand that you were on duty during last night's low-level test," continued Alexandrov. "Did all go smoothly?"

"That it did, sir. During the entire sequence, we generated barely a tenth of the power that we're capable of producing. Were the results satisfactory?"

"Dr. Petrov is still working to determine the actual results," revealed Alexandrov. "So stand by. There's a good chance that we'll have to repeat the test, sometime this afternoon."

The technician nodded and returned to his log, while Alexandrov exited by way of the forward hatchway. This brought him directly onto the catwalk that surrounded the moonpool. The only evidence of the adjoining reactor consisted of the twin rubber cables that protruded from a hole cut into the bulkhead, just on top of the waterline. The cables extended into the depths below, and he was fully confident that they would be ready to relay all the power needed.

Both diving saucers lay securely moored alongside the forward portion of the moonpool. Two technicians were attending to them, and as Alexandrov walked over to check the condition of these vessels, a sudden disturbance in the water beside him caught the corner of his eye. He looked to his left, and watched as a bottlenose dolphin broke the surface of the moonpool. The sleek grey creature had a latex strap wrapped around its snout, and attached to the strap a small, steel pressure cooker.

With a deft movement of its head and neck, the dolphin deposited the pressure cooker upon the steel-latticed catwalk, directly in front of Alexandrov. The senior lieutenant was no stranger to this efficient creature, who saved wear and tear on their minisubs by acting as a messenger between the support ship and the habitat below.

"Well, Comrade Dolly, what have you brought us?" remarked Alexandrov as he walked over to grasp the object that the dolphin had conveyed from the depths.

Dolly reacted with an excited outburst of whistles and clicks. Ignoring this high-pitched chatter, Alexandrov prepared to open the pressure cooker to see what lay inside. Yet Dolly was not about to go unnoticed, and the dolphin stood up on its tail, then dove beneath the water and shot to the surface, leapt through the air, and came down in a frothing splash that quickly gained Alexandrov's attention.

Now finding himself with his uniform partially soaked, Alexandrov redirected his line of sight back to the moonpool. "All right, Comrade, I hear you loud and clear. Let's see what kind of treat Viktor can find for you."

An ice-filled bucket of mullet sat on the forward portion of the catwalk for just this purpose. Alexandrov picked up the largest of the partially frozen fish by its tail, and held it out, high above the water.

"Come and get it, Comrade," he teasingly offered.

Not to be denied, Dolly circled the entire moonpool. After disappearing beneath the surface, the dolphin spiralled upwards in a graceful leap, snatched the mullet in its mouth, and fell back into the water with a resounding splash.

Satisfied that the insistent marine mammal would leave him alone now, Alexandrov turned his attention back to the pressure cooker. The lid was tightly sealed, and it took a bit of effort to unscrew it and pull the rubberized gasket apart. It opened with a loud, popping noise, and he reached inside and removed a large manila envelope that contained several supply requisitions and a sealed letter addressed to Dr. Harlan Sorkin, the head of the U.N. observer team. Marked *Personal and Confidential,* this piece of mail immediately caught the naval officer's attention. Yet before delivering it, he decided to share its presence with his superior officer.

He found Admiral Valerian in his stateroom, in the midst of a shave. The one-eyed veteran still used an old-fashioned, pearl-handled straight razor, which he honed to a fine sharpness on a rawhide strop. Clad only in a T-shirt and his skivvies, Valerian greeted his guest while staring into the mirror and carefully scraping the shaving cream from his neck.

"To what do I owe the honor of your presence this early in the morning, Senior Lieutenant?"

"I'm sorry to disturb you, Admiral. But I found an unusual item in the habitat's morning mail."

With several dextrous strokes of his razor, Valerian completed his shave. He then took the time to wipe his face dry with a terry-cloth towel before turning to impatiently address his guest.

"So Senior Lieutenant, just what is this unusual item that you speak of?"

Alexandrov pulled out the letter that he had taken

from the mail envelope. "This is the item, sir. It's addressed to Dr. Sorkin, and is marked personal and confidential."

Valerian roughly grabbed the letter, and wasted no time picking up his razor and cleanly slicing open the envelope. It held a single sheet of white paper that he hastily skimmed, then slowly reread.

"You'll never believe it, Senior Lieutenant. But it seems that our brave aquanauts have managed to stumble upon our secret. Somehow they got their diving saucer operational, and as fate would have it, witnessed our submersibles at work on the bottom of the trench last night."

Alexandrov appeared genuinely shocked by this revelation. "Does this mean that our operation is over?"

"Why of course not!" replied Valerian firmly. "It's only going to demand a bit more resourcefulness on our part. Let me see their supply requisition. I have a feeling that calamity is about to strike the inquisitive occupants of Starfish House."

Twelve

It took Mimi Slater an entire day and night to make her final decision. Beyond the monetary expense that a trip down to the Bahamas would incur, was the ever important emotional cost involved in such a questionable excursion. Still not absolutely certain if Dr. Elizabeth was legitimate or not, Mimi couldn't help wondering if she wasn't merely prolonging her period of mourning by holding onto this last hope of contacting her husband. Unlike the other family and wives of the crew of the *Lewis and Clark,* she alone could not accept her loved one's death, and she was even willing to search the vastness of the universe in an effort to locate him.

Was she deceiving herself? Or was the psychic's story true after all? Because these questions would haunt her for the rest of her life, she had no choice but to turn a deaf ear to logic, and follow the call of her heart.

With her tear-filled stare locked on the photograph of Peter that crowned the fireplace's mantel, she picked up the telephone and informed Dr. Elizabeth of her decision. The psychic had been anticipating her call, and she readily agreed to meet Mimi at the Miami airport Marriott the next evening. Meanwhile, she was to proceed down to Southern Florida, and arrange to charter a boat for the voyage to the waters off Andros Island. With the fall equinox only three days away, there was no time to waste, and Mimi hung up the phone feeling that she had made the proper choice.

She made a quick call to her travel agent, and reserved a one-way ticket on a noon flight to Miami. This gave her less than two hours to shower, pack, and close up the house. She drove her car to the Charleston airport, and left it parked in the short-term lot. A flight delay gave her an extra thirty minutes. She used this time to find an automatic teller machine and get a five-hundred-dollar cash advance. With Peter gone, she had no one to call to say good-bye, and she walked onto the plane feeling as if she were leaving her old life behind.

The aircraft was half empty, and she sat alone above the right wing. Minutes after takeoff she fell soundly asleep, and slept until the stewardess shook her to inform her that they were about to land at their destination.

She looked out the window in time to see the clear blue waters of Biscayne Bay passing down below. The Miami Beach skyline colorfully beckoned in the distance, and beyond stretched the surging Atlantic. It had been almost twenty years since she had last visited Miami, and she noted the dozens of newly built high-rise skyscrapers that gave the sprawling city a vibrant, modern look.

Since she had only carry-on luggage, she didn't have to stop at the crowded baggage-claim area after landing. She went right to the Hertz counter and rented a car.

A short drive brought her to the Marriott, where she got a double room overlooking the pool. She ate a sandwich in the coffee shop, then stopped to see the concierge to get help finding a reliable boat-charter outfit.

As it turned out, the nearest charter boats could be found on Key Biscayne. Also home to the Miami Seaquarium, Key Biscayne was less than a fifteen-minute-drive away, and Mimi had no trouble finding the proper causeway. This roadway conveyed her to a small, exclusive, condo-filled island, located immediately south of Miami Beach.

Because the concierge couldn't recommend a particular boat to rent, Mimi would have to make that decision on her own. She found the charter docks easily enough, and after parking the car, walked out onto the pier to see what she had to choose from.

Most of the boats moored at the marina were sleek fishing vessels, designed for day trips out into the Gulf Stream. These fiberglass cabin cruisers featured stern-mounted fighting chairs, where fishermen could go after sailfish or marlin from the upholstered comfort of a leather-lined perch.

One of these boats had just pulled in. Mimi joined the crowd assembled beside this vessel's stern as the crew opened the fish locker and began throwing more than a dozen shiny grey bonitos onto the dock. This solidly built fish was of the tuna family, and each one weighed well over thirty pounds. The two proud fishermen responsible for this catch climbed out of the cabin with bottles of beer in hand. Both were slightly overweight white men in their mid-forties. They wore tennis shorts, Polo shirts, and New York Mets baseball caps, with their exposed skin reddened from the sun.

"I'll take odds that they won't even bother takin' home a single filet," broke a gravelly voice on Mimi's right.

She looked over to see who had uttered these words, and set her eyes on a silver-haired black man, with a weather-beaten face and kind brown eyes. He wore a yachting cap on his head, of the type made popular by the famed band leader, Count Bassie, and when he saw that he had an audience, succinctly added, "Looks like I'll be eatin' good tonight."

"You don't mean to say that they're merely going to give these fish away, after all the expense of catching them," asked Mimi.

"It sure appears that way, missy," replied the old-timer, who grinned and displayed two prominent front teeth made from glistening dental gold.

"What a waste," reflected Mimi as the crowd began to thin out when the last bonito was pulled from the locker.

The captain of the vessel could be seen shaking hands with his satisfied passengers. He was a big man, with solid, muscular shoulders, and long, curly blond

221

hair, and Mimi decided to wait until the fishermen had departed before asking him the price of a charter.

She stood there on the pier, and watched as the black man who had spoken to her earlier asked one of the vessel's crew members a question. He must have gotten a positive response, for he broke out in a warm smile and proceeded to pick up a bonito by its tail. He then dragged this fish to an adjoining slip, where a battered, thirty-foot-long wooden trawler was moored. With a light step, he boarded this ship, ducked into its interior cabin, and emerged seconds later holding a knife.

He broke out whistling as he climbed back onto the dock. Mimi recognized the melody as "Summertime," from Gershwin's *Porgy and Bess*. This had always been one of her favorite tunes, and she watched him bend down beside the bonito and begin expertly filleting it.

"You look like you've done this kind of work before," remarked Mimi casually.

"I guess you could say that I have, missy. You see, my pappy taught me da proper way of cuttin' up a fish, not long after I first learnt to talk. And I sure been puttin' this lesson to work ever since, 'specially since the good Lord saw fit to provide me with my very own fishin' boat."

Mimi looked to the wooden trawler and responded to this. "Do you mean to say that this is your boat?"

"It sure is, missy. I call her *Sunshine,* for her warm disposition. Charter trips down into da keys are my specialty, and if it's tarpon you'd be want-

222

in' at a fair price, you've come to da right place."

Though Mimi had her mind set on a more modern vessel, she liked this old-timer's style and once more she went with her instincts. "I'm not interested in fishing, though I am looking for a boat to take me and a friend to Andros Island."

"I know those waters well, missy. My cousin Sherman runs a fishin' camp outside of Nicholls Town. It's nothin' fancy mind you, but on a clear night you can see all da way over da Tongue of da Ocean, to the lights of Nassau."

"Is the *Sunshine* available tomorrow evening?" asked Mimi.

"As luck would have it, that she is, missy. If da weather cooperates, we can have you and your friend at your destination by sunrise. And we'll even take you back for the same three-hundred-dollar fare."

Mimi felt as if a heavy weight had just been taken off her shoulders. "Mister, you just made yourself a deal."

"The name's Alphonse Cloyd, missy. But you can just call me, Al. And don't worry about packin' your supper, 'cause I'll supply all da grilled bonito you can eat, and even throw in some red-eye to wash it down with."

Thomas Moore's first full day spent aboard a nuclear-powered attack submarine had been most interesting. After the tiring effects of the seasickness patch had finally worn off, he felt rested and refreshed as he began a tour of the three-hundred-and-sixty-foot-long

223

vessel. His guide was the sub's personable supply officer.

Hop had been stationed aboard the *Rickover* for the last one and a half years, and he knew every member of the crew by their first name. Hop was the only officer not nuclear-qualified, so he rushed Moore through the reactor spaces, preferring instead to concentrate his tour on more familiar areas such as the boat's galley.

In a space the size of an average apartment kitchen, three men cooked for a crew of one hundred and forty. Four meals were served each day, with menus ranging from turkey with all the trimmings, to steak, fried chicken, and everyone's favorite, pizza.

Moore found this food excellent. Because of the rote nature of submarine duty, mealtimes were looked forward to, as special occasions. Finding adequate storage space for foodstuffs was a real problem, and on extended deployments, Hop and his boys had to utilize every available nook and cranny. Canned goods were often stored on the floor, and then covered with plywood planks so that the crew could walk over them. The galley had a single walk-in freezer, which had to be crammed to overflowing when two-month-long patrols were undertaken.

Another problem unique to submarines was trash management. A group of one hundred and forty men could produce an amazingly large amount of waste each day, and Hop made certain to give Moore a quick rundown on how they managed to dispose of this garbage. The investigator was especially interested when his knowledgeable guide took him into the room where

224

the trash disposal unit was situated. No stranger to the TDU after his previous experience on the *Lewis and Clark,* Moore listened with interest as Hop explained how the day's trash was compacted into corrugated metal shells. The TDU itself operated much like a torpedo tube, and could hold up to five of these slugs before having to be flushed out into the sea below. Moore paid close attention when Hop described the system's pitfalls, including torn gaskets and jammed ball valves.

With vivid memories of Homer Morgan's nightmarish confrontation with a malfunctioning TDU ever in mind, Moore followed Hop down into the torpedo room. A young black torpedoman from Kansas City was on watch here, and he readily showed Moore around while Hop took a telephone call.

The *Hyman G. Rickover* was outfitted with four bow-mounted torpedo tubes capable of firing the Mk 48 ADCAP torpedo, and the Harpoon and Tomahawk missiles. The weapons themselves were stored on a trio of double-layered steel racks, that nearly filled the relatively large, dimly lit compartment. Because of space constraints, several members of the crew used this same rack as a bunk. Two sailors were currently sleeping here, and Moore's guide kept his voice low as he pointed out the various weapons, and described how they were maintained and prepared for firing. The loading system was totally automated, and Moore noted that only two of the tubes were currently loaded.

From the torpedo room, Hop led Moore up to the wardroom for dinner. Captain Walden had already arrived here, and waited for his guest from his customary place at the head of the table. Moore was seated to Walden's left, with the XO directly across from him and Hop at the table's far end. The rest of the places were filled with the officers who weren't currently sleeping or on watch.

Moore pulled out his blue cloth napkin from a silver ring that had his name stencilled on it. This same napkin was carefully folded after every meal, and returned to its holder, for use the next time around.

"How are you getting along, Mr. Moore?" asked Walden as he passed him the server holding three types of salad dressing.

Moore answered while covering his lettuce, tomato and cucumber salad with a spoonful of french dressing. "I'm doing just fine, Captain. Hop's been taking good care of me."

The XO turned to his left, and put a tape into the cassette player. The pastoral sounds of Beethoven's Sixth Symphony soon filled the wardroom, and Moore contentedly munched his salad and accepted the next course of veal parmigiana, spaghetti, and steamed broccoli.

"We'll be surfacing at 2100 and arriving at Port Canaveral two hours later," informed Walden between bites of his veal. "You're more than welcome to join the XO and his watch party on the sail, Mr. Moore, though I'm afraid the visibility will be a bit limited at that late hour."

Moore was in the midst of a mouthful of spaghetti, and could only nod in response to this offer. Quick to

226

continue the conversation was Lieutenant Carr, the handsome, blond-haired officer seated to Moore's left.

"I can't wait for dawn, so that we can get our first good look at *Seawolf*."

"Too bad that we won't have the time to tour her, Weaps," added the bespectacled navigator, who sat across from Carr.

"What's *Seawolf* doing down in Port Canaveral?" managed Moore after washing down his spaghetti with a sip of milk.

It was the captain who answered him. "Sea trials, Mr. Moore. Because of the radically new nature of *Seawolf*'s operational systems, the Navy has decided to break her in beneath the waters of our Tongue of the Ocean test range."

This revelation was news to Moore, who thoughtfully responded. "And when will that be?"

"Though the exact time of embark is classified, from what I gather, things are progressing a bit ahead of schedule for a change, which means that *Seawolf* could be setting sail as early as next week."

Moore was uncharacteristically quiet during the rest of his meal, his thoughts instead focused on the implications of this surprise revelation. And it was during his dessert of apple pie a la mode, that he finally realized why Admiral Proctor was so adamant on sending him on this rushed cruise. The *Rickover* was being used to scour the waters of the Andros test range, to determine if any unknown man-made dangers could possibly interfere with *Seawolf*'s upcoming sea trials.

227

The Navy could not risk having *Seawolf* share the *Lewis and Clark's* fate, for if *Seawolf* were to be somehow spirited away to an enemy port, one of the greatest intelligence losses in history would befall the country.

It would soon be time to share his suspicions with the *Rickover's* CO. Still not certain how Walden would react to his incredible tale, Moore patiently waited for the proper opportunity. Meanwhile, he would continue getting familiar with the platform and crew that Command had given him to work with.

Over coffee, Moore learned that it would take the better part of a day to fit the DSRV that they had come to Florida to pick up, onto the *Rickover's* hull. And if all went smoothly, they'd be leaving Port Canaveral sometime tomorrow evening, to begin the three-hundred-mile journey to the Tongue of the Ocean. Moore was anxious to get to their destination and see what mysteries the depths held for them.

Every evening after dinner, the wardroom was turned into a theater. Over hot popcorn and drinks, a picture was shown from the boat's rather extensive film catalogue. Moore was asked to choose from this list, and after careful consideration, he decided that an action-adventure flick was in order. He chose *Predator,* staring Arnold Schwarzenegger.

As it turned out, no one was disappointed with his choice. This included the captain, who sat through most of the movie before being called away to handle a minor problem in engineering.

After the film was over, Moore decided to visit the

control room before turning in for the evening. Declining Hop's offer to show him the way, he made it to the red-lit compartment all on his own.

The *Rickover* was about to go to periscope depth, and it took Moore several minutes for his eyes to adjust to the lack of direct lighting. He felt a bit more at ease as he identified the current OOD as Lieutenant Clark, the boat's communications officer. Clark wore a dark green, woolen sweater over his coveralls, and displayed his usual, tight-lipped, no-nonsense personality.

The boat's diving officer was Chief Ellwood. The COB had the unlit stub of a cigar in his mouth, and greeted Moore without taking his eyes off the dials and gauges of the main control panel.

"Evening, sir. Are you ready for that driving lesson that I promised you? If you want, I'll ask the officer of the deck if you can take us up to periscope depth."

"That's not necessary, Chief," replied Moore. "I'm content just to watch."

"Just holler if you change your mind," said the COB, who suddenly sat forward and tweaked the helmsman's ear with his right index finger.

"Hey, Kowalski, watch your course!" he gruffly warned. "And put both your hands on that steerin' yoke, son. You're sittin' there like you was drivin' your dad's Chevy. Don't forget, you're steerin' a billion-dollar submarine."

Moore couldn't help laughing. Because of the total absence of windows aboard, he had almost forgotten their current method of transport. Where else could a kid barely twenty be responsible for driving a costly vessel such as the *Rickover* through the black depths?

A stop at the navigational plot allowed Moore to see their current position off the coast of central Florida. The precise coordinates were determined by constant updates from the boat's SINS equipment. As the quartermaster called out his suggested course changes to the OOD, Moore continued on to sonar.

Petty Officer Tim Lacey was the current watch supervisor here. He smiled when Moore entered, and Lacey beckoned to the newcomer to have a seat beside the broad-band CRT console.

"Welcome to the house of pain, sir," said Lacey warmly.

Lacey perched on a stool behind three seated junior technicians. Each wore headphones, and faced a glowing monitor screen. Their job was to monitor the variety of sounds being conveyed through the sub's passive sensors. These hydrophones were positioned throughout the hull, and could also be deployed on a towed array. They were accessed by manipulating a thin black joystick that was mounted into each console, and by addressing a square keyboard positioned beside the CRT screen.

"I've got a new contact in our baffles, Tim," revealed the young sailor seated at the middle console. "Designate Sierra nine, biological."

"Good work, babe," said Lacey, who reached up for a bulkhead-mounted microphone. "Conn, sonar, we have a new contact, bearing three-three-zero, designate Sierra nine, biological."

"Sonar, Conn, designate Sierra nine biological, aye,

sonar," returned a voice from the intercom speaker.

"Would you like to have a listen, sir?" asked Lacey, who pulled off his own headphones and handed them to the newcomer.

Moore readily placed these headphones over his ears, and listened to a distant crackling noise.

"They're shrimp, sir," revealed Lacey. "They always remind me of a bunch of out-of-control castanets."

Moore grinned with this comparison, and handed the headphones back to his host.

"I've always had a genuine respect for anyone sharp enough to make sense out of the sounds of the sea," said Moore. "It's an amazing science."

"It's more than that, sir," replied Lacey. "Sonar's an art form all its own."

"Contact, Chief," interrupted the seaman monitoring the broad band screen. "Bearing two-two-eight, designate Sierra eleven, merchant."

"Thata way, babe," responded Lacey, who relayed this information to the Conn, then reached up into a hole cut into the overhead air vent.

Moore watched as Lacey proceeded to pull out a bag of Hershey's Kisses. Like a mother bird feeding her chicks, he handed each of his men a handful of candies, making certain to include Moore.

"I always take care of my boys, when they take care of me," added Lacey, who bit into a candy himself.

"You never did say why you call this room the house of pain," remarked Moore.

Lacey shook his head. "Stop by and see us if we should happen to cross paths with an unfriendly, and

231

trade a sonar lashing," he explained. "Then the answer to your question will be all too obvious."

Moore watched the sonar team at work for another half hour. In that time period they tagged a number of biologicals, and tracked a trawler that passed almost directly overhead. The *Rickover* was on its way to periscope depth when Moore fought back a yawn and decided to turn in.

He left the hushed confines of the dimly lit control room, and exited by way of the aft accessway. This brought him directly down into the crew's mess. The atmosphere on the deck above had been tense, but to enter the brightly lit mess was like arriving at the neighborhood malt shop. Mid-rats were in the process of being served, and Moore passed by a line of hungry enlisted men waiting to fill their plates with freshly cooked hamburgers and french fries. The smell was enticing, and the overweight investigator had to fight the temptation to fill up a plate.

His bunk was awaiting him in the adjoining corridor. The berthing compartment was dark, and most of the bunks had their curtains closed. Moore did his best to make as little noise as possible. He slid open his own curtain, and decided that it would be easier to sleep right in his coveralls.

It took him several tries to maneuver himself into his bunk. He awkwardly tucked himself beneath the blanket, and after resealing the curtain, did his best to stretch out on his back. His feet just touched the narrow bulkhead, and without bothering to switch on his overhead light, he tucked his wristwatch under the edge of his mattress and closed his eyes.

One of his bunkmates was contentedly snoring, and in the distance he could just hear two sailors talking in the hallway. Hop had mentioned earlier that the compartment had been designed to hold computer equipment. A special ventilation system had been installed to keep this machinery cool. Yet when it was decided to fill the space with bunks instead, the ventilation system remained, resulting in ideal sleeping conditions. Thankful for the warmth of his blanket, Moore drifted off into a dreamless slumber.

Boris Dubrinin couldn't believe their good fortune. For well over twenty-four hours now, the *Pantera* had been able to follow in the unsuspecting American attack sub's baffles. This was a great accomplishment, considering that sonar confirmed this vessel to be one of the top-of-the-line 688 class vessels, and that the pursuit was taking place practically right off the U.S. coastline.

The zampolit knew that this only served to prove the excellence of the *Pantera*'s sensors and of the noise abatement systems. At long last, the people's Navy could field a submarine that could rival the best underwater warship of the capitalist fleet.

In the past, Russia's nuclear-powered submarines had been notoriously noisy and prone to frequent accidents. To rectify these faults, great efforts had been made to acquire the latest technologies. Many of these high-tech advances came out of the *rodina*'s own labs and research facilities, the by-product of hard, exhausting work and great monetary sacrifice. Other technology was acquired abroad, through legitimate purchase, and when this avenue was blocked, through industrial espionage. A well-placed spy could save the *rodina* billions of rubles in research and development expense. Spies could also reveal what the competition was up to.

The *Pantera* class was proof that Russian industry could compete with the very best that the West had to offer. But how long would this state of parity exist? This question was especially relevant now that the new *Seawolf* was about to enter the American fleet.

Economic conditions inside what was left of the Soviet Union made it all but impossible for them to produce a next-generation platform equivalent to the SSN-21. The great social upheavals of the 1990s signaled the end of the socialist state, with the U.S.S.R. being replaced by a group of separate republics, alienated by ethnic rivalries and a loss of direction. Such a weakened coalition could never hope to muster the resources needed to produce a rival to *Seawolf*, meaning that they would have to accept a future position of undersea inferiority. This was the greatest tragedy of all, to work so hard and sacrifice so much, and have all this effort be in vain.

Thankfully, several key members of the red banner fleet would not allow such a dangerous imbalance to come into being. Boris had the privilege of meeting this group's ringleader, in the days before the *Pantera* put to sea on their current patrol. Admiral Igor Valerian was a decorated hero of the Great Patriotic War, and Boris was pleasantly surprised upon receiving an invitation to meet with the legendary, one-eyed veteran during his visit to the *Pantera's* homeport in Polyarny.

The political officer supposed that this meeting had something to do with his outspoken views concerning the *rodina's* current course. As far as Boris was concerned, the decision to abandon communism and convert the economy to a free-market system signaled the beginning of the end of Lenin's dream. Stripped of its power, the Party could no longer insure the motherland's integrity, and Boris feared for their future security.

When the Komsomol was banned from Russian warships, Boris dared to speak up. He bravely challenged this decision in a series of blistering memos sent directly to fleet headquarters. The Komsomol was an official Party organization, created as a forum for political discussion and debate. It was an integral part of every ship in the Russian Navy, with the *zampolit* acting as its official head.

In the recent past, over ninety percent of all naval officers were members of the Komsomol. Demonstrating one's Party loyalty had always been essential to a successful Navy career, and few non-Party officers ever obtained their own commands.

Soon after the October Revolution, it was decided to assign each Soviet warship a political officer. The *zampolit's* duties included monitoring the political reliability of the crew, directing their ideological indoctrination, and insuring that Party decisions were

235

properly carried out. The political officer also enforced discipline and promoted morale by assuming the dual roles of social worker and chaplain.

The decision to abandon the Komsomol could only mean that the ship-borne *zampolit* would also soon be a thing of the past. This had dangerous implications, for without the strict supervision of the political officer, the Navy would no longer be completely subordinate to the state, and would be in a position to exercise military power for its own political ends.

Boris's thoughts came to the attention of a group of high-ranking flag officers who shared similar beliefs. Much to his relief, these officers were able successfully to convey their fears to Moscow, and a decision was made temporarily to continue deploying *zampolits* to the ships of the fleet, with one major condition — each political officer would need to have had practical experience as a line officer as well.

Because Boris had previous training as a navigator, he was spared the indignity of having to go back to technical school. His assignment to the *Pantera* was a great honor, and he wondered if his outspokenness had something to do with this high-profile assignment. Supposing that this was the topic that Admiral Valerian wanted to discuss, he went to his meeting with confidence and pride.

Boris would never forget the morning this meeting took place. Igor Valerian was every bit as imposing as he thought he would be. The distinguished veteran was tall and erect, and had a way of looking into one's eyes as if he were gazing into one's soul. Before getting

236

down to business, he produced a bottle of gold-tinted vodka, and together they toasted the continued security of the motherland. Only then did he get around to explaining the reason for this meeting.

As it turned out, Valerian didn't want to discuss their shared political beliefs at all. Rather, he had matters of a much more practical nature to divulge to Boris, who sat back and listened as the one-eyed mariner sketchily revealed the details of a top-secret operation that he would soon be directing. This operation's lofty goal was no less than to guarantee the *rodina's* future competitiveness in the important field of undersea warfare, by securing the technology needed for this next step with a single, bold move. Because the *rodina* would never be able to develop these technological advances on their own, they would get them in another manner, by stealing the most advanced underwater warship of all — *Seawolf.*

Though Valerian never explained the exact details of how he would go about doing this, Boris did learn that the operation would take place during *Seawolf's* initial sea trials. The relevance of this disclosure came into focus as the *Pantera* continued with its current duty.

Boris had just returned to his stateroom after a six-hour watch in navigation. During this time, he was part of the team who plotted their course and that of their unsuspecting quarry. The 688 class submarine's destination was becoming evident as they continued to cruise southward down America's eastern coast. Only an hour ago, the twinkling lights of St. Augustine, Florida were barely visible through the *Pantera's* attack scope. The 688 then began a slight course change to the southwest, which brought it ever closer to the shallower waters above the continental shelf. This meant that the vessel would soon be surfacing, with the only submarine base in the vicinity less than a couple of hours distant.

Even their most junior navigator was able to determine that the 688 was headed for Florida's Port Canaveral. Yet what his crewmates didn't know was that this same port was the current home of the one warship that could irrevocably tilt the balance of naval fighting-power forever in favor of the imperialist West. For it was here that *Seawolf* was being prepared for its sea trials.

Was it merely the hand of fate that had led the *Pantera* into these sensitive waters? Boris couldn't help wondering as his thoughts returned to his morning spent with Igor Valerian. The Admiral had informed him that *Seawolf* would be putting to sea in late summer or early fall. This meant that its sea trials could be starting any day now, and that the 688 that they had been following from Norfolk could be a part of this test run. Excited with this possibility, Boris retired to his bunk. It was time now to get as much rest as possible, for there was no telling what the days ahead had in store for them.

Thirteen

The team was just assembling for breakfast, when the bell began ringing inside the ready room of Starfish House. From his wooden perch beside the dining room table, Ulge was the first to respond audibly to this unexpected call.

"Dolly's here! Awk. Dolly's here!" animatedly squawked the parrot. "Hello, Dolly!"

With a rush of flapping green feathers, Ulge then streaked into the ready room, prompting Lisa Tanner to put down her napkin and scoot back her chair.

"I wonder if Dolly's brought us a response from Dr. Sorkin," she remarked while standing. "Everyone sit tight while I go and see."

Her four seated co-workers readily accepted this offer, and watched as Lisa followed Ulge into the adjoining room. Less than a minute later she was back holding an open envelope and a single piece of paper.

"It's a message from topside alright," she said with a hint of disappointment. "But it's not from Dr. Sorkin."

Lisa handed the dispatch to Pierre Lenclud, who read it while sipping a glass of Irish breakfast tea.

"We've been notified to be ready to accept a shipment of helium tanks this morning at 0900," he reported. "The rest of our requested supplies will be sent down later in the day."

"I wonder why there's no word from Dr. Sorkin," remarked Ivana Petrov. "At the very least, he should have acknowledged the receipt of our memo."

"Maybe he hasn't even read it yet," offered Tomo, between bites of his waffle.

"Not Dr. Sorkin," countered Lisa. "If he received the envelope, he'd open it and read its contents at once."

"I think all of us should give the man a chance to do some preliminary investigation first," said Karl Ivar.

"I agree," concurred Lenclud. "After all, he's only had twelve hours to act on our warning. Dr. Sorkin impressed me as the type who wouldn't waste time contacting us until he had some solid information to pass on. In the meantime, we have to be patient."

Ivana Petrov pushed away her food and impatiently voiced herself. "Even if we do hear from him soon, I still think we should return to the bottom of the trench and catch those minisubs with *Misha's* video camera. And if the saucers aren't still there, at least we can get close-up proof of just what it is that they're working on."

"No, *mon amie,*" returned Lenclud. "Until we hear from Dr. Sorkin, such an excursion would be far too dangerous. Those two vessels could be involved in a clandestine military operation for all we know, and I think it's best that we stay far away from the floor of the trench until we hear otherwise."

Karl Ivar looked at his watch, then hurriedly chewed his last section of waffle. "Who wants to help me convey the helium back to Hangar One?" he asked, before gulping his milk.

"I'll give you a hand, Karl Ivar, if you'll assist me in putting up the new wall to the fish pen," offered Tomo.

"You've got yourself a deal," replied the Norwegian, who stood, adding, "In fact, I'll even throw in the services of *Misha*. We can use the saucer's articulated manipulator arm to do most of the manual work for us."

"Good idea," said Tomo as he also stood and followed his muscular, blond-haired co-worker to the ready room.

This left only Pierre Lenclud and Ivana Petrov still seated at the table. They shared a moment of thoughtful silence, as Lisa began clearing the dishes.

"My instincts warn me that something is not right on the floor of the trench, Comrade," reflected the Russian. "The *Academician Petrovsky*'s commanding officer is a crafty old Communist fox, and if he's indeed using this mission as a cover, there's a very good chance that the members of the U.N. observer team will never know about it. Why, I wouldn't put it beyond Admiral Valerian to intercept our dispatch to Dr. Sorkin, which means that even as we speak, he knows of our suspicions."

"Though I seriously doubt that's the case, *mon amie,* we must nevertheless be prepared for just such a possibility. And if we don't hear from the good doctor by tomorrow this time, I'll seriously reconsider your request to return to the floor of the trench and film this machinery that you discovered. In fact, I'll even accompany you aboard *Misha* myself."

While the occupants of Starfish House continued with their discussion, Karl Ivar and Tomo climbed down the stairs of the ready room. From the protection of the shark-proof grill, they halted a moment to survey the coral clearing before them. The only evidence of the world above was the morning sunlight that filtered down from above, illuminating the crystal water with a soft blue radiance.

It didn't take long for the rightful occupants of this undersea realm to make themselves known. The first noticeable sea creature was a familiar, tough-looking brute, with a long tapering body and a jawful of razor-sharp teeth. Uncle Albert raced past them with lightning speed, and he needed a mere second to notice that Lisa Tanner was not one of these wet-suited newcomers. Quick to continue his patient vigil beside the kitchen porthole, the barracuda disappeared beneath one of the habitat's telescopic legs.

It was Tomo who pointed out a moray eel in the distance. The snakelike creature was on its way to a nearby clump of brain coral, and its undulating, four-foot-long body passed right by them. In reality, it looked more menacing than it was, though its powerful jaws and sharp teeth could produce a nasty bite. Most often, such an injury was inflicted upon a diver's hand, as it reached into the dark recesses of a reef, accidentally provoking the eel's anger.

A group of angel fish darted in and out of the iron bars comprising the sharkproof grill. These colorful, gentle creatures seemed to be trying their best to hide themselves from a quartet of lurking snappers. A family of grunts swam by, as well as a group of squirrel fish, and a brilliantly colored, spiny-finned wrasse.

Though he was more than content to watch this never-ending procession, Karl Ivar glanced down at his waterproof watch. The luminescent hands showed it quickly approaching 9:00 A.M., and he signaled this fact to his diving partner. Tomo nodded that he understood, and together they left the shelter of the grill and began their way towards a sand-filled clearing located on the far side of Habitat One. This was the preplanned drop-off zone for items that were either too bulky or heavy for Dolly to carry down to them.

This portion of the sea floor was located from above by means of a small, battery-powered, sonic emitter, moored to the sand at the center of the circular clearing. When the supply ship wished to find this target, the crew could switch on the emitter with a remote control device, and this portion of the seabed was readily recognizable.

The two divers were just swimming by Habitat One when Karl Ivar spotted a disturbance topside. The objects responsible for this turbulence soon became visible as the Norwegian reached the edge of the clearing and glanced upwards.

To transfer the habitat's breathing gases in the most efficient manner, six metal tanks filled with helium had been tied together with a nylon strap. When dropped overboard, these heavy tanks quickly went plummeting to the bottom.

As the tanks struck the sea floor near the center of the clearing, a cloud of sandy sediment rose upwards. Quick to penetrate this milky veil, Karl Ivar pulled out his knife and cut the restraining strap. Each tank weighed over forty pounds, and he wasted no time grabbing one by the neck and carrying it off to Habitat One. With Tomo's help, they were able to get all of the shipment stowed away in half an hour.

"It looks like we could use some fresh helium in the main compressor," remarked Tomo as he helped his fellow-aquanaut position the last of the newly arrived tanks in Habitat One's storage room.

"Let's go ahead and use up what's left of our old stock," replied Karl Ivar.

"If you'd like, I'll load the compressor while you get *Misha* ready," offered Tomo. "It would be great if we could get the walls of the fish pen up by lunch."

"I don't see why we can't," said the Norwegian. "Why don't you meet me in the hangar as soon as you're finished here."

Karl Ivar was surprised to find Dolly waiting for him in the pool of water of Habitat One's accessway. The dolphin seemed strangely agitated, and nervously jerked its head from side to side, while calling out in short, high-pitched cries.

"What's the matter, Dolly? Did Uncle Albert eat your breakfast again?"

The dolphin seemed to shake its head that this wasn't the case, and made several short dives into the water below.

"I hear you, Dolly," said Karl Ivar as he strapped on his air tanks. "And I'm coming down to join you as soon as I can get my diving gear in order."

Dolly impatiently waited while he spat into the inner glass plate of his face mask to keep it from fogging up,

244

and pulled on his flippers. Then after putting the air hose in his mouth and testing the flow of the regulator, he climbed into the water and dropped into the depths below.

Dolly seemed to be relieved when he turned towards the hangar and began swimming. The dolphin made several short sprints to the hangar, to emphasize where she wanted her human companion to end up.

Having no idea what Dolly was up to, Karl Ivar passed by the large clump of brain coral that lay halfway between Habitat One and his goal. There were no sharks in the area, and remembering Ivana Petrov's near miss with death beside this same coral clump, he followed his marine mammal escort all the way to the hangar's accessway. Dolly never left his side as he climbed up the ladder and broke the water's surface.

Long before he was able to reach up and flick on the overhead lights, he knew that something was seriously wrong here. The air had a foul, acrid stench to it, and when the lights failed to activate, he was forced to reach to a supply chest and pull out a flashlight. Then he spotted the reason for Dolly's behavior.

The entire bottom portion of their diving saucer was blackened by scorch marks. With unbelieving eyes, Karl Ivar knew that *Misha* had been the victim of a fire. This smoldering blaze must have started sometime in the early hours of the morning. Only a lack of oxygen prevented it from spreading to the rest of the hangar.

With Dolly chattering away in the background, he determined that the fire had started in *Misha*'s battery compartment. Of course, he immediately blamed him-

245

self for this accident. Most likely, his recent work on the minisub's alternator had created an internal electrical short. This short had somehow escaped his most recent inspection of the system only last evening. And now they would have to pay the price for his incompetence. For even with help from above, *Misha's* days of exploring the depths were over.

Thomas Moore was awakened by the blaring voice of a public address announcement. He groggily fumbled for his watch, and had to do a double take upon finding it well past 10:00 A.M. Once again, the *Rickover* had encouraged a sound night's sleep, and he felt almost guilty as he yanked back his curtain and planned the best way to extricate himself from his bunk.

To reach the deck, he awkwardly rolled over on his stomach and pushed himself backwards until his feet struck the floor. Still in his coveralls, he pulled his brown leather topsiders from the corner of the bunk, and unlatched the small locker to get to his shaving kit.

As he rolled back the compartment's sliding door, a shaft of bright light hit his eyes. Two sailors dressed in blue dungarees passed, on their way aft to the crew's mess. Moore nodded hello and directed his steps to the nearby officers' head.

He was thankful to have this space to himself. He relieved himself at the urinal, and felt like a veteran submariner as he properly flushed it by pulling down the steel lever that opened a ball valve positioned in its stainless-steel bottom. After washing it out with a slug of water, he turned to the sink.

A hot lather machine was mounted beside the mirror, and after washing up, he spread the warm cream over his face and neck. He shaved, brushed his teeth, then headed for the shower. Ever mindful of Hop's directions, he turned the water on until the right temperature was attained. Then he ducked inside and hastily soaked his body before halting the flow of water by pushing closed the steel pin located above the shower head. He lathered up, washed his hair, and slid open the pin, causing a torrent of tepid water to issue forth from above.

Once his shower was completed, he wiped the stall with a squeegee, stored on the wall for just this purpose. He felt much better as he slipped back into his coveralls and shoes, and returned to his berth to stow away his shaving kit.

He had long ago missed breakfast, but knew that he could always get some coffee and cereal in the crew's mess. Lunch would shortly be served, and the galley was empty except for the ever-present cooks and several sailors who were using the vacant tables to study.

Not wishing to disturb them, Moore filled a bowl with Rice Krispies and milk, and shoveled down this combination while standing. Then, with a mug of coffee in hand, he climbed the ladder across from the milk dispenser. This put him immediately aft of the control room, where the SINS navigational equipment was stored. The perpetually locked door to the radio room lay further aft, yet Moore headed in the opposite direction.

The control room was brightly lit, and had but a smattering of junior personnel present at its various stations. Moore stopped by the vacant navigation plot, and all too soon found out the reason for this partial watch. The topmost chart showed that they were no longer at sea, but had reached Port Canaveral, the first stop on this patrol. Anxious to check out this facility, he continued to the forward accessway. As he peered up the hatch, a patch of blue sky invitingly beckoned, and he readily climbed upwards.

Moore's first impression upon reaching the deck, was that he had just emerged from the netherworld. The fresh air was like a tonic, its warm, tropical essence rich with the scent of the sea. The sun greeted him like a long-absent friend, and he momentarily closed his eyes and angled his face upwards to absorb its rays.

He was soon brought back to reality by a loud, grinding mechanical noise. This sound emanated from the adjoining pier. Here a huge crane was in the process of lifting the DSRV *Avalon* from the back of a flatbed truck. The DSRV itself was almost fifty feet long, and looked like a fat, oversized torpedo. It was painted black, with a pair of thrusters cut into its rounded bow, and a large white circular shroud protecting its stern-mounted prop.

Moore joined the collection of enlisted men and officers who were gathered aft of the *Rickover*'s sail. This included the captain and his XO, who anxiously orchestrated the DSRV's placement with miniature two-way radios. The tension was thick as the crane swung its special cargo over the *Rickover*'s stern. A four-legged cradle had been bolted to the deck directly above the aft access trunk, and the *Avalon* was slowly lowered into its protective grasp. Only when the DSRV was firmly in place did the tense atmosphere lighten. The crane's transfer sling was detached, and while the crew gathered around the *Avalon,* Moore took this opportunity to go ashore.

A narrow gangway led him to the pier. It felt a bit strange to be on dry land once more. His legs were shaky, and he could have sworn that the solidly anchored dock was bobbing up and down beneath him.

It took a bit of effort, but he managed to find his landlegs and walk to the far end of the pier, away from the mass of machinery and humanity gathered beside the *Rickover's* stern. From this new vantage point, he was able to view yet another submarine, docked in the slip directly opposite them. Appearing to be the same size as the *Rickover,* this vessel had one unique design feature that set it apart from the 688 class. Its hydroplanes, instead of being mounted on the sail, were set into the hull, giving it a sleek, streamlined appearance.

"Hello, Commander," broke a voice from behind.

Moore turned his head and identified this newcomer as the *Rickover's* supply officer.

"Good morning, Hop," replied Moore, who watched his grinning shipmate join him at the end of the pier.

"What do you think of SSN-21?" asked Hop, in reference to the sub that lay on the opposite slip.

"Do you mean to say, that's *Seawolf?*" questioned Moore, while turning his gaze back to the vessel that he had been previously admiring.

"That's her, all right," answered Hop. "Too bad we won't have time to take a tour below deck. That's

249

where the differences between *Seawolf* and the previous classes are really supposed to be noticeable.

"Well I'll be," reflected Moore. "To tell you the truth, I really didn't know what class of vessel she belonged to."

"That's nothing to be embarrassed about, Commander. Except for its hull-mounted hydroplanes and slightly redesigned sail, *Seawolf*'s exterior isn't all that different from a 688's. But that's as far as the similarities go. Why even its hull is formed out of a radically new type of steel that allows *Seawolf* to penetrate depths that we can only dream about."

"So I understand, Hop. And if my memory serves me right, the folks back at EB sure had a hell of a time getting those hull welds up to spec."

"That's all part of the learning process, my friend," said Hop, whose glance didn't leave the prototype warship.

"I'm glad I got up in time to get topside and see all this, Hop. The way I've been cutting Z's, I could have slept right through our port visit. How soon until we return to sea?"

"We'll be setting sail as soon as *Avalon* is secured, which should be within the hour. Scuttlebutt has it that we're taking the DSRV with us in case we should happen upon the *Lewis and Clark* stranded on the bottom."

"Hop, I wish that were the case, but unfortunately the *Avalon*'s presence has nothing to do with a possible underwater rescue. Right now, all that I can really tell you is that I'll be using the DSRV for a vastly different purpose."

"That's too bad," replied the supply officer as he looked to his watch and added. "We'd better start back for the *Rickover,* Commander."

"Very well, Hop," said Moore, who took a last glance at *Seawolf* before following his shipmate back down the pier.

Waiting for him alongside the *Rickover's* gangway was Captain Walden and a short, barrel-chested lieutenant, with a square jaw and grey sideburns.

"Ah, Commander Moore," welcomed Walden. "We were just talking about you. I'd like you to meet the *Avalon's* pilot, Lieutenant Barnes."

"Please call me Ned," said the deep-voiced veteran, who was in his late forties.

Moore accepted a vicelike handshake, and noted the way the pilot stared directly into his eyes as he responded. "Pleased to meet you, Ned."

"The captain here was just tellin' me that you'll be callin' the shots aboard *Avalon,*" remarked Barnes. "Where are we headin', and what's our mission?"

Moore hesitated a moment before guardedly replying. "I'll be using the *Avalon* to explore the depths of the Tongue of the Ocean."

"Does this have anything to do with the search for *Lewis and Clark?*" asked the pilot.

"Not directly," returned Moore.

Sensing that Moore knew more than he was admitting, Barnes questioned Walden. "Captain, how long is it going to take us to get to the Tongue of the Ocean?"

"We'll be rounding the northern tip of Andros Island early tomorrow morning," answered Walden.

"You know, I'm still curious to find out more about this operation myself, Commander."

"All in due course, sir," said Moore, who was saved any further explanation by the arrival of the *Rickover's* XO.

Moore excused himself, and headed for the submarine's forward access trunk. After filling his lungs with a last breath of warm, tropical air, he climbed down into the vessel's cool, darkened interior.

To sort out his thoughts, he proceeded straight for his berth. This was the only portion of the crowded ship that could guarantee him any semblance of privacy. His pledge of secrecy had put him in a most awkward position, and as far as he was concerned, they couldn't get to the waters of the Andros Trench fast enough.

It had all sounded simple enough when Admiral Proctor had explained his mission back in Washington. But now that other people were involved, it was getting much more complicated.

How could he tell his current shipmates that he still didn't know exactly what he was looking for? Like a confusing jigsaw puzzle, the mystery that he had been asked to solve would take both patience and an extreme amount of focused concentration. He would also need an open mind to sort out the facts in a case that pushed beyond ordinary conditions of reality.

From the shelter of his bunk, Moore was able to go over the facts as he knew them. He recalled the first time he laid eyes on the *Lewis and Clark,* and the moment they cracked open the hatch and climbed inside. He would never forget the discovery of the redheaded seaman, and the amazing tale he told while under hypnosis.

Proof that the *Lewis and Clark* had begun its tragic voyage in the Atlantic, lay in the boat's log, and the sargassum that Moore had pulled from the sub's sail. Yet many questions remained — how had the vessel travelled halfway around the world in a virtual blink of an eye? And what happened to the rest of its crew along the way?

And then there was the Philadelphia Experiment to consider. The theory behind this legendary project provided the most logical explanation of all. The explanation gained credence since Moore knew that Russia's equivalent of Albert Einstein currently waited for them in the waters above the Andros Trench.

Had Seaman Homer Morgan indeed been saved by a cover of water, as appeared to be the case with the USS *Eldridge*'s sole survivor? This would mean that the devices that caused their warships to dematerialize had been very real ones, and that one of them actually waited for Moore off the coast of Andros Island.

Chilled by this realization, Moore readied himself for the coming confrontation. In less than twenty-four hours, his time for supposition would be over. Reality would then rule the day, in his quest for the solution to this perplexing mystery.

Fourteen

Mimi Slater spent her free day in Miami at her hotel. She slept well, for the first time in recent memory, and treated herself to a late brunch. She passed her afternoon reading the newspaper around the pool, and even had a chance to join an aerobics class in the exercise room. She was in her room getting ready for dinner when the telephone rang, and a familiar female voice greeted her.

"Hon, it's the doc. How the hell are you?"

"I'm doing just fine, Dr. Elizabeth. Where are you calling from?"

"I'm down in the lobby of your hotel. Why not join me in the lounge for a cocktail, and you can tell me what you've been up to."

"I'll be down in a couple of minutes," replied Mimi, who was grateful that she had already showered and needed only to throw on some clothes.

She found the psychic seated in the lobby lounge, beside a potted palm tree. Dr. Elizabeth was dressed in a brightly colored, loose-fitting Hawaiian shift, and wore sunglasses and a big, straw hat. An animal carrier lay on the ground beside her, and Mimi could just see the black fur of the psychic's Persian cat inside.

"Have a seat, hon, and name your poison," greeted Dr. Elizabeth, after putting down the coconut shell that she had been sipping from. "But be careful, these rum smoothies are wicked."

Mimi sat down, and after ordering a glass of white wine, got right to business. "I chartered us a boat yesterday afternoon. The captain seems like a real nice fellow, and is prepared to get under way practically any time we'd like."

"What do you feel about takin' off tonight, hon?"

"That's fine with me, Dr. Elizabeth."

"Good. I'm always excited when I'm about to go on a cruise, and couldn't sleep now even if I wanted to. How are you really feelin', hon? You certainly look a bit more rested since last time I saw ya."

"To tell you the truth, Dr. Elizabeth, all this activity seems to be good for me."

"There's nothin' like travel to make ya forget all your cares. You needed this break, lady."

"I just hope that we're doing the right thing," said Mimi thoughtfully.

Dr. Elizabeth tenderly reached out and took Mimi's hand in her own. "Quit feelin' so guilty, hon. Those doubts of yours are only natural. When we get out there on the open seas, you'll soon enough know that you made the right decision. Say, you don't get seasick, do ya?"

Mimi shook her head that she didn't, and Dr. Elizabeth smiled. "That's good to hear, hon. Because all

255

that medication can dull your psychic powers, and I'm gonna need you fully alert to help me contact the entity."

"How do you go about doing that?" questioned Mimi, not really certain just what an entity was.

"I've got a little ritual, hon, that helps me focus my powers and make the connection. When this channel is opened, my psychic guide will be there to lead us along the path to our goal."

"I still can't believe that I'm going to get a chance to talk to my husband, and that he's in another universe."

"You've gotta believe, hon. Remember, it's your faith that's gonna make this thing possible. I'm only the conduit."

In the background, a piano began playing. Mimi recognized the music as Gershwin's, "Summertime." She had heard this same song very recently, but couldn't remember exactly where. Seemingly picking up on her thoughts, Dr. Elizabeth began softly humming along with the melody.

"That's sure a fittin' song," said the psychic. "This bein' the last full day of summer and all."

Mimi had almost forgotten the date, and looked down to the floor when the cat began to meow. "Sounds like Isis wants to sing along also," she said with a grin.

"What about some chow before we hit the seas?" asked Dr. Elizabeth.

Mimi readily accepted the offer, yet excused herself to make a single phone call to Virginia Key first. Only when she was satisfied with the results of this call did she join Dr. Elizabeth in the dining room.

The evening buffet included seafood specialties, and Mimi and Dr. Elizabeth put away their fair share of boiled shrimp, scallops, grilled red snapper, and succulent lobster tails. Isis had her portion of this feast during the drive that followed, and all were content as they passed over the Rickenbacker Causeway and took in the sparkling lights of Miami to their left.

The wharf area was for the most part empty of other cars, and Mimi parked her rental vehicle and led the way onto the nearby docks. Carrying the cage holding Isis, she passed by the sleek cabin cruiser that had been responsible for yesterday's catch of bonito, and halted alongside the rather decrepit wooden trawler that lay beside it. This vessel's owner could be seen on his hands and knees, at the stern, over the open engine hatch. With the assistance of a flashlight, he was in the process of exploring the compartment's innards, and failed to note the presence of newcomers.

"Excuse me, Captain Al. It's Mimi Slater."

The silver-haired old-timer looked slightly embarrassed as he switched off his flashlight and quickly looked up. "Hello, missy. I was just makin' some last minute adjustments to *Sunshine*'s carburetor."

"Don't let us stop you," said the psychic as she climbed onto the boat's fantail and set down her suitcase. "Hi, I'm Dr. Elizabeth."

Al stiffly stood, and made a point of wiping his grease-stained right hand on his coveralls, before pulling down the bill of his sailor's cap and issuing a mock salute. "Pleased to meet ya, Doc. The name's Alphonse Cloyd. But please, call me Al."

Dr. Elizabeth scanned the wooden stern and curiously peered into the engine compartment. "How's she been runnin', Al?"

"*Sunshine*'s a lot like her master, Doc. She just keeps movin' right along, slowly but surely. So don't you worry none, she'll get us there sure 'nough."

"I believe she will," said the psychic, who read the truth of this promise in the black man's honest face.

Mimi boarded the boat, and carefully handed the cage to its owner. Dr. Elizabeth wasted no time opening the wire-grill door, and Isis strolled onto the deck. The cat contentedly stretched, and then was kept busy with the assortment of scents that permeated her new home.

"My, what a beautiful pussycat," commented Al. "When I was a lad, we once had a big white cat who used to hang out down by da docks. Boy, did it ever get friendly when it got to be time to cut up da day's catch."

"Isis just loves fish, Al," replied Dr. Elizabeth.

"Then she certainly came to da right place, Doc, because I've got a locker just plumb full of fresh bonito fillets, just waitin' for her."

Mimi returned to the dock for her bag, then stowed it away in the boat's interior cabin. The cramped compartment featured a tiny private bathroom, a small galley, complete with a hot plate, a table with four wooden chairs, and two bulkhead-mounted sofas that doubled as beds. The only artwork present was a poster, tacked to the wall beside the kitchen area. It

258

showed a large, swampy expanse of water, with a flat-bottomed John boat floating on it. A pair of shabbily dressed black fishermen occupied this vessel, and it was Al who explained this poster's significance while he was preparing them some tea.

"That's a scene right outta my childhood, ladies."

Mimi and Dr. Elizabeth were gathered around the table, and it was the psychic who politely probed. "Where were you raised, Al?"

"Florida's Lake Okeechobee," answered Al proudly. "I was born in Port Mayaca, just a stone's throw from da water. My, oh my, was that some wild place in those days. We had gators comin' right up to da front door, and you never saw so many snakes in all your life."

"Sounds dangerous," remarked Mimi.

"Not really," returned Al. "My pappy taught us to respect nature, and da only critters we had any trouble with were da mosquitoes. I soon enough learned that skunk oil would take care of them, and I spent my childhood without so much as a snake bite."

"I envy you," said Dr. Elizabeth. "I grew up in the wilds of Brooklyn. A city of that size didn't have much nature to offer — an occasional songbird and plenty of rats and roaches."

"I don't mean to be nosy, or anything, but what's callin' you to da waters off Andros?" asked Al, as he wiped chipped ceramic mugs, none of which matched. "I know dat it's not for da fishin'."

"That's for sure," answered Dr. Elizabeth with a chuckle. "The closest that I ever want to get to a fish is my dinner plate."

"Then why go to all da expense of charterin' this boat?" continued the old-timer.

"Al, you look to me like you're a man of some religion," observed Dr. Elizabeth.

Al pointed to the ceiling and replied to this. "I respect and fear da Lord—if dat's what you mean, Doc?"

Dr. Elizabeth nodded and directly met the black man's curious stare. "Al, I guess you could say that we've chartered your boat for some very special prayers. All that we ask is that you leave us alone when these prayers begin, and that you guarantee us absolute quiet."

"I can certainly handle dat, Doc," replied Al, who poured a spoonful of loose tea into each of the mugs and then filled them with hot water.

"I thought you could," said Dr. Elizabeth, while catching Mimi's furtive glance.

Al served them their tea, and began whistling as he proceeded to pull a dented pewter flask from his pocket. To the melodic strains of "Summertime," he poured a good portion of the flask's contents into his tea, then looked up and smiled.

"I've got some tasty red-eye sweetener here, if you'd care to join me."

"Pour away," instructed Dr. Elizabeth as she anxiously held out her mug.

Mimi declined this offer, but she recognized the song she'd heard in the hotel's piano bar. It had been from Al's lips, just yesterday.

* * *

Captain Alexander Litvinov spent most of his afternoon inside his cabin aboard the *Pantera,* working on his personal log. He had started keeping a diary shortly before entering the Nakhimov Naval Academy in Sevastopol. The early days of his military career had been exciting, and he was glad that his father had recommended that he document this portion of his life. He had kept on writing, and he couldn't count the number of small, spiral notebooks that he had filled with his impressions and exploits.

Alexander hoped someday to combine these books into a cohesive account, and then have it published. For he was living proof that no matter how humble one's beginnings were, there was always the opportunity to better oneself.

Forty-two years ago, he had been born in the small Siberian town of Bratsk. His parents were both Kiev-bred engineers, who had volunteered to work on the Angara River hydroelectric facility. This was in the days when the pioneer Communist spirit swayed the hearts of young and old, and his parents spent the rest of their lives attempting to harness the wild rivers of Siberia, to obtain clean, inexpensive electrical power.

Alexander's fate was sealed the day his father took him on a weekend fishing trip to the shores of Lake Baikal. Never had the impressionable youngster seen anything like this lake, the largest fresh-water body on the entire planet. The surging waves entranced him, and when his father told him of other bodies of water

261

called oceans, which made Lake Baikal look like a mere pond in comparison, Alexander knew that his destiny lay at sea.

Soon after entering middle school, he joined the All-Union Voluntary Society for Assistance to the Navy, otherwise known as the DOSAAF. This paramilitary club did much to prepare him both physically and mentally for his chosen career. Because of his excellent grades and spotless disciplinary record, his application for enrollment in the Nakhimov Academy was accepted, and on the eve of his eighteenth birthday, he left Bratsk to become a man of the world.

He then broke the seal of his first diary, to record his journey on the Trans-Siberian Railroad. This was a great adventure, and he fought the urge to sleep, so eager was he not to miss a sight.

His father's stories did little to prepare him for the immensity of their country. It took a week just to reach the Ural mountains. From there a rail journey of several more days was needed to reach Stalingrad, Dnepropetrovsk, and finally, Sevastopol.

The Nakhimov Academy was situated on the shores of the Black Sea, and Alexander initiated his studies with one eye on the sparkling blue waters. Four years later, he graduated number one in his class, and received his first junior assignment, aboard a diesel-powered training submarine, based on the Baltic Sea, outside of Leningrad.

To get there, he boarded another train, and saw yet more of the *rodina* with memorable stops in Odessa, Kirov, and Moscow itself. Though he had only a day to spare, his hasty tour of the capital brought him to the Kremlin and the grave of the Soviet Union's founder. Viewing Lenin's mummified body was a great inspiration, and Alexander reboarded the train anxious to defend the socialist principles to which Lenin had dedicated most of his lifetime.

Alexander's summer in the Baltic whetted his appetite for more submarine duty, and after attending nuclear-power school in Leningrad, he became a reactor specialist aboard an Echo class attack sub. After distinguishing himself as a loyal, hard-working line officer, he served with distinction aboard the latest nuclear-powered attack and ballistic-missile-carrying submarines.

A year ago, he had been teaching physics at the Academy, and didn't know if he'd ever be sent to sea again — when the most exciting assignment of all was given to him. At long last, he was to have his very own command. And what a command this turned out to be!

The *Pantera* was the most advanced undersea warship that the *rodina* had ever produced. Its sensors and electronics were first class, and easily rivaled those of their primary adversary. Unfortunately, the world's changing political climate made this a most confusing time to take such a prototype vessel to sea, and he often wondered if this great expense was necessary.

With the breakup of the Soviet Union and the fall from power of the Party, went the end of the infamous Cold War. Today the enemy wasn't the United States, but internal strife within the

263

boundaries of the motherland.

As one of the new generation of naval officers who hadn't seen service in the Great Patriotic War, Alexander was participating in one of the greatest demobilizations in history. Half of the *rodina*'s submarine fleet had already been retired, with more to come. This would leave them with a vastly decreased force level of mostly newer, more capable vessels, with class names such as Akula and Pantera. These were the undersea warships that would take the *rodina* into the twenty-first century.

Alexander's current diary segment was a discussion of the new geopolitical climate, and *Pantera*'s place in it. As far as he was concerned, their present patrol was nothing but a friendly exercise in hide-and-seek. Following the USS *John Marshall* across the Atlantic was only a game, as was their current assignment.

The chances of actual hostilities with the Americans were improbable. The United States was now a firm ally, whose grain filled their bellies and whose clothing kept them warm.

Russia's experiments with a free-market economic system were promising, and America's guidance was invaluable. Communism was dead and buried, and the sooner his countrymen accepted this fact, the better off they'd be.

But how hard it was to break the socialist spell. Years of propaganda had ingrained a tangled web of lies deep into the *rodina*'s collective psyche. Even today, in these so-called enlightened times, the endless suspicions persisted, resulting in missed opportunities, and so much wasted effort.

Alexander knew that some aboard the *Pantera* would label his thoughts traitorous. Their *zampolit* was one of them.

Boris Dubrinin was a prime example of all that was wrong in today's Russia. He was a living anachronism, whose gospel was an irrelevant state Party line. Frustrated by his own personal shortcomings, he was an advocate of a step backwards, to a time when a tyrannical central state had ruled every aspect of one's life.

The fall of the Berlin Wall showed mankind that no dogma lasted forever, and that freedom of choice was every man's prerogative. Once set free, democracy swept through Eastern Europe, and soon made itself known on the streets of Moscow.

What Boris Dubrinin and his cronies failed to comprehend was that once the *rodina* had tasted such freedoms, a return to the blind subservience of the past would be impossible. They were still fighting yesterday's war, with the true enemy being themselves.

It proved to be the growl of the intercom that redirected Alexander's thoughts to more mundane matters. His hand shot out to pick up the nearest telephone handset.

"Underwater sonar contact, Captain!" said an excited male voice on the other end of the line. "Bearing two-six-zero."

"I'm on my way," replied Alexander.

The *Pantera*'s attack center was conveniently located only a few meters from his stateroom. A tense atmosphere prevailed here, as Alexander strode past the helm and approached the bearded figure seated behind the sonar console.

"What exactly do you have out there, *Misha*?" he breathlessly asked.

The senior sonarman pulled back one of his bulky headphones and pointed towards the repeater screen. "I've got a solid underwater transient, sir. But for the life of me, I can't quite place it."

To hear for himself, Alexander put a set of auxiliary headphones over his ears, and listened to a clearly audible, pulsating, whirring noise.

"You know, this signature reminds me a bit of that produced by the *John Marshall*," he surmised.

"I thought that was the case," said the sonarman. "But how can that be, when we left the *Marshall* behind in Norfolk, with the only other American sub similarly outfitted with a hull-mounted swimmer delivery shell whose home port is in the Pacific?"

"Perhaps the USS *Sam Houston* has transited the Panama Canal and is currently operating out of Port Canaveral," offered Alexander. "Or maybe what we're hearing is the signature of another submarine, that's carrying a deep submergence rescue vehicle on its back. Whatever it may be, make certain that you get plenty of tape on it for further analysis."

"That I will, sir," replied the sonarman as he returned his attention to his console.

From the other side of the attack center, a familiar bald-headed figure urgently beckoned Alexander to join him at the navigation plot. Though he was in no mood to tangle with Boris Dubrinin right now, he reluctantly crossed the compartment to see what was so important.

"Captain, what do you make of this new contact?" asked the concerned *zampolit*.

"My best guess is that it's either a converted Ethan Allen class vessel, or another class of attack sub that's been outfitted with a DSRV," answered Alexander.

The political officer responded to this news while patting his soaked forehead dry with a handkerchief. "Then for all we know, it could be the same 688 that we tailed from Norfolk."

"That it could, Comrade *Zampolit*," returned the captain.

Dubrinin looked down at the navigational chart that lay before him. "Captain, it's urgent that we follow this sub to learn its intentions."

"What's the reason for this urgency?" asked Alexander. "My operational orders say absolutely nothing about such a thing."

The *zampolit* pulled a folded piece of paper from his breast pocket and handed it to Alexander, who read its contents while Dubrinin spoke out in a bare whisper.

"This communiqué arrived only minutes ago, Captain. As you can see, the *Pantera* has been temporarily assigned to Special Development Group Thirteen, and is now under the direct command of Admiral Igor Valerian. Since our new orders implicitly direct us to monitor all American naval traffic headed into the Bahama Islands, we have no choice but to follow this new contact."

Alexander carefully reread the dispatch and shook

267

his head in confusion. "This is certainly a strange turn of events, Comrade. What is this Special Development Group Thirteen, and why have we been assigned to them?"

The *zampolit* sardonically grinned. "Your guess is as good as mine, Captain. And until we hear otherwise, what else can we do but follow these new orders as directed?"

Fifteen

Shortly after leaving Port Canaveral, the *Rickover* turned on a southeasterly course. They would continue in this direction for the next eighteen hours, passing by the western shores of Grand Bahama Island and entering Providence Channel sometime around dawn. This would put them at their desired destination shortly thereafter.

Thomas Moore spent his afternoon in seclusion. Tucked away in his bunk, he carefully read all the material that he had collected since his initial discovery of the *Lewis and Clark*. This event seemed to have taken place long ago, and he found it hard believe that he had been involved in the case for less than a week.

At 1650 hours, one of the mess stewards quietly entered the compartment and peeked around Moore's curtain.

"Excuse me, sir," he politely whispered. "But will you be joining the captain for dinner?"

"I sure will," answered Moore, who had skipped lunch and was ravenously hungry.

After stowing away his notes beneath his mattress,

and sealing the locker shut with a padlock, he proceeded to the head to wash up. Hop was in the process of drying his hands when Moore entered.

"Evening," said Hop, while Moore shuffled past him to get to the sink. "I hope you'll be having dinner with us."

"Wild horses couldn't keep me away," said Moore. "I'm starved."

"You picked the right meal to have an appetite, Commander. While in Port Canaveral, one of my men was able to get us a couple of fresh turkeys. They've been cooking all day, and the last time I checked, they looked perfect for eating."

Moore washed his face and hands, and gratefully took the towel that Hop handed him.

"Thanks, Hop. You know, there's a question that I've been meaning to ask you. How do you manage to keep so trim with all the good chow that they serve around here?"

Hop patted his belly and grinned. "I guess it's genetic, because no matter how much I eat, I always seem to remain the same weight."

"It must be nice, Hop, because I just look at food and put on the pounds."

"I hear you, my friend, and if it's any consolation, the *Rickover*'s got a Lifecycle and rowing machine available back in engineering. So this evening you can chow down all you want, and ease your guilt with a little exercise later on."

"I just might do that, Hop," said Moore, who followed his shipmate out of the head and into the nearby wardroom.

Captain Walden was already seated at the head of the table, with his XO on his right. Moore's position was to the captain's left, with a square-jawed newcomer seated beside him. Lieutenant Ned Barnes, the *Avalon*'s pilot, was all business as he passed the dressing to Moore and went back to work on his salad.

Tonight's background music was Aaron Copland's, *Appalachian Spring*. Its spirited melodies evoked an American mood, and provided the perfect accompaniment for the traditional meal that soon filled their plates.

As Moore was learning, submariners did things right, and the evening's menu was no exception. After a salad of fresh lettuce, with sliced tomatoes, cucumbers and green peppers, the steward arrived with the main course. Beginning with the captain, he circled the table with a silver-plated platter of sliced turkey. Then came the trimmings, including corn-bread dressing, yams, mashed potatoes, string beans, cranberry sauce, and pumpkin pie for dessert.

During dinner, conversation was at a minimum, with comments confined to the excellent food. During coffee afterwards, they were able to learn a bit more about the newcomer in their midst. It was Hop who got the ball rolling.

"Lieutenant Barnes," he said in a serious tone. "I don't want you to think that we eat this way every evening. In your honor, our cook was able to appropriate a couple of turkeys while we were picking you up."

"I'm always scared when you use that word appropriate, Hop," interrupted the captain. "I sure hope those birds were purchased legitimately."

"It's nothing the Admiral won't miss," deadpanned Hop. "At least, not until Thanksgiving."

A chorus of laughter was followed by the deep voice of Ned Barnes. "That was one fine meal, gentlemen. Where I've been for the last month, the only safe chow we had to look forward to were MRE's."

"Where was that?" asked the captain.

Relishing the spotlight, Barnes scanned the faces of his audience before answering. "Between you and me, *Avalon* was doing a little salvage job off the coast of Nicaragua. A type TR-1700 diesel-powered attack sub hit a reef there, and sank in a hundred feet of water. We were flown down to determine the nationality of this vessel, and to check on survivors."

"What did you find?" asked the XO, who spoke for all present.

Barnes took his time answering. "A chlorine leak in the battery well sealed the fate of the boat's twenty-nine crew members, who wore no uniforms and didn't appear to be from an organized military unit. Other than the original warranty papers from the German factory that constructed the sub, we couldn't find any evidence of its owners, though we did make an unusual find in five of the vessel's six torpedo tubes. Instead of weapons, they were stuffed with several thousand pounds of pure opium. Shit, there was enough poppy in there to addict half the population of New York City!"

"So now the drug cartels are using submarines," reflected the captain. "I wouldn't be surprised if the *Rickover* was to make a little visit to those waters sometime in the near future."

272

Moore had heard rumors that drug-smuggling submarines had paid America's shores a visit, and this story seemed to prove that they were true. While the *Rickover*'s officers discussed the best tactical way to counter such a threat, Moore carefully rolled up his napkin and excused himself.

In an effort to digest his meal, he began an extensive walking tour of the boat. He started off in engineering, passing by the vacant exercise machines. The reactor and power plant occupied a full two-thirds of the *Rickover,* and he was able to stretch his legs in relatively uncrowded passageways.

After paying his compliments to the cooks in the galley, he climbed to the deck below and walked around the torpedo room several times. The dimly lit compartment was quiet, as usual, and the watch team was content to let him take his stroll, without bothering him with any questions.

He concluded his evening in the control room. The excellent chow seemed to have put everyone in a good mood, and Moore spent an informative hour at the navigation plot, learning the intricacies of keeping a modern attack submarine on course.

Petty Officer Lacey wasn't on duty in sonar, but Moore did find the COB fulfilling his watch as the diving officer. Chief Ellwood had half of an unlit cigar in his mouth, and wouldn't let Moore leave until he tried his hand at driving the *Rickover.*

Lieutenant Carr was the current OOD, and the easygoing Californian readily approved this unscheduled switch of helmsman. Moore was a bit uneasy as he settled into the upholstered chair and grabbed the control

273

yoke. It was stiffer than he had imagined, and with the COB close beside him, he initiated several minor depth changes, careful to keep the boat on course.

"How's she handle?" asked the COB, after relighting his cigar and putting his feet up on the center console.

Needing both hands and the combined strength of his arms to pull the sub out of a slight three-degree descent, Moore replied. "It's not quite up to 'Vette standards."

"Hell, she can turn just like a Jet fighter if needed," informed the COB. "And that ain't bad, considerin' that we're pushin' almost seven thousand tons of boat through the water."

Moore was grateful when the helmsman relieved him several minutes later. And after thanking the COB for his driving lesson, he left the control room, with a new respect for its men and machinery.

He caught the last half of a Clint Eastwood spaghetti Western in the wardroom, and by the time the film's final frame faded, he was ready for bed. Sleep was quick in coming, with his food-induced dreams taking him on a hike into the Highlands of Scotland with Laurie, and a frightening visit to a pitch black tunnel whose walls seemed to be closing in on him.

He awoke seven hours later, with the urge to relieve himself his number one priority. To get to the head, he had to pass the wardroom, where he encountered the XO, hurriedly filling a mug with coffee.

"You got up just in time," called the XO, who was clean-shaved and ready for work. "We've got a sighting on the periscope that I think you'll be interested in."

"Just give me time for a pit stop, and I'll be right with you," replied Moore as he continued to the head.

The XO was faithfully waiting to escort him up to the control room. He found the compartment lit in red, and the captain anxiously huddled over the boat's attack scope.

"Commander Moore's here, Captain," announced the XO.

Walden stepped back from the scope, and scanned the room until his gaze locked on Thomas Moore.

"Mr. Moore, please have a look," offered Walden.

The investigator climbed onto the slightly elevated bridge and joined the captain beside the periscope. A neophyte at this business, he tentatively grabbed onto the scope's twin handles and peered into the rubber lens coupling.

The dawn was breaking topside, and thankful that his night vision was intact, he spotted a surface ship floating in the distance.

"Use that left handle to increase the magnification if you'd like," informed the captain.

Moore rotated the handle downwards, and the surface vessel seemed to jump into closer view. The ship had a pointed bow, with a sleek, modern superstructure and a single stack. He had seen a picture of this same boat only recently, while sorting through his notes, and knew that he was looking at a live shot of the *Academician Petrovsky*.

The captain's voice lowered to a whisper. "Did you get a look at those flags flying from her stern?"

With the amplified assistance of the scope, Moore spotted the crimson red hammer and sickle banner of the Soviet Navy blowing in the breeze beside the ship's fantail. Next to it fluttered the blue and white insignia of the United Nations.

"Those flags sure make strange bedfellows," said Moore as he backed away from the scope.

Walden lowered the periscope, then turned to address Moore. "Now that we've made it to our destination, I believe that you're supposed to be calling the shots, Commander. How do you want to proceed?"

Moore had been dreading this moment, and he had to clear his throat before being able to express himself. "Captain, I'm going to need to board that vessel. Can we contact her?"

"She's as close as a call on our underwater telephone," answered Walden. "Things would sure go a lot smoother if I knew her name."

"It's the *Academician Petrovsky*," Moore said without missing a beat.

Impressed with the investigator's knowledge, Walden reached up to the ceiling and pulled down a coiled cord, which was attached to a large hand-held microphone. Walden placed this device to his lips and spoke out clearly.

"*Academician Petrovsky*, this is the American warship, USS *Hyman G. Rickover*. Do you read me, over?"

Walden had to repeat this message three more times, before a somewhat scratchy response resounded through the intercom speakers.

"This is the *Academician Petrovsky*. What nature of vessel are you?"

Walden didn't look all that happy as he responded.

"We're a nuclear-powered attack submarine, positioned beneath the water three thousand yards off your port bow."

"One moment, please," said the amplified voice with a hint of excitement. "I must get my superior officer."

Two minutes passed before another voice projected from the intercom speakers. "This is Senior Lieutenant Viktor Ilyich Alexandrov at your service, Comrade. To whom do I have the honor of speaking?"

"This is Captain John Walden of the USS *Hyman G. Rickover.*"

"And how can I help you, Captain Walden?" asked the Russian.

Walden looked at Moore for help, and the investigator alertly pulled out his notebook and scribbled out an appropriate response for the captain.

"Senior Lieutenant Alexandrov, one of my crew members, Commander Thomas Moore, would like permission to board your ship to speak to the U.N. observer team."

"Such a surprise request is highly irregular, Captain," retorted Alexandrov. "And before I can approve it, I must clear it with my superior, Admiral Igor Valerian."

"Very well, Senior Lieutenant. We'll await your reply."

Walden stowed away the microphone and looked the investigator straight in the eyes. "Commander, I believe I'm long overdue for that briefing that you've been promising me."

"That you are, Captain," returned Moore. "And

277

you'll have it, right after you get me on that ship."

It took ten minutes before the intercom speakers once again crackled alive. "Captain Walden, this is Senior Lieutenant Alexandrov. In the spirit of peaceful coexistence that underscores our current mission, Commander Moore's request has been approved. Please surface at once, and we'll send out a boat to initiate the transfer."

Moore's relief was instantaneous, and he hurried down to his bunk to prepare himself. A quarter of an hour later, he was climbing up the *Rickover*'s forward access trunk.

The sun was breaking the eastern horizon as Moore approached the sailors gathered on the sub's deck. One of these was the captain, who took Moore aside and pointed towards the small, wooden gig headed towards them from the direction of the *Academician Petrovsky*.

"About how long will you be needing over there?" questioned Walden.

"I shouldn't be gone more than an hour, Captain."

"Very well, Mr. Moore. We'll wait for you topside. Don't hesitate to call us if you should run into any lengthy delays."

"Will do, Captain."

Still not certain what he'd be encountering aboard the Russian ship, Moore tried his best to look as confident as possible. Because the sea was almost dead flat, the transfer over to the gig took place without incident, and the investigator soon found himself surrounded by four brawny Russian sailors, wearing blue-and-white striped tunics. It was evident that none of them

278

spoke English, and because Moore's Russian was equally limited, the short voyage took place in utter silence.

He boarded the *Academician Petrovsky* by way of a ladder. Waiting for him on the deck was an immaculately uniformed Russian naval officer, and a heavyset, ruddy-cheeked, middle-aged fellow, dressed in a baggy seersucker suit. It was this portly fellow who stepped forward and initiated the introductions.

"Good day, Commander Moore. I'm Dr. Harlan Sorkin. On behalf of the United Nations, I'd like to welcome you aboard the *Academician Petrovsky*. May I introduce Senior Lieutenant Alexandrov, our host vessel's executive officer."

Moore politely nodded towards the Russian, noting that Dr. Sorkin's accent indicated that he was most likely either from Australia or New Zealand.

"Dr. Sorkin," said Moore in an easygoing, informal tone of voice. "I'm sorry to drop in on you like this, but I've been sent to check on your team's comfort and on the adequacy of this vessel to provide support for the habitat."

"You have nothing to worry about on either account, Commander," returned the doctor. "The *Academician Petrovsky* has provided us with all the comforts of home, and it's been the ideal support ship for our program."

"I don't believe that I've ever seen a vessel quite like this one," remarked Moore.

"That's because it's unique on all the seven seas," said Alexandrov proudly. "It was originally designed for oceanographic research, and is one of the newest research ships in the Russian fleet."

Moore approvingly scanned the spotlessly clean deck. "It's most impressive. Would you mind a quick tour before I return to the *Rickover?*"

"I'd be glad to show you around myself," offered Dr. Sorkin. "That is, if Senior Lieutenant Alexandrov doesn't mind."

Though the Russian didn't look exactly thrilled by this prospect, he nevertheless beckoned towards a hatchway leading below. "Go ahead and enjoy yourself, Commander Moore. And when you're done with your tour, perhaps you'll join us in the wardroom for some breakfast."

"Thanks for the offer," replied Moore. "But all I have time for is that tour before I have to start back."

The Russian looked disappointed with this news. "That's too bad, Comrade. I'm certain that the other officers would enjoy meeting you."

"Perhaps another time," said Moore, who allowed Dr. Sorkin to take him by the arm and lead him to the ship's interior.

They went below and began their way aft down a long central passageway.

"I'm flattered that your government thought enough about our project to send you out here to check on us," remarked Sorkin as they passed by several spacious staterooms. "By the way, these are our cabins. Pretty luxurious, aren't they?"

"I'll say," replied Moore. "This sure beats the nine-man berthing compartment I'm currently sharing."

Sorkin went on to show him the vessel's well-equipped laboratory, which easily rivaled that of a small university. Moore met two other members of the U.N. team, an Indian scientist studying plankton dispersal, and an Italian, whose specialty was hydrography. A trained oceanographer himself, Sorkin was studying the local reef corals, and determining how pollution was affecting their growth.

He seemed to take special pride in that portion of the ship positioned aft of the laboratory. A large rectangular opening to the sea had been cut into the hull. Called the moonpool, it was surrounded by a latticed-steel catwalk, and currently held a pair of bright yellow, saucer-shaped minisubs floating on its surface.

Moore was interested to learn that one of the habitat program's goals was self-sufficiency, and therefore these diving saucers were available only for emergencies. Dr. Sorkin and his team had their services for research, and utilized this unique mode of exploring the sea floor whenever the crew's schedule permitted.

Fascinated by the moonpool, Moore walked down the catwalk until he reached a closed hatch cut into the after bulkhead. When he went to open this hatch, he found it locked, and his guide was quick to explain the reason. On the other side of this bulkhead was the reactor room, and for the safety of the team, this portion of the *Academician Petrovsky* was off limits.

Moore spotted a pair of thick rubber cables penetrating this same bulkhead and extending into the sea via the moonpool. He kept this discovery to himself, and told his escort that he had seen enough.

During the trip topside, he couldn't help pondering two disturbing thoughts. Because the *Academician Petrovsky* was powered by a diesel-electric propulsion plant, why was it outfitted with a nuclear reactor? And there were those twin cables to consider. Since the Mir habitat was supposed to be self-sufficient, they couldn't be used as a power conduit, unless it was for a vastly different underwater project that even the U.N. observer team wasn't aware of.

Though Moore would have liked to share his suspicions with his guide, he wisely held his tongue. Declining Sorkin's offer of tea, he gratefully climbed to the outer deck, where he found two officers waiting for him beside the ladder leading to the gig. One was the ship's senior lieutenant. The other was a tall, erect, distinguished-looking veteran, with a patch covering his left eye.

"Commander Moore, I'm Admiral Igor Valerian," greeted the velvet-voiced flag officer. "I understand that Dr. Sorkin has been giving you a tour of my ship. I do hope you found everything satisfactory."

"That I did, Admiral. This vessel is most impressive, and it appears that you have been taking excellent care of Dr. Sorkin and his staff. I'll make certain to pass on this fact to my superiors, and also relay the warmth of your hospitality, considering that this spur-of-the-moment visit took you by surprise."

"It's always nice to have visitors while at sea," returned Valerian. "Though it's not often that they arrive on such a specialized mode of transport."

Looking out to sea at this point, Valerian focused his gaze on the *Rickover* and added. "I see that you're carrying a DSRV, Commander. I hope that one of your submarines isn't missing in the area."

Quick to pick up the intentional irony in these

words, Moore did his best to smile. "The *Rickover's* only carrying it for an exercise, Admiral. I wish that I could invite you aboard to have a closer look, but we'll be sailing as soon as I return."

"That's too bad," returned Valerian. "I always did want to visit the vessel named after the father of your nuclear navy. Hyman G. Rickover was a great visionary, and from what I understand, a man who could get things done. Our own Admiral of the Fleet Sergei Georgiyevich Gorshokov, had similar talents. It's tragic that neither of them lived to see this day of mutual military trust between our two great nations."

"That it is, Admiral," replied Moore, who went on to thank Dr. Sorkin for his time, and then began the short climb into the awaiting gig.

During the trip back to the *Rickover,* he pondered his impressions of the one-eyed Russian flag officer. Admiral Igor Valerian had a supercilious, haughty manner. He seemed to be deliberately teasing when he made reference to the DSRV, and Moore got the distinct impression that he was referring to the *Lewis and Clark,* with his remark about a missing submarine in the area.

It was as he made the transfer over to the *Rickover,* that he decided how best to continue the investigation. First he would give Captain Walden an intense briefing. It could be dangerous to keep the *Rickover's* CO in the dark any longer. Then his next move would be to take advantage of the *Avalon's* presence. With the DSRV's invaluable assistance, he'd be able to find out just what it was that the *Academician Petrovsky's* reactor was supplying power to.

"Down scope!" ordered Alexander Litvinov as he backed away from the periscope well.

"So, now we know the precise nature of the contact whose mysterious signature led us all the way from Port Canaveral," said the grinning *zampolit,* who stood beside the nearby navigation plotting table. "This is a momentous day, Comrade. To follow an American 688 class vessel, and have it completely unaware of our presence!"

"I'd be in a much better mood to celebrate if that 688 hadn't been burdened with a DSRV on its back," returned Litvinov.

"You're being much too hard on yourself, Captain," countered Boris Dubrinin. "The moment we raised our scope and captured that Yankee attack sub on film, signaled a new era in the history of the red banner fleet. No longer are we disadvantaged by technological backwardness, for today, the hunter has become the hunted!"

Alexander Litvinov's eyes couldn't help gleaming with pride in response to this observation.

"I must admit that when I first looked through the scope, that surfaced 688 looked like an inviting target," he thoughtfully reflected. "In all my years of naval service, I never dreamed that I would be privileged to see such a remarkable sight."

"I always said that the highly vaunted 688 class was overrated," added Dubrinin.

"Captain," interrupted the senior sonar technician, "I'm picking up internal noises inside the American

284

sub. It sounds as if they're getting ready to dive."

Both Litvinov and his political officer raced to sonar, where the *zampolit* emotionally voiced himself.

"Your vigilance is needed more than ever, Misha, because we've come too far to lose them now. And besides, Admiral Valerian himself is presently monitoring our efforts."

Sixteen

Ever since the fire in the hangar, a somber, almost funereal atmosphere prevailed inside Starfish House. The aquanauts took the loss of the minisub like that of a co-worker, and the team's leader took it upon himself to boost their badly sagging morale. It was during lunch that Pierre Lenclud directly confronted the group, who had gathered around the dining room table.

"*Mes amis,* it's time for all of us to come to terms with the fact that we will no longer have the services of our diving saucer. I know that all of us have grown dependent upon *Misha,* but now that must change. Until this great experiment is ended, we will have to get used to doing things ourselves, with no more excursions into the depths, and no additional muscle but our own. Can you live with that?"

"It doesn't sound like we have much of a choice in the matter," remarked Ivana. "I relied on *Misha* more than any of you, yet I certainly don't want to give up. Even though I still think we've been the victim of deliberate sabotage."

"I disagree," countered Karl Ivar. "I'm the only one to blame for that fire, and I take full responsibility for it."

Ivana snickered. "Comrade, your sentiments are noble, but your perceptions naïve. It's obvious that you don't understand the ruthless nature of the forces that we're dealing with."

Before the Norwegian could respond to this, Pierre Lenclud slapped the palm of his hand hard against the table. "Enough of this senseless bickering! It will get us absolutely nowhere. If this team is to survive intact, then we must put this incident behind us."

"I'm with the Commandant," concurred Lisa Tanner. "So we've lost a valuable piece of machinery. Big deal. We've still got our life-support system, and all the other features of this underwater city. So let's not go and lose our perspective, or we'll ruin this once-in-a-lifetime opportunity."

Tomo quickly got on the kiwi's bandwagon. "Well said, Lisa. I was looking forward to using the saucer to help me put up the walls of the fish pen. But I've been waiting five long years to attempt this experiment, and I'm quite prepared to do all the manual labor myself. I say forget *Misha*, and let's continue with this great adventure while we have the opportunity to do so."

"You won't have to work on the fish pen by yourself, Tomo," said Karl Ivar. "I think I've figured out a way to raise those steel frames by utilizing a simple lever and our underwater winch."

Pierre Lenclud appeared delighted with this news, and he exclaimed, "Now that's the spirit!"

"Spirits?" squawked Ulge, from his perch at the

Frenchman's side. "Where's the spirits? Where's the spirits?"

"See what we get for having a lush for our mascot," joked Lenclud, who broke out in laughter along with the rest of his teammates.

This served to break the tension, and even Ivana Petrov seemed to have her spirits lightened. For the first time in over a day, she smiled. And when she spoke, her very tone had changed.

"I guess that I have been taking this entire incident much too seriously, Comrades. I apologize, and promise to look beyond my own selfish goals, and reapply myself for the good of the project as a whole. Who knows what may be discovered right outside the doors of Starfish House."

"Before we go and get too involved with a new project, *mon amie,* I'm going to need you to assist me in Habitat One. It's time to recharge the compressor with helium, and then there's another inventory to begin."

Ivana warmly responded to this request. "Lead the way, Comrade Lenclud. And this time you can be my lookout for any prowling sharks in the area."

"With pleasure, *mon amie,*" said the Frenchman with a relieved grin.

Thomas Moore didn't know which would be the harder of his two tasks, briefing Captain Walden on his mission, or summoning the nerve to crawl into the *Avalon.* Much to his relief, he got through both of them with a minimum amount of stress.

288

No sooner did Moore return to the *Rickover* from this visit to the *Academician Petrovsky,* when the captain called him into his stateroom. To make things as easy as possible, Moore stuck to the truth, and told Walden everything, from the first time he set eyes on the *Lewis and Clark,* to his encounter with Homer Morgan, and all that he had learned from Admiral Proctor back in Washington. He concluded by reaffirming his skepticism, but emphasizing the necessity of keeping an open mind and following every available lead to its end.

Walden had been a physics instructor at the Naval Academy, and had a previous knowledge of the Philadelphia Experiment. Also a skeptic, he nevertheless expressed his belief that the scientific principles behind Einstein's theories were sound, and that a device that could render matter invisible, then teleport it to another location, was well within the boundaries of scientific possibility. Like Moore, he immediately dismissed the black-hole story as pure science fiction, and agreed that it was in the best interest of the investigation to deploy the DSRV with all due haste.

One factor that Moore hadn't anticipated was that John Walden had been a personal friend of the *Lewis and Clark's* skipper. They had served together on a past command, and Walden had even had dinner at his house several times. Genuinely saddened by his disappearance, Walden pledged his full support, and Moore left the stateroom ready for the next challenge.

He found the *Avalon's* pilot in the wardroom, reading a worn copy of the Navy League magazine, *Sea Power.* Ned Barnes didn't flinch as Moore explained to him just what he needed from the DSRV. To guarantee this operation's secrecy, Barnes recommended that they deploy the *Avalon* while submerged, a good ten thousand yards from the *Academician Petrovsky*. That way it would be all but impossible for them to be discovered. He also advised Moore to bring along a sweater, and a thermos of coffee if he so desired.

Moore took his expert advice on both counts, and ten minutes later was making his way up the stern access trunk. This was his first visit to a DSRV, and he was all eyes as he climbed through the transfer skirt and entered the main pressure capsule. Waiting for him was a skinny, bald-headed sailor with a drooping brown moustache and deep sunken cheeks.

"Afternoon, sir. I'm Chief Ollie Draper, the *Avalon*'s sphere operator. I'll be operating the life-support system and manipulator controls."

"Pleased to meet you, Chief. Is Lieutenant Barnes on board?"

"That he is, sir. You'll find him in the cockpit, where you'll also be sitting."

The pressure capsule was dominated by a large sphere that could hold up to two dozen tightly packed crewmen in the event the DSRV was called upon to evacuate a distressed submarine. With only one way to go but forward, Moore crawled through a tight hatch, and found himself in an equipment-packed compartment which reminded him of an airplane's cockpit. Seated in the left-hand position, completely surrounded by dozens of glowing dials and gauges, was Ned Barnes. The grizzled pilot wore a set of blue coveralls, and a matching cap with the insignia of the Dallas Cowboys football team emblazoned on its bill. The seat to his right was vacant, and Barnes addressed the newcomer while going over his "preflight" checklist.

"The only way to get yourself properly settled is by going in feet first. Grab those handholds above your head, and maneuver in that way."

Moore did as instructed, and it took him several awkward seconds to line up his body in the right position. Climbing into his berth on the *Rickover* was child's play compared to this, and trying his best to ignore a cramp in his foot, he managed to lift up his lower torso and ease himself into the spare seat.

"You're going to be my copilot during this mission," informed Barnes. "There are some functions such as sonar and communications that only you can access. I'll talk you through, so don't worry, it's nothing you can't handle. And please, we're on a strict first-name basis here on *Avalon*. Do you go by Thomas or Tom?"

"Thomas is just fine."

"Very well, Thomas it is."

Barnes went back to his checklist, while Moore studied the complicated console that lay before him. The only piece of equipment that looked familiar was a green-tinted CRT monitor, that appeared to be a condensed version of the screens found in the *Rickover*'s sonar room.

"Thomas, I'm going to need you to activate the echo sounder," informed Barnes. "To do so, push up on those two green toggle switches located to the right of your sonar repeater."

Moore scanned the console and spotted the twin switches beside the CRT screen. As he pushed them upwards, a constant, hollow pinging noise began sounding in the background.

"Delta, Zulu, Foxtrot, this is Alpha, Omega, Bravo, do you read me?" spoke Barnes into his miniature, chin-mounted radio transmitter.

"That's affirmative, Alpha, Omega, Bravo," spoke an amplified voice from the elevated P.A. speakers. "We copy you loud and clear."

"Am initiating unlock sequence, Delta, Zulu, Foxtrot," informed Barnes.

"Alpha, Omega, Bravo, you are cleared to unlock."

After this announcement the pilot's hands addressed the various switches of the console with practiced ease. There was a loud clicking noise, and the muted, humming sound of an engine turning over.

"Here we go, Thomas," said Barnes, as he gripped the thick, black plastic joystick that was situated between his knees.

The *Avalon* momentarily shuddered, and its pilot yanked back on the joystick, causing the DSRV's bow to angle sharply upwards. This movement was accompanied by a rolling sensation, as the *Avalon* canted over hard on its left side, and Barnes readdressed his chin-mounted microphone.

"Unlock completed, Delta, Zulu, Foxtrot. We're proceeding to target."

"That's affirmative, Alpha, Omega, Bravo. Good hunting."

Barnes pulled back the microphone and exhaled a deep breath of relief. "We're on our way, Thomas. Now I'm going to need your help activating the video camera. We might not have any windows in this little lady, but I'm about to show you the best underwater view in town."

"Captain," said the concerned voice of the *Pantera*'s senior sonar technician, "I'm picking up another transient coming from the direction of our target. I believe it's the DSRV."

This information caused both Alexander Litvinov and his *zampolit* to rush over to the sonarman's side. Litvinov anxiously put on the auxiliary headphones, and he momentarily closed his eyes to focus his concentration on the sounds coming from the sea.

"Well, Captain, what do you hear?" quizzed the impatient political officer.

Litvinov held up his hand to silence Dubrinin, and didn't vocally respond for another thirty seconds.

"It's the DSRV all right, and it appears to be going somewhere in a great hurry."

"We must inform Admiral Valerian of this fact," replied the worried *zampolit*. "Because the DSRV's most likely destination is the *Academician Petrovsky* itself!"

Igor Valerian was in his stateroom, in the midst of his morning tea, when a knock sounded on his door.

"Enter," said Valerian curtly.

The door swung open, and in walked Senior Lieutenant Alexandrov, looking pale and perturbed.

"Excuse me, Admiral. But we just received a priority-one communiqué from the *Pantera*."

Valerian looked surprised by this revelation. "The

Pantera, you say? This is certainly an exciting turn of events, Comrade. What does the *rodina's* most advanced undersea warship have to say?"

"It concerns the *Hyman G. Rickover,* sir. It seems the *Pantera* has been successfully shadowing the American sub for sometime now. Minutes ago, the *Rickover* was monitored as it released its DSRV. And the *Pantera* fears that it's headed back our way."

"You sound surprised by this news, Senior Lieutenant. Did you expect anything different?"

Alexandrov appeared perplexed, and Valerian compassionately added, "It was obvious from the very beginning that the American naval officer who visited us was nothing but a spy. And now our Yankee comrades are about to stick their ever-curious noses where they don't belong."

"And what can we do about it?" asked Alexandrov.

"We have several options available to us, Comrade. The fact that the *Pantera* has been able to secretly tail the *Rickover* gives us the advantage. And now it's time to use our submarine to convey our displeasure."

Valerian momentarily halted and thoughtfully stroked his chin, before continuing. "If I remember correctly, the *Pantera's* current captain was quite an accomplished strategist while at the Nakhimov Academy. His *zampolit,* Boris Dubrinin, is a crafty old fox, and together they should be able to get our message across to the Americans."

"And how will they do that, short of launching a torpedo salvo?" questioned the senior lieutenant.

"I see that you've never had duty aboard a submarine, Comrade," observed Valerian with a wise grin.

"The Cold War taught us a variety of so-called peaceful ways to rid the seas of an unwanted trespasser. One of my very favorites is a sonar lashing. And then there's always an old-fashioned love tap. Comrade, you'd be surprised how much damage the *Pantera's* specially reinforced bow can do to the unsuspecting American vessel. The *Rickover* will soon enough be limping back to port, and the ironic part is that they'll never know what hit them!"

Completely oblivious to the underwater confrontation that was unfolding in the sea around them, the crew of the Mir habitat went about their day's business with an innocent naïveté. To the five aquanauts, the habitat was their entire milieu, with the evil machinations of the outside world all but forgotten.

This state of innocence was especially apparent in Starfish House's galley, where Lisa Tanner went about preparing for dinner with her usual exuberance. In honor of the first day of autumn, she was cooking a special meal. Back home in New Zealand, it was customary to greet the equinox with either fresh game or local fish. Since neither were readily available, she had to make do with sauteed orange roughy filets, that she had been saving in the freezer for just this occasion. She also planned to serve canned yams, her mom's famous broccoli-rice casserole, and jellied cranberry sauce. Pumpkin custard would replace the traditional mincemeat pie, with plenty of caffeine-free, apple-spice tea to wash it down.

Her only companion during the entire afternoon

had been Ulge. The rest of her co-workers stayed busy with chores that took them out of the central habitat. Even Uncle Albert had abandoned her, the barracuda being conspicuously absent from his usual haunt outside the galley's porthole. Certain that he'd be back in time for leftovers, she breaded the defrosted fish filets in cornmeal, and went to work on the casserole.

It was while cooking the rice that she became aware of a gathering headache. Beginning in her temples, it quickly expanded, until her whole head seemed to be throbbing with pain. She felt slightly dizzy, and decided that a couple of Tylenol were in order. This medication was stored in the bathroom, and as she left the kitchen, she spotted a small green object on the floor beside the dining room table. Her pain-clouded thoughts were unable to identify it at first, and it wasn't until she bent down that she realized what she was looking at.

"Oh my God, Ulge!"

The parrot was gasping for breath, and seemed to be barely hanging onto life. With Lisa's exclamation, it opened its eyes wide, then began shaking uncontrollably. Seconds later, it was dead.

Lisa's first instinct was to pick up and cuddle the poor creature. But then a sudden realization dawned in her consciousness. Ulge hadn't been there just for his company, but had been included with a definite purpose in mind. She suddenly found herself panting for breath, and knew in an instant what had killed their mascot. The air had gone bad!

Every couple of days, Commandant Lenclud would surprise them with an unannounced drill. The sce-

296

narios ranged from fire to a loss of their life-support systems. The Frenchman had insisted that these training sessions be adhered to with the strictest of realism, and they were constantly repeated, until they could practically react to each worst-case scenario in their sleep.

Though the constant throbbing pain in her head made the mere process of thinking difficult, the long hours of repetitive training paid off, and she instinctively dragged herself into the ready room. She was fighting for each breath as she reached for her scuba tanks, turned on the regulator, and put the rubber mouthpiece of the air hose into her mouth. The relief was almost instantaneous. She no longer had to struggle to breathe, and even her headache seemed to dissipate.

With her thoughts now clearing, she proceeded to put on her wet suit, weight belt, and dual tank harness. Then with mask and fins in hand, she began her way into the water to warn the others.

Lisa found her four scuba-clad associates outside, working on the fish pens. Dr. Petrov held a white plastic clipboard in hand and waterproof pen, that they used to communicate with, and Lisa borrowed these objects to spell out the warning.

Air Emergency!!! Ulge dead!!!

This dreaded message prompted an immediate response. It was the Frenchman who led the way over to Habitat One. With their air tanks still in place, they climbed inside to check the compressor. They found it in perfect working order, which meant only one thing. It was the air mixture itself that was at fault.

While Karl Ivar and Tomo went back into the store-room to see what they could do to rectify this cata-strophic problem, Lenclud grabbed the clipboard. He expressed himself with a frantic scrawl.

Gather all emergency scuba tanks. Am returning to Starfish House to issue SOS.

Lisa signaled with a thumbs-up, and she worriedly watched the Frenchman as he turned for the accessway to get on with this task.

Thomas Moore had been pleasantly surprised at how easy it was to locate the submerged cables. They located them on active sonar, at a depth of two hun-dred and fifty feet, almost directly beneath the *Acade-mician Petrovsky*. With the invaluable assistance of the *Avalon's* bow-mounted video camera, they verified this find, and began following the snaking cables into the black depths below.

At four hundred and twenty-seven feet, the *Avalon* appeared to stop dead in the water, and it was Ned Barnes who surmised that it was the thermocline that was most likely impeding their way. To penetrate this dense liquid barrier, additional salt water ballast was brought aboard, and the DSRV was able to continue its descent.

The depth gauge was just about to pass five hundred feet, when the radio activated with a burst of static, followed by a firm male voice.

"Alpha, Omega, Bravo, this is Delta, Zulu, Foxtrot. Do you read me, over?"

Barnes pulled down his chin-mounted microphone

and responded. "Delta, Zulu, Foxtrot, this is Alpha, Omega, Bravo. We copy you loud and clear. How can we help you?"

"Alpha, Omega, Bravo, we need you to break off your current op at once, and head to chart coordinates three-five-zero-one. We've just been notified of an emergency aboard the Mir habitat that requires your immediate presence."

"I copy that, Delta, Zulu, Foxtrot. Let them know that the cavalry is on its way."

"Well don't that take the cake," added Ned Barnes as he pushed the microphone out of his way. "Looks like it's a good thing that we were down here snooping after all."

He yanked back on the joystick, and the *Avalon* pulled out of its descent, until its bow was steeply angled upwards.

"Thomas, I need you to access the navigation plot. If I remember right, that habitat is located almost due west of us, at a depth of about sixty feet. It's well within our range, and I can only wonder what in the hell's happening to warrant this abrupt change in orders."

"Captain, I've got increased propeller revs on the DSRV," reported the *Pantera's* senior sonar technician. "I believe they've just pulled out of their dive."

"Right now that's inconsequential, Comrade," returned the *zampolit,* who stood directly behind the sonarman, with Alexander Litvinov close beside him. "Because as the captain here will attest, our proper quarry is not the DSRV, but its mother vessel. What is the status of the 688?"

The bearded sonar operator readjusted his sensors, and answered Dubrinin somewhat tentatively. "I believe it's turning on a new course, bearing two-five-zero."

"Why weren't we made aware of this course change sooner?" barked the enraged *zampolit*. "While you wasted your efforts on that DSRV, our prey almost slipped right out of our fingers!"

"Please get control of yourself, Comrade Dubrinin," interjected Litvinov. "Raising your voice like that will accomplish us nothing."

Redirecting his remarks to the technician, the captain spoke out in a calm, reassuring tone. "Isolate the 688, Misha, and interface its signature directly into the fire-control system."

"Will we be launching a torpedo at them, Captain?" asked the concerned technician.

"I certainly hope not," returned Litvinov. "Though all six of our tubes are currently loaded with weapons, our intention here is not to start World War III, Misha. We've only been ordered to scare the American submarine away. And to accomplish this, I think that our first task should be to let them know that we're here. We shall do this by hitting them with a deafening burst of active sonar, that's bound to get their attention and put fear in their hearts."

Seventeen

"I sure am sorry about da delay, Doc," apologized Al from the open confines of the *Sunshine*'s wheelhouse. "It sure ain't like *Sunshine* to fail me like that."

"All that matters is that we safely made the crossing, Al," returned Dr. Elizabeth, who stood beside him, with her hands on hips.

Andros Island was passing on their right, and the psychic looked out at the low-lying mass of mangrove trees and sand. The sun was already inching towards the western horizon, yet it still radiated unmerciful warmth. With the brim of her straw hat long since soaked, Dr. Elizabeth redirected her gaze to the boat's interior cabin, when Mimi Slater emerged into the sunlight. Appearing pale and unsteady, Mimi held onto the edge of the hatchway as if for dear life.

"Feelin' better, hon?" asked Dr. Elizabeth, her concern most genuine.

Mimi shook her head. "I'm afraid not. No matter what I do, I still feel sick to my stomach."

"We's out of da Gulf Stream now, missy, and da waters here are usually as calm as a bathtub. So you can relax, knowing dat da worst is over."

"Al's right, hon. We've come such a long way to get here, it would be a pity to give up now. Come join me in the sunlight, and breathe in some of this good clean air."

Mimi somewhat reluctantly took the psychic's suggestion, letting go of her handhold and unsteadily proceeding into the wheelhouse itself. Isis could be seen lazily sunning herself on the boat's fantail, where a card table and three chairs had been set up.

"So that's Andros Island," managed Mimi, in reference to the passing landmass.

"Are you sure dat you don't want to stop at Nicholl Town?" asked Al. "My cousin Sherman will take good care of us there."

Dr. Elizabeth looked at Mimi while answering. "I'm sure that he would. But unfortunately, we've got another date to keep."

Al shrugged his skinny shoulders, and quickly reached down to inch back the throttle when the trawler's engine began sputtering. A thick plume of blue gray smoke billowed from the stern, prompting Al to lift up his head in mock prayer.

"Come on, *Sunshine*. Don't fail me now, ole gal."

Seemingly in response to this petition, the engine loudly wheezed a single time, before finally returning to normal.

"Dat's my baby," said Al with a satisfied grin.

Dr. Elizabeth walked over to Mimi, and gently guided her by the arm to one of the chairs.

"You have a seat right here, and everything will be

302

just fine. Can I get you some water? Or maybe you'd like some of my herb tea."

"I'm fine for now," said Mimi, as she sat herself down and absently peered out to sea.

"Hon, you look like you just lost your best friend," observed the psychic, who also sat at the table.

Mimi looked close to tears as she responded to this innocent remark. "I have, you know. Without Peter, I have no one."

Dr. Elizabeth reached over and grasped Mimi's hand. "Come now, hon, you know that's not entirely true. You can count on me for a friend. And besides, who says that your husband still doesn't have some say in the matter? I've got a feeling that he's gonna be influencing your life for some time to come."

"What do you mean by that?" asked Mimi, her interest piqued. "Do you really feel that Peter is close by?"

The psychic firmly nodded that she did, and with her finger to her lips, she beckoned Mimi to look towards the fantail. Still stretched out on the fish locker there, Isis had awakened, and was now anxiously searching the blue heavens, like someone was calling to her from above.

"She senses something," whispered Dr. Elizabeth. "I tell you we're close, hon. I can feel it in my bones."

"Surface contact, Chief, smack in our baffles," reported the most junior sonarman in the *Rickover*'s crew. "Sounds like it could be a small fishing trawler."

Tim Lacey had been checking on the depth of their

towed array, and he swung around to inspect his young shipmate's CRT monitor.

"Nice work, babe," said Lacey as he reached up for the microphone and his direct line to the control room. "Conn, sonar. New contact bearing three-three-zero. Classify Sierra six, trawler."

"Sonar, conn. Aye," returned the amplified voice of the OOD.

As Lacey reached up into the ventilation shaft and pulled out a bag of miniature Snickers bars, Captain Walden entered sonar. Unaffected by the CO's presence, Lacey reached into the bag and casually handed Walden a candy bar.

"Enjoy it, sir. I know Snickers are your very favorite."

"Thanks, Mr. Lacey," replied Walden as he pulled the candy bar out of its wrapper and devoured it in a couple of bites.

"We're just picking up the *Avalon* on the broad band, Captain," informed Lacey. "She's tearin' up the water something fierce, and headed due west."

Walden held back his response until he had checked the monitor screen. "I still find it strange that the *Academician Petrovsky* has yet to respond to that SOS. Commander Moore reported sighting two diving saucers in their moonpool, and you'd think they'd send them down when those aquanauts called for help."

Lacey tapped the upper portion of the middle CRT screen. "We've been isolating the Russian vessel ever since we left them, sir, and so far we haven't heard a peep out of them. That's some support ship."

"I'm afraid that's what we get for letting the wol

guard the chicken coop," offered Walden, who looked up when a loud, hollow pinging noise sounded inside the sonar room.

This same noise generated a painful chorus of shouts from the three technicians. As they tore off their headphones, blood could be seen running out of their ears.

"Son of a bitch!" cursed Lacey, while rubbing his own throbbing ears. "Someone out there just lashed the shit out of us!"

Spurred into action by this unexpected sonic attack, Walden's first concern was his men. "Get your boys down to the doc, and call in the next watch. It's evident that we've got company down here. And I smell a Russian rat."

"I'd like to remain on duty, if that's all right with you, Captain," pleaded Lacey. "I know the score out there, and if there's another submarine close by, all I need is another bearing to tag 'em."

Walden turned for the aft doorway. "Do it, Lacey. And I'll go and see what I can do about flushing them out for you."

The captain was furious with rage as he stormed into the control room.

"What in the hell hit us, sir?" asked the OOD, from his position beside the periscope well.

"Someone's playing hide-and-seek with us," revealed Walden. "And we're not leaving this damn quadrant until we find out just who it is. So let's start the ball rolling with a nice, quiet turn to clear our baffles. And if we should happen to encounter any visitors out there, we'll say hello with a sonic lashing of our own!"

"Well, Comrade Petrokov, how did they react to our little greeting?" quizzed the *zampolit* with his usual air of impatience.

The *Pantera*'s senior sonar technician held back his reply until he had a chance to check out each of his sensors.

"I don't understand it, sir. So far, we haven't heard a peep out of them."

"Maybe they didn't hear us go active," offered a junior associate.

"They heard us all right," returned his bearded superior. "In fact, I wouldn't be surprised if they didn't hear us back in Murmansk."

Quick to join them after a hasty visit to the helm was Alexander Litvinov. The *Pantera*'s CO had only to scan the faces of the sonar team to know that their tactic had failed.

"Do you mean to say that the 688 isn't hightailing it for open waters?" he asked against hope.

"That they aren't, Captain," answered the senior sonarman. "Not only have they gone completely silent, but they don't appear to have heard us."

Litvinov began massaging the technician's shoulders. "But we know differently, don't we, Misha? They got an earful, that you can bet your pension on. And instead of making them run for cover, we've ignited their ire."

"Do I hear fear in your voice, Captain?" ventured the red-faced political officer.

"What you mistake for fear, Comrade *Zampolit*, is

306

one professional naval officer's respect for another," retorted Litvinov. "I inwardly doubted that the Americans would be so easily intimidated, and now we must pay the price."

"But Admiral Valerian has ordered us to remove them from this sector at once!" countered Dubrinin.

"That could be a little difficult, if we can't even manage to find them again," said the captain, who was finding it hard to hide his loathing for the ignorant political officer.

The *zampolit* couldn't believe what he was hearing. "But we must locate them, and do so with haste. Admiral Valerian is relying on us, and no matter the risks involved, we have to rid the sea of this 688."

"And how do you propose that we do this, Comrade *Zampolit?*" asked Litvinov angrily.

"How should I know?" replied Dubrinin. "You're the trained naval expert. Apply yourself, Captain!"

Litvinov sardonically commented, "One course that they unfortunately didn't teach at the Academy was how to handle a pretentious political officer."

"Your impertinence is noted, Captain," spat the *zampolit*. "I shall make certain to describe it in full when it comes time to record my official log."

"You just do that," returned Litvinov. "And please don't forget to include one more thing. If it had been up to me, the rank of *zampolit* would have been abolished years ago. Your kind do nothing but waste space and precious resources, and cause dissension among the crew. You are a living symbol of all that was wrong in our past — a system that has left the *rodina* a nation of bankrupt beggars. Shame on you, Boris Dubrinin.

And shame on your precious Party!"

Stunned into silence by this unexpected outburst, the *zampolit* was spared further comment by the remarks of the senior sonar technician.

"We continue to monitor the DSRV, Captain. It's well above the thermocline, and any minute now, they'll be arriving in the quadrant where the Mir habitat is located."

This news caused a sudden idea to dawn in Litvinov's mind. "Why of course, the DSRV! All we have to do is close in on it and use it as bait to draw out the 688. Then when we know their location once again, we'll challenge them to a little game of chicken. Soon they'll be limping back to port with a dented hull to repair."

The *zampolit* failed to share the captain's enthusiasm. "I hope this tactic, is more effective than your sonar lashing, Comrade. I say, enough of these childish games. Once we locate them again, let's hit them with an acoustic homing torpedo and be done with it."

"Our orders are to scare them away, not start a war," reminded Litvinov.

"Who said anything about starting a war, Captain? A well-placed torpedo will guarantee no survivors. And all the Americans will ever know is that one of their submarines lies scattered on the bottom of the Andros Trench, the apparent victim of a defective weld."

"Such talk scares me, Comrade *zampolit*. It's indicative of what a blind fool you really are."

Fighting back the urge to slug the captain, Boris Dubrinin swore to himself that he would revenge this insult. The exchange took place in the public confines of the *Pantera*'s attack center, so it would soon be common knowledge. Unless the *zampolit* did something drastic to redeem himself and show the extent of his power, he'd lose the crew's respect, with no hope of ever again regaining it.

As fate would have it, the opportunity presented itself shortly after *Pantera* changed course to close in on the DSRV. No sooner did they start up the reactor and turn to the west, when an ear-splitting, resounding sonic blast penetrated their hull. It instantly shattered the eardrums of the sonar team, and the confidence of the men gathered around them.

Yet of all those assembled inside the attack center, only Boris Dubrinin looked at this lashing as a great opportunity. At long last, the American sub had exposed itself.

It was as Alexander Litvinov attended to the bleeding senior sonar technician, that Dubrinin casually made his way to the vacant fire-control console. With a key that only he and the captain had copies of, the *zampolit* proceeded to arm the sonic homing torpedoes stored in tubes one and three. These weapons were targeted on the source of the powerful sonic burst that they had just received, and with a casual push of his index finger, he released them into the sea.

The *Pantera*'s deck shuddered twice as the torpedoes streamed from their tubes, and Boris Dubrinin calmly stood back and watched their progress on the flashing monitor screen. Satisfied now that he had shown his shipmates where the power lay, he turned his glance back to the sonar room. There Alexander Litvinov stood speechless in the doorway, his shocked gaze locked on the man who had just abruptly changed their destinies.

Tim Lacey was monitoring the hydrophones placed inside the *Rickover*'s towed array, when a muted, buzzing sound caught his attention. His first impression was that it was nothing but a biological anomaly. But when the noise persisted, and seemed to actually intensify, he knew that it warranted his complete attention.

"I've got a transient, Chief!" informed one of the new members of the sonar watch. "Bearing two-five-five. Could it be the *Avalon*?"

"I've also got it on the towed array," replied Lacey. "It's the wrong frequency for *Avalon*. Let's boost the volume gain to the max and see what we come up with."

With the hope that they wouldn't be the victim of another sonic lashing at this inopportune moment, Lacey further amplified the mysterious sound. The familiar buzzing whine continued, and he searched his memory for the last time that he heard a similar signature. He had to go back all the way to sonar school, and when it suddenly dawned on him what it was that they were hearing, his pulse quickened and his voice shouted out in warning.

"Incoming torpedoes! Maximum range, on bearing two-five-five!"

In the adjoining control room, these words of warning were greeted with instant dread. John Walden heard them while huddled over the navigation plot,

310

and he quickly joined the OOD on the bridge.

"I've got the conn. Battle stations, torpedo!" ordered Walden firmly.

It was the chief of the watch who reached up and triggered a loud alarm that penetrated every corner of the *Rickover,* informing the crew to man their action stations. Rushing in to join the captain was his XO, who had been shaving when this alert came down, and still had some lather covering his face and neck.

"What the hell's coming down, Skipper?" he breathlessly asked while taking up a position beside the attack scope.

Walden answered as he scanned the instruments above the helm. "Looks like whoever lashed us didn't appreciate it when we returned the favor, and now they've gone and expressed their displeasure by taking a potshot at us."

"You've got to be kidding me!" remarked the startled XO, his tone tinged with utter disbelief.

Walden reached up for one of the microphones that hung from the ceiling, and secured a direct line into sonar.

"Chief, do you have a definite on those torpedoes?"

"That's an affirmative, Captain," shot back Lacey. "They're still well outside the twenty-thousand-yard envelope, though both appear to be emitting."

Walden clicked off the microphone and addressed his XO. "We've got plenty of time to lose them. Have Weaps ready a MOSS. If we're livin' right, our decoy will take care of the threat for us."

"But what about that cowardly bastard out there's who's responsible for this unwarranted attack?" the

XO asked.

"We'll take care of him as soon as we've neutralized those oncoming torpedoes," replied Walden. "But first, we've got one hundred and forty lives to get out of harm's way. And only after that's accomplished, and we've ensured the safety of our DSRV, will we turn our thoughts to revenge."

Eighteen

The crew of the *Avalon* received word of the attack on the *Rickover* via their underwater telephone. Captain Walden himself was on the other end of the line, and he urged them to continue with their current mission of mercy before returning to the safety of the depths to await further orders.

Thomas Moore couldn't really say that this shocking news caught him by surprise. He knew that there was a chance that these waters were home to an enemy military operation. And his suspicions were proved right. Sorry that they hadn't been able to inspect the device that most likely prompted this attack, Moore readied himself for the unscheduled part of their mission.

Beside him, Ned Barnes carefully manipulated the joystick, and guided the *Avalon* up towards the coral shelf where the Mir habitat was located. The grizzled pilot was still upset by the report from the *Rickover*, and he voiced himself while readjusting the DSRV's thrusters.

"Damn, I can't believe that anyone's stupid enough to think that they could possibly get away with such a thing. It's not every day that someone goes and takes a shot at a nuclear attack sub. What the hell were they trying to prove?"

Thomas Moore had yet to brief Barnes, and he responded somewhat guardedly. "I just pray that we can contain this whole thing."

"Do you think this emergency that we're responding to is somehow related?" asked the pilot.

"I don't know, Ned. But it sure seems like a weird coincidence that all of this is happening at the same time."

The DSRV's sphere operator poked his bald head into the cockpit to voice his own concern. "How much longer until our ETA at the habitat?"

"Hang in there, Ollie," replied the pilot. "It looks like you'll be havin' some company in another couple of minutes."

"Then what?" continued the senior enlisted man, while nervously twisting the pointed ends of his moustache.

Barnes held back his answer until he had completed a minor course change. "The *Rickover*'s skipper recommends that we head for deep water to wait this whole thing out. And I'm all for that. The *Avalon* sure doesn't want to get in the way of a torpedo."

The digital depth gauge broke seventy feet, and Barnes redirected his remarks to his copilot. "We should have the habitat complex on visual now, Thomas. Hit the spotlights and activate the video camera."

Thomas Moore did as ordered, and watched as the central monitor screen filled with a distant collection of strangely-shaped, underwater structures. Lights glowed from inside the largest of the buildings, which looked like they belonged to a futuristic space colony.

"Holy cow! Will you just look at that," said Ollie Draper. "For the life of me, I never thought I'd see the day when folks would be actually livin' on the sea floor."

Thomas Moore was equally impressed, noting that one of the structures seemed to be configured like a star, with several tubular appendages, while the others were single-pieced domes, shaped much like the top half of an onion. All of them stood on telescopic legs, with a flat coral shelf providing their solid foundation.

"Looks to me like there's a tiny flickering light out there in the open water between the two domes," observed the sphere operator, whose eyes never left the monitor screen. "Maybe that's one of the aquanauts."

"By George!" said Barnes as he inched back the throttle. "Get ready for that company, Ollie. It won't be long in comin', and I can't wait to hear their story."

For the first time since childhood, Karl Ivar Bjornsen experienced true fear. Though he had certainly had had his fair share of close calls with death while working in the North Sea as an oil fields service diver, his current situation was different. Soon they would run out of breathable air, and be forced to the surface, to face a deadly enemy.

When they reloaded the air compressor to purge the

315

system of the gases that had killed Ulge, it soon became apparent that all of the newly arrived tanks of helium were tainted, so they were forced to survive by breathing the air in their scuba tanks. In less than a half hour, this supply would be exhausted, and then they would have to ascend and face the people responsible for this attempt on their lives.

As Karl Ivar left Habitat One to join his teammates in Starfish House, he realized that Ivana Petrov had been right all along. The fire that had destroyed *Misha* had not been an accident. The same persons who had sent the poisoned helium had been responsible for the blaze. All that he lacked to complete the puzzle was their motive.

The only logical explanation was that it had something to do with the discovery that they had made on the bottom of the trench. They had obviously stumbled upon some sort of clandestine military operation at that time, and now these operatives were trying to kill them.

With the slim hope that Commandant Lenclud had come up with a plan to see them safely past this deadly predicament, Karl Ivar passed by the coral clump, which marked the halfway point of his present swim. Not even bothering to keep a lookout for prowling sharks, he concentrated his line of sight solely on the glowing lights of Starfish House. And it was only as he reached the protective shark grill and climbed up onto the first rung of the ladder, that a distant flickering light caught his attention.

The Norwegian's initial concern was that their mysterious enemy was returning to finish them off. He expected that this light was coming from one of the diving saucers, and was genuinely surprised when an underwater vessel of a much different design glided into view. This fifty-foot-long, black, sausage-shaped submersible had a distinctive white transfer skirt set into the bottom of its hull, and Karl Ivar wanted to shout with joy when he spotted an American flag painted on its side.

"Our decoy continues to emit loud and clear, Captain. I think one of the torpedoes has taken the bait!"

Tim Lacey's hopeful observation was met by a moment of constrained silence, as the two senior officers gathered behind the sonar console anxiously awaiting further news. The next update came soon, and was delivered by Lacey with great relief.

"Scratch one torpedo, Captain! That makes one down and one to go."

"There goes half our problem," said John Walden solemnly.

His XO grunted. "We've still got time to shake the other one, Skipper. Shall we try another fist in the water?"

"Let's do it, XO. And this time I want that water in our wake so shaken up that the remaining torpedo will never be able to find us!"

Admiral Igor Valerian stood in the sheltered confines of the *Academician Petrovsky*'s bridge, listening to the assortment of sounds being conveyed by their hydrophones. With his senior lieutenant close at his side, the one-eyed veteran shook his head in wonder, when one of the underwater microphones relayed a growling, low-pitched signature that could have only one source.

"I tell you, Viktor Ilyich, that's a torpedo all right. I'd know that distinctive sound anywhere."

"But Admiral, what does such a thing mean?" asked the grim-faced Alexandrov.

Valerian's words flowed with great emotion and pride. "I'll tell you what it means, Comrade. In the dark seas beneath us, a brave crew of our fellow countrymen have taken it upon themselves to carry out their orders like true patriots. And because of the actions of Alexander Litvinov and his crew, the *rodina* has a chance to be great once more!"

"When the *Pantera* was directed to divert the American 688 from these waters, I didn't realize that such extreme means would be needed," reflected Alexandrov. "Why, we could have a full-scale nuclear war on our hands as a result of this attack."

"Such are the risks that one must pay for greatness, Viktor Ilyich. We must give Litvinov the benefit of a doubt. Obviously, he wouldn't go and attack the Americans unless he had no other option. Besides, don't you think that if the Americans were to discover the equipment that we have stored on the sea floor of the trench below, that this same war that you speak of would be precipitated? Of course it would, Comrade. And the *Pantera*'s desperate actions saved us from such an embarrassment."

The sonar speakers filled with an agitated whirring

318

sound, which prompted the senior lieutenant to comment, "Of course, there's always the possibility that the attack will succeed, and that the United States will never learn the cause of the loss of their submarine."

"A detonating torpedo does have a way of hiding evidence," added Valerian, whose thick eyebrows arched upwards in sudden thought. "You know, there's another way to remove the 688, even if they should manage to escape the *Pantera's* torpedoes. And what better time to give Dr. Petrov that full power test that he's been insistent on."

"Do you mean to say that you're going to try to dematerialize the American 688?" asked the unbelieving senior lieutenant.

"Why not?" returned Valerian. "All we need to do is lock in its signature and then pray that it gets within range. And if the fates are with us, the USS *Hyman G. Rickover* might soon be spending the rest of its days in the icy Arctic waters off Siberia, divulging its many secrets, with *Seawolf* soon to follow!"

"Prepare for a series of thirty-degree snap turns!" ordered Walden, who had moved back into the control room to direct the evasion maneuvers. "Diving officer, is the helm ready to initiate the sequence?"

The COB was in the process of pulling a fresh cigar from his pocket and he answered without hesitation. "Aye, aye, Captain. Helm is standing by for orders to initiate."

The strained voice of Tim Lacey echoed from the elevated intercom speakers. "Torpedo continues its ap-

319

proach. Range is nine thousand yards and continuing to close."

Walden reached up to grab a handhold, and briefly met the concerned glance of his XO before calling out firmly. "Initiate evasion sequence! Flank bell! Thirty degree starboard rudder!"

The harnessed helmsmen were quick to carry out this directive, and as they turned their steering yokes, the *Rickover* canted over hard on its right side. A lone ruler slid across the sharply angled deck, and the crew struggled to keep from falling over because of this unexpected movement.

"We're cavitating, Captain," informed the COB, in reference to the glowing green light set directly above the helm's digital depth meter.

Not concerned by this report, Walden watched as the speed indicator shot upwards in response to the flank bell. The angle of the deck began to lessen, and the captain was quick to convey his next order.

"Take us to one hundred feet at full angle. Then bring us back down to max depth, while initiating thirty-degree snap turns to port."

"One hundred feet at full angle it is, Captain," repeated the COB, who anxiously sat forward with his cigar clenched in his teeth.

It took both hands for the helmsmen to pull back on their yokes, and the *Rickover* crisply responded. As the bow angled almost straight upwards, the crew once more fought the inertial forces of gravity, and it took a maximum effort to remain standing.

"One hundred and ninety feet . . . One hundred and eighty . . ." observed the COB, whose job it was to relay the figures on the rapidly decreasing depth gauge.

"Torpedo's coming down with us," warned Tim Lacey over the intercom. "Range is down to eight thousand yards."

At a depth of one hundred and thirty-five feet, Lacey's voice once more sounded, yet this time his tone was noticeably different. "We've got a narrow-band transient contact, Captain, bearing three-zero-zero. I think we just chanced upon the SOB who fired at us!"

John Walden looked over at his XO and grinned with this news. "What do you think, Mr. Laycob? Shall we give them something to think about?"

"By all means, Skipper," returned the XO, who couldn't help grinning as he struggled to follow Walden over to the fire-control console.

Alexander Litvinov couldn't think of a worse time for the *Pantera*'s reactor steam-release valve to stick. Whenever this problem occurred, it automatically corrected itself, creating a great deal of noise along the way. Inwardly cursing the design fault that was responsible for this unwanted racket, he tensely addressed his senior sonar technician.

"Well Misha, what's their status?"

The bearded sonarman held back his response until his current sensor sweep was completed. "After a rapid ascent, the 688 has levelled out well short of the surface. And now they appear to be diving once more."

"And our torpedo, Misha?" asked Litvinov.

"It remains right on their tail, sir."

Senior Lieutenant Yuri Berezino entered the attack

center from the forward accessway and joined Litvinov beside sonar.

"The *zampolit* has been securely locked inside the wardroom, Captain. I had the corpsman give him a powerful dose of tranquilizer as well. That should keep him quiet for the next couple of hours."

"Good work, Yuri," replied Litvinov. "Boris Dubrinin has caused us enough trouble for one day."

"Sonar contact, Captain!" exclaimed the senior technician, while pressing his headphones tightly over his ears. "It's a single torpedo, and definitely not one of our own!"

"We should have expected as much," said Litvinov bitterly. "That stuck valve was a dead giveaway, and somehow the alert Americans must have managed to get off a quick shot."

"All ahead full!" he added to the helmsman. "And take us deep. Like the 688, we too shall take advantage of the depths to lose this weapon before it can get a definite lock on us."

Nineteen

Ivana Petrov couldn't believe their good fortune. The American DSRV was like a gift from heaven, and it was with few regrets that they left Starfish House for the safety of this unique undersea vessel.

A thin, bald-headed sailor dressed in blue coveralls welcomed them aboard the submersible named *Avalon*. Primarily designed to rescue other submarines, the *Avalon* was constructed around a central sphere, where the rescuees were to be held. The craft was operated from a small, two-man cock-pit.

The team's leader, Pierre Lenclud, was the first to be invited to visit the control compartment. While the Frenchman scooted down a tunnel-like accessway to meet the *Avalon*'s commanding officers, Ivana and her teammates settled themselves into the main sphere.

The air was blessedly sweet, and it was wonderful not to have to rely on their scuba tanks to breathe. The sphere operator proved to be a colorful character, who appeared to have taken an immediate liking to Lisa Tanner. He apologized for not having any food for them, though he did manage to pull out a large thermos filled with coffee. Then, with only a single cup available, the steaming hot brew was passed around for all to share.

Ivana was in the process of enjoying a sip from this communal mug when Lenclud crawled back into the sphere. The Frenchman looked drawn and tired, and he gratefully accepted the coffee from Ivana and softly addressed her.

"They'd like to see you next, *mon amie.*"

With Lenclud's help, she entered the narrow accessway from which he had just emerged. Crawling forward on her hands and knees, she didn't have to go far until her head and upper torso emerged into a cramped, dimly lit compartment, designed much like a space capsule.

She found herself positioned between two seated men, who were surrounded by glowing gauges and instruments. Both appeared to be middle-aged, and dressed in identical blue coveralls.

"I understand that you're Dr. Ivana Petrov," said the heavy-set man seated to her right. "I'm Commander Thomas Moore. Welcome aboard the *Avalon.*"

"It's good to be here," replied Ivana, who noted that Moore didn't wear a baseball cap like his square-jawed associate.

"Dr. Petrov," continued Moore. "Commandant Lenclud mentioned that your emergency might have been prompted by a discovery that you made on the bottom of the trench beneath us. Was the machinery that he told us about by any chance connected to a dual power cable that extended towards the surface?"

"It certainly was, Comrade. In fact, I saw this cable with my very own eyes."

Moore seemed satisfied with her answer and probed still further. "If we were to continue to the floor of the trench, could you show it to us?"

"I'd be happy to, Comrade. But under our current circumstances, isn't such a visit dangerous?"

"Not any more than staying around here," returned the quick-talking American, who instructed her to give his tight-lipped co-worker a description of the exact portion of the sea floor where her discovery had been made.

Thomas Moore pulled out a detailed bathymetric chart, and the two Americans shared a muffled conversation before Moore readdressed Ivana.

"Hang on, Doctor. We're going down."

She braced herself with a hand placed behind the back of each seat, and she watched as the pilot expertly manipulated his joystick. The DSRV's rounded bow angled sharply downwards in response, and she sensed a certain urgency guiding the Americans onwards.

"Dr. Petrov, are you aware of the fact that your father is currently aboard the *Academician Petrovsky*? And that he could very well be responsible for that machinery that we're going down to inspect?" revealed Moore on a spur-of-the-moment impulse.

Moore's intense glance never left Ivana's face as it lit up in pained confusion.

"But my father can't be up there. He's in forced exile!"

"He's aboard that support ship all right. And from

what I understand, that machinery could belong to a device that your father invented over five decades ago."

Ivana's expression turned to horror, and Moore prepared to set the hook.

"Dr. Petrov, do you know anything about your father's work in the field of antimatter? Is it true that he actually invented a device that could make solid objects invisible, and then teleport them to different locations?"

"This can't be happening," she managed, her voice trembling with emotion. "He promised the world that he'd never put his theories into practice. He knew better than anyone that if such a device were to fall into the wrong hands, the resulting danger to mankind would be too great to contemplate."

Stunned by the reality of this shocking revelation, Thomas Moore knew that Admiral Proctor's suspicions had been correct. Now he had to destroy this device, before it was responsible for more tragedy.

"Torpedo has just broken the three-thousand-yard threshold, sir," reported a very worried Tim Lacey. "It's comin' right down with us."

Walden was standing almost directly behind the helm, tightly gripping a ceiling-mounted handhold when he received this bad news. Still in the midst of a spiraling dive, the *Rickover's* bow was steeply angled downwards, making the mere act of standing almost impossible.

"Let's try a couple of snap turns, Chief," suggested Walden. "And make 'em crisp."

"You got it, Captain," returned the COB, who passed on additional instructions to the helmsmen.

The deck rolled over hard on its left side, while continuing the descent. Then like a jet fighter in a dogfight, the *Rickover* abruptly changed course, causing the deck to cant over in the opposite direction.

"What's our sounding?" called out Walden forcefully.

"That last turn put us almost directly on top of the trench, Captain," informed the navigator. "We've got a good thousand feet of water between us and the bottom."

Since they had already descended well over seven hundred feet, the sea floor was just at the outer limit of their crush depth. Not wishing to push their luck too far, Walden conveyed his strategy to all within voice range.

"I want to take us all the way down to fourteen hundred feet before pulling us up. I know we're going to be close to the walls of that trench, but that's where I want to lead that damn torpedo!"

A tense, somber atmosphere prevailed inside the *Pantera*'s attack center, where Alexander Litvinov and his second-in-command anxiously stood behind the senior sonarman. Also in the midst of a desperate crash dive, the *Pantera* had just broken through the thermocline, at a depth of four hundred and twenty feet.

"Why not try another series of roll turns, Captain?" offered Yuri Berezino in a bare whisper.

"Noise alone won't lose this pesky Mk48, Yuri," remarked Litvinov. "But if we can combine it with speed and depth, then we stand a real chance of escaping this threat."

"Torpedo continues to close," said the bearded sonarman in a dull monotone. "Isn't there any way of losing it?"

"Easy, Misha," cautioned Litvinov, who reached out to massage the back of the technician's neck. "We have plenty of ocean beneath us to play with, and many things can happen to that torpedo along the way."

"I curse that damn *zampolit* for ever getting us in this fix!" swore the sonarman.

Litvinov calmly replied while increasing the pressure of his massage. "Come now, Comrade. Quit getting your blood pressure worked up for such an insignificant matter. The *Pantera* shall see us to safety, and then we'll let a firing squad take care of our dear political officer."

"What do you mean he refused to activate the power grid?" screamed Igor Valerian in a near rage. "He must do as ordered!"

The *Academician Petrovsky*'s senior lieutenant rather sheepishly responded to this outburst. "So I told him, Admiral. But he just sat there, and said that it would be much too dangerous to recharge the system."

"The good doctor will soon enough learn the meaning of danger, Comrade," returned Valerian bitterly. "For now he has provoked a whirlwind!"

Squaring his shoulders with this remark, the one-eyed veteran stormed out of his cabin, with his second-in-command close on his heels. With a brisk, angry stride, Valerian raced down the long central passageway that took him past the engine room. Not stopping to return the greetings of the group of men huddled around the moonpool, he hurriedly entered his security code into the keypad beside the sealed aft hatchway. In his mad rush he entered the wrong sequence, and had to wait for the system to reset itself before he impatiently tried it again. This time he succeeded, and the door popped open with a loud click.

The laboratory where Dr. Petrov had been working was located beside the reactor compartment. Its door was closed, and Valerian burst into the room without even bothering to knock. He found the silver-haired physicist huddled over a samovar of tea, and the admiral wasted no time venting his wrath.

"Andrei Sergeyevich Petrov, I demand that you prepare the system to be activated at once!"

Senior Lieutenant Alexandrov entered the lab in time to hear Petrov calmly voice himself.

"You can demand all you want, Admiral. But it will make little difference to me. I will not activate the power grid until the design faults that I recently discovered are rectified."

Valerian was surprised by this revelation. "What design faults are you talking about, Doctor?"

"That is the reason that I was sent here, wasn't it, Admiral?"

Halting a moment to stir his tea, Petrov added, "After a careful analysis of the data that I collected during my visit to the floor of the trench, I believe I know why your initial experiment failed. The fault lies not with the magnetic generators, as we first suspected, but with the electrical source that powers them."

"Whatever do you mean, Doctor?" questioned Valerian in a calmer tone.

Petrov took a sip of his tea before answering. "My calculations indicate that we will need an additional power surge of at least ten percent to ensure complete success. Only then will the dematerialized object end up at the target location."

Valerian appeared relieved by what he was hearing. "That's easy enough to correct, Comrade. All we need to do to produce this additional power is operate our reactor at full capacity. That should generate the ten percent additional surge that you say is needed."

"As you very well know, Admiral, such a thing is much too dangerous. The reactor on board this ship is not designed to run at full capacity. We risk a partial meltdown or even worse."

Valerian abruptly changed tactics, and replied with a gentle almost brotherly concern. "Unfortunately, we have no choice, Comrade. There is no time to install a new reactor, and for the sake of the *rodina's* future security, we must make do with our present capabilities."

The wall-mounted telephone began ringing, and Senior Lieutenant Alexandrov answered it. A brief conversation followed, after which he hung up the handset and briefed his superior.

"That was the *michman*, Admiral. He reports that the signature of the 688 is quickly approaching the capture zone. It will be within range in another three and a half minutes. He also indicates that radar has picked up a small surface vessel in the area. It is believed to be a fishing trawler."

"That radar sighting is not important at the moment, Viktor Ilyich," returned Valerian. "What concerns me is that we are about to lose an opportunity to try the system before *Seawolf* puts to sea. Please Doctor, I implore you. Supervise this final test, and I promise you that I will scrap the entire project if it should fail."

"That will mean absolutely nothing if our reactor explodes," retorted the physicist.

"But it won't!" replied Valerian.

"I wish that I could share your optimism, Admiral. But I'll tell you what. If you agree to see to it that the U.N. observer team immediately leaves the ship, I will attempt a single full power surge. After fifty years of merely pondering a theory, I too am curious to finally see if it belongs in the realm of reality or not."

Valerian's face broke out in the warmest of smiles. "Of course I'll agree to this condition. And thank you, Comrade. I guarantee you that you won't be disappointed."

From the open bridge of the *Sunshine*, Al peered through a pair of binoculars, and took in the large ship that lay motionless in the water due south of them. This vessel was painted white, and had sleek, modern lines. Though it displayed no deck guns, Al sensed that it was a military ship of some sort, and he decided to give it a wide berth when it came time to pass it.

331

A gull cried harshly from above, and Al put down the binoculars. The rich scent of incense filled the gentle sea breeze with an alien odor, and he slowly redirected his gaze to his boat's fantail.

His two passengers remained seated at the card table, with their hands tightly linked, and a thick, white candle flickering between them. Al had seen wise women like Dr. Elizabeth before, while growing up in the swamps of Okeechobee. His mama had called them healers, and Al would never forget visiting one such elder who spoke in strange, frightening tongues and was known for her love spells that she wrote out in gator blood.

Still not certain why the two white women had gone to the expense of chartering his boat, Al left the bridge and headed aft. The setting sun did little to relieve the oppressive tropical heat, and as he slowly walked out onto the open stern, the large black cat sprinted between his legs. He watched as this creature excitedly leaped up onto the gunwales, and stared down into the sparkling blue depths with eyes wide with wonder.

"Even Isis knows what's going on in the water beneath us," said Dr. Elizabeth, her voice unnaturally deep and guttural. "I tell you, it's nothing less than the battle between good and evil!"

"But what about Peter?" asked Mimi Slater, her tone tinged with worry. "Will we be able to contact him?"

Al watched as Dr. Elizabeth proceeded to take off the straw hat that she had been wearing, and throw it on the deck. Then with a reverent slowness, she looked into the powdery blue sky and spoke forcefully.

"With the coming of the equinox, the Tuaoi stone

shall awaken. The crystal capstone will be activated, and the link reestablished between Mother Earth and its cosmic swan. Woe to those who attempt to divert the force for their own selfish gain. For we are witnessing a struggle as old as man himself. Only if the powers of the white light prevail, will the lovers be reunited to sanctify this greatest of all victories."

Twenty

"Torpedo has just broken the five-hundred-yard threshold. It's got capture!" exclaimed Tim Lacey.

John Walden listened to these dreaded words from his perch behind the helm. His pulse quickened, and he scanned the gauges before him for any sign of redemption.

"Thirteen hundred and fifty feet, and continuing the dive, Captain," tensely reported the COB on their current depth.

With the deck angled sharply downwards, and the hull plates moaning in response to the pressure at these depths, Walden glanced up at the speed indicator. Somehow the engineering crew had managed to squeeze out another precious knot of forward speed. But this effort would all be in vain, unless their pursuer could be countered.

"I've got a clear picture of the walls of the trench on the fathometer, Captain," informed the navigator. "At our present course and speed, we'll impact the lower portion of the western ridge in another two minutes time."

"Torpedo range is down to three hundred yards," added Lacey, his somber voice scratchy from use.

"Thirteen hundred and seventy feet," reported the Cob, who had chewed his unlit cigar down to a bare stub.

Walden allowed the depth meter to fall another ten feet before calling out forcefully. "Take us up, helmsmen! Full rise on the planes!"

Having anticipated this order, the helmsmen yanked back on their steering yokes, and the depth gauge fell yet another ten feet before it momentarily stopped, then began turning in the opposite direction. The deck was now angled sharply upwards, and as Walden regrasped the steel handhold, his glance returned to the speed indicator.

"Come on, *Rickover.* I know you've got it in you," he softly urged.

Over at the sonar console, Tim Lacey tried his best to sort out the cacophony of sounds being conveyed through his headphones. With the torpedo due to strike them any second now, he bravely turned the volume gain to maximum amplification, and searched the roiling depths for any sign of the weapon. And it was then he heard the distinctive buzzing signature of the torpedo, that seemed to momentarily intensify, before steadily lessening. Yanking off his headphones, he excitedly cried out into his microphone.

"That sucker just passed right by us, Captain! It's lost capture!"

"Brace yourself, gentlemen," warned Walden, after issuing a brief sigh. "That baby's gonna smack into the wall of the trench, and all hell's gonna break out down here!"

* * *

Rocketing downwards through the same depths that its adversary had just penetrated, the *Pantera* was in the midst of its own desperate dive. The vessel's attack center was unusually hushed, its assembled crew members were content to lose their anxieties in the glowing instruments of their individual consoles.

With his own gaze locked on the broad-band sonar screen, Alexander Litvinov monitored the weapon that relentlessly followed in their wake. His sense of hopelessness was only intensified by the somber reports of the senior sonarman.

"The Mk48 continues its pursuit. Impact will take place any moment now."

With nothing left to do but pray for a miracle, Litvinov found his thoughts going back in time. He was a cadet once more, nervously anticipating his first full day at the Academy. That had been the day that he took an oath to surrender his life if necessary for the defense of the motherland. It had all seemed so unreal at the time. But now he knew differently. Life was the most precious gift of all, and to waste it in this manner was the ultimate tragedy.

Doing his best to contain his fears, Litvinov looked away from the flashing monitor screen, to take one last fond look at the men who awaited death beside him. They were a brave, admirable lot, and before he could voice his pride, a deafening, gut-wrenching explosion diverted his attention back to sonar. The deck began to shake wildly beneath him, and he blindly grabbed onto the senior sonarman's arm to keep from falling over.

"What in heaven's name is happening, Misha?" he managed. "Have we been hit?"

The bearded technician ignored his pain-racked ears and valiantly struggled to monitor his headphones. "I don't believe so, Captain. That detonation took place in the waters directly before us."

"I bet it was our very own torpedo!" observed Litvinov, with a new sense of hope. "And we shall continue to penetrate its shockwave to the very floor of the trench, and lose our relentless pursuer along the way!"

In the adjoining waters, the occupants of the *Avalon* also heard this booming explosion. Wildly tossed from side to side by the agitated wall of water that accompanied the blast, the DSRV found itself spiraling downwards, completely out of control.

"It's no use," reported Ned Barnes as he ineffectively addressed the joystick. "We've lost all thruster power and ballast control. Right now, there's nothing that I can do to keep us from being sucked into the floor of the trench."

"What do those readings on the monitor screen indicate?" asked Thomas Moore, who was not the type who easily gave up hope.

"That data is coming from our external sensor pod," revealed the pilot. "It must be malfunctioning, because it's showing an extreme amount of magnetic resonance outside."

"Could this be a result of that blast?" continued Moore.

"No way," replied Barnes firmly. "The only time I ever saw a reading that high was when *Avalon* was being degaussed, to counter its magnetic signature."

This matter-of-fact revelation caused Thomas

337

Moore to gasp. "Damn, they're activating the device!"

"What device?" asked the confused pilot.

"It has to do with the reason that I was sent down here," explained Moore, who shuddered to think what would happen to them if *Avalon* were to share the *Lewis and Clark*'s fate.

"Jesus, will you just look at that magnetometer reading," instructed Barnes with utter disbelief. "It's goin' off the damn scale!"

Moore didn't have to look up at the monitor screen to recognize the extreme peril that surrounded them. He knew that the magnetic field would continue to intensify, until the DSRV and its unfortunate occupants were torn apart by a cosmic implosion that would vaporize the very substance that matter was based upon. Well aware that only two men had ever survived such an encounter and lived to tell about it, Moore could think of only one way they could save themselves.

"Ned, can the *Avalon* be internally flooded?"

Barnes looked at his associate like he didn't hear him properly. "What the hell are you askin' that for?"

Moore didn't flinch. "You're just going to have to trust me, Ned. Can this vessel be filled with water with us still safely in it, or not?"

The steely-eyed pilot seemed momentarily flustered. "Jesus, Thomas. Sure, I can pull the plug on the *Avalon*. But the only way we can keep breathin' is through the EBA's."

"Then you'd better get on with it, Ned. Or I can guarantee you that you'll never live to see those Cowboys of yours play in another Super Bowl."

338

"The explosion has temporarily masked our hydrophones," reported the *Academician Petrovsky*'s sensor operator.

"Then use your low-frequency filters and unmask them," ordered Valerian from the adjoining fire-control console.

Seated beside the flag officer, Dr. Andrei Petrov looked up from his computer keyboard.

"Perhaps that blast indicates that the 688 has been destroyed. Then this test is all for naught. And there's always the chance that it could affect our own submarine that's prowling these waters."

Unable to respond to this remark, Valerian vented his frustration on the sensor operator. "Well, Comrade. Is it out there?"

The technician nervously addressed his console. With his hands shaking so badly that he had trouble hitting the proper keys of the input panel, he turned up the volume gain and readjusted the graphic equalizer.

"There appears to be some kind of man-made signature down there," he tentatively observed. "But I still can't be certain if it's emanating from the 688."

"Let me listen," said Valerian disgustedly.

With a sweeping motion, he yanked the headphones away from the startled technician, and cupped them to his ears. Barely thirty seconds passed before he came to a conclusion based more on hope than on firm evidence.

"It's the 688 all right. For the glory of the motherland, reactivate the power grid to one-hundred-percent capacity, Andrei Sergeyevich!"

The physicist obediently addressed his keyboard, and as the reactor pile went critical, he visualized the series of events taking place on the sea floor below. Energized by the power of the interacting atoms that he had just released, the series of magnetic generators placed alongside the walls of the trench would begin throwing out intense resonating pulses of electromagnetic energy. Any solid object within range would be captured by this field, its own atoms pulled apart by the gravitational forces that ruled the universe.

"It's started! The crystal capstone is activating!" exclaimed Dr. Elizabeth, who followed this news with a detailed description of the battle between good and evil that had taken place in the water directly beneath them.

Al remained skeptical of this entire story, yet he asked, "And just who won this battle, Doc?"

"Why the powers of good, of course," answered the psychic.

"Now can we contact Peter?" asked Mimi, her patience all but exhausted.

"There's just one more test to pass, hon. Then the door will be wide open."

The *Sunshine* picked this inopportune moment to shudder to an abrupt stop. Al seemed to know just what caused this problem, and he left the open wheelhouse where he had been standing, passed by his two seated passengers, and peered over the square transom.

"Just like I thought, ladies. Gulf weed's gone and wrapped up the prop."

"Is there anything you can do about it?" asked Mimi. "Maybe we can radio that white ship we passed for help."

"No need for that, missy," remarked Al as he pulled off his hat, shirt, and shoes. "Just hang on and I can cut us free in no time."

Al whipped out a pocket knife and began climbing overboard.

"Be careful down there," warned Dr. Elizabeth.

"No need to be worried," offered Al before disappearing completely. "I needs to cool off anyway. See ya in a bit, ladies."

As Al plopped into the water, Isis unexpectedly let out a shrill, high-pitched screech. Both Mimi and Dr. Elizabeth looked to the starboard gunwale, where the cat was perched with its back arched and its head pointed out to sea.

"What in the world do you see out there, Isis?" asked the psychic.

Only moments ago, the dusk sky had been clear, with hardly a cloud visible. But now they saw a mean-looking bank of quick-moving clouds that veiled the sky in a cloak of swirling green mist.

"Looks like we got us a storm comin'," observed Dr. Elizabeth.

Just as she pulled Isis off her perch and put the cat down at her feet, the deck began to vibrate. This was accompanied by a sudden drop in the air temperature, and the arrival of a howling, gusting wind.

A thunderous boom sounded overhead, prompting Mimi to turn towards the transom and call out. "Al, you'd better get out of the water. We've got a storm on its way!"

"Don't bother, hon," said the psychic. "You see, this ain't no ordinary storm. This is nature's way of tellin' us that it's time to make the contact!"

Also watching this swirling green bank of clouds take form was John Walden. Yet he did so from a depth of sixty-five feet, with the amplified assistance of the *Rickover*'s periscope.

"Looks like a real nasty one's brewing topside," said Walden, as he rotated the scope and took another look at the wooden fishing trawler that he had been previously studying. "I sure hope those folks up there have battened down the hatches."

Any further comment on his part was cut short by the frantic voice of the chief of the watch.

"Engineering reports a partial electrical failure! The reactor is being automatically scrammed."

As if to emphasize the seriousness of this report, the lights suddenly dimmed. The deck seemed to shudder, and then angle down slightly by the bow.

"I've just lost neutral buoyancy," informed the chief of the watch.

"Blow emergency and get us on the surface!" ordered Walden, who was about to return to the periscope, when the chief of the watch replied to this directive.

"Can't do, Captain. Ballast pumps are inoperable."

"What the hell?" remarked Walden, genuinely puzzled by this entire sequence of events.

To get some kind of handle on the situation, he lowered the periscope and quickly turned for the helm. The COB was standing over the diving console, with the current chief of the watch close beside him. Together they studied the various instruments, with the assistance of a hand-held flashlight.

"Sound general quarters!" ordered Walden. "COB, I want you to get on the horn with engineering, and find out what the blazes is going on back there."

As the electronic alarm sending the crew to their action stations sounded throughout the *Rickover,* the sub began sinking into the same depths that only minutes ago they had climbed out of. Unable to get the engines started and reverse this descent, Walden gripped an overhead handhold and watched as his men frantically tried to restore full power.

One of the few operational stations that remained online was sonar. Here, in the midst of his second consecutive watch, Tim Lacey found his attention locked on a hypnotic, humming sound that seemed to emanate from the floor of the trench itself. On a mere hunch, he informed the captain of this transient. Much to his surprise, he was instructed to play this mysterious signature over the control room's intercom speakers.

From his position beside the helm, John Walden carefully listened to the sounds that had gained Lacey's attention. With the assistance of the navigator, he was able to determine that they indeed originated from the bottom of the trench, at a depth of approximately seventeen hundred feet.

Earlier, Commander Thomas Moore had shared with him details of an amazing man-made device, that the NIS feared could be anchored on the floor of this very trench. Unable to believe in the existence of a machine which could dematerialize matter, Walden initially had been skeptical. But now he was beginning to wonder if he had been too hasty in his judgment.

With the slim hope that the device Moore spoke of

was real, and that it was the cause of the *Rickover's* current problems, Walden ordered the fire-control team to ready a pair of Mk 48 wire-guided torpedoes. The source of the unexplained humming noise was then precisely determined, and with this information keyed into the boat's fire-control system, the torpedoes were fired.

As they streaked from their tubes, the deck once more shuddered. And Walden found himself crossing his fingers, all the while praying that this dive to oblivion would soon be halted.

Twenty-one

Igor Valerian remained in the *Academician Petrovsky*'s reactor compartment, anxiously awaiting word of the experiment's success. He knew that this would most likely come in the form of a satellite-relayed telephone call from Pacific Fleet headquarters in Vladivostok. If all worked out as planned, he would be notified that the *rodina* now had the services of the USS *Hyman G. Rickover*. This would be a great achievement in itself, but it would serve as a forerunner for an even greater feat to come.

Much to his disappointment, the call came from the bridge, informing him of an approaching storm. This news soured his mood, and he wondered if he could spare the time to return to his stateroom for a little liquid refreshment. A good drink of vodka never failed to fortify him, and just as he was about to excuse himself, the sensor operator kept him from doing so.

"Sonar contact, Admiral. It appears to be another submarine."

Rushing to the man's side, Valerian worriedly asked, "Can you classify the signature, Comrade?"

While the technician addressed his keyboard, Dr. Petrov sauntered up to the console. The physicist calmly sipped from a cup of tea, and casually commented:

"I wonder who it could be down there."

"Most likely, it's just the *Pantera*," offered Valerian, whose glance nervously scanned the broad-band frequency monitor.

It seemed to take forever for the technician to complete his signature analysis, and the news he relayed was far from heartening.

"I don't really understand it, sir. But the analysis shows an eighty-seven-percent probability that this vessel is an American 688 class attack sub."

"That can't be!" retorted Valerian. "Could the device have failed completely?"

"That's highly unlikely," replied the physicist. "You just saw the preliminary reports yourself, Admiral. And the one thing that we know for certain is that a submarine definitely crossed into the force field and never left it."

"But the 688 is still down there," countered Valerian.

Andrei Petrov dejectedly shook his head. "I told you that we should have waited. But you wouldn't listen, and now we've gone and possibly destroyed one of our very own submarines.

"I won't accept that!" shot back Valerian. "Maybe this 688 is a vessel other than the *Rickover*. Or perhaps our sensors are inaccurate. Whatever be the case, we must act on this find. Prepare to recharge the power grid, Doctor."

"Absolutely not!" shouted Andrei. "This insanity has gone too far already."

"You fool!" spat Valerian disgustedly as he roughly pushed the physicist aside and made his way to the fire-control console. "If you won't do it, Doctor, then I'll hit the switch myself."

Ignoring the spilled tea that had scorched his hand, Andrei rushed over to stop Valerian.

"Please, Admiral," implored the physicist. "You're only opening us up to yet more tragedy."

Igor Valerian attacked the keyboard with a vengeance, and as the atoms of the nuclear pile once more went critical, he triumphantly voiced himself.

"The only tragedy here is your cowardly recalcitrance, Doctor. Because your inaction could have very well cost the *rodina* another chance at future greatness."

Before pressing the final input key to trigger the power grid, the one-eyed veteran looked up at Andrei Petrov and cried out boldly.

"What you're about to witness is history itself in the making. For the glory of the motherland!"

At the moment that Admiral Igor Valerian pressed the final input key, the first of the *Rickover*'s Mk48 torpedoes slammed into the wall of the trench with a blistering blast. The torpedo that followed made a direct hit on the lead generator, and as the concussion from this explosion tore apart the power coupling, a reverse surge of electricity shot up the frayed cable. In a microsecond, this ultrapowerful burst of raw energy made its way to the surface, where it streamed into the *Academician Petrovsky*'s engineering spaces. No one there even had the time to know that anything was wrong, when a tremendous explosion tore the ship apart at the waterline.

No sooner did this secondary detonation fade on the tropical wind, when the *Rickover*'s electrical systems returned to normal. No one was more relieved than John Walden, who wasted no time ordering his submarine to the surface.

By the time they completed their ascent, and Walden made his way up onto the open sail, the *Academician Petrovsky* was nothing but a torn hunk of smoldering debris. Yet hopes for survivors from this unexplained tragedy brightened when one of the lookouts spotted what appeared to be the captain's gig floating in the distance.

Expectations were high as Walden ordered the *Rickover* to rendezvous with this vessel. They found only three survivors, confused members of the U.N. observer team. Walden took them aboard and sent them below, thus freeing the *Rickover* for yet another search. Somewhere below, the depths held the secret of the DSRV *Avalon,* its valiant crew, and the five aquanauts that it had been sent to rescue.

Epilogue

Al pulled himself over the *Sunshine's* transom and plopped onto the deck feeling chilled to the bone and momentarily dizzy. The fog was so thick that he could barely see his hand in front of his face, and as his dizziness passed, he heard in the background a strange sound that was disturbingly familiar. The air itself smelled alien, and he couldn't help being reminded of his childhood.

His hand brushed up against a large straw hat that lay on the wooden deck before him. Having completely forgotten about his two passengers, he stiffly stood and tentatively called out.

"Doc? Missy? Where are ya?"

The only sound to greet him was the monotonous humming noise that he had initially heard as he pulled himself out of the water. This steady, pulsating chorus reminded him of the racket produced by the swamp frogs and crickets, and with this odd comparison in mind, he began a thorough inspection of the trawler.

It didn't take him long to find out that he was all alone. He searched everywhere, including the galley, storage locker and engine spaces. The only evidence that he found of his passengers was their luggage, and a few personal items such as toiletries and clothing.

As he returned to the open stern he realized that even the cat was missing. Fearing that they had fallen overboard during the brief storm that had engulfed them, he peered out into the fog-enshrouded waters and called out forcefully.

"Doc! Missy! It's Captain Al. Are ya out there?"

His words reverberated throughout the veiled dusky twilight, only to be answered by a strong male voice.

"Hello over there!" cried this nearby stranger.

The powerful beam of a light cut through the fog, and Al anxiously leaned over the port gunwale as the ghostly outline of another vessel took form. It was a strange-looking ship, shaped much like a fat cigar. An open hatch was situated on its rounded upper deck, where the upper torso of a man could just be seen. He held a flashlight in his hand, and used this source of illumination to scan the *Sunshine*.

"Boy, are we ever glad to see you!" he shouted. "Our engines are out of commission, as well as our communication and navigational systems."

"What kind of vessel is that, mister?" asked Al. "And where ya headed?"

"This is a U.S. Navy Deep Submergence Rescue Vehicle, and right now our destination is the nearest port."

Supposing that this was some kind of newfangled submarine, Al readily responded. "That would be Nicholls Town, mister. My cousin Sherman runs a fishin' camp there, and he'll take care of ya. If you'd like, I'll give ya a tow."

"That would be most appreciated."

Before turning for the wheelhouse to crank over the engine, Al asked one more question. "Say mister, you didn't happen to pick up two women and a cat out of the water? It looks like I lost a couple of my passengers during that storm that just passed."

"I'm sorry to say that we haven't seen any sign of them," returned the crew-cut stranger. "Though with all this fog and all, they could have floated right by us and we'd never have known it."

With his heart heavy with disappointment, Al turned for the wheelhouse. He was in the process of passing by the card table, when a warm, humid breeze hit him full in the face. The scent of this gust had a fetid ripeness that smelled vaguely of decaying vegetation. With its arrival, the fog momentarily lifted, and he spotted another vessel floating in the water directly in front of the *Sunshine*'s bow. This sleek ship was of tremendous size, and sported the distinctive sail of a submarine, with a five-pointed red star emblazoned on its side. There was an unusual-looking pod on the protruding rudder, and not a soul visible on its wide deck.

The breeze also temporarily uncovered a patch of tree-covered shoreline beyond. Supposing that they had drifted to the eastern shore of Andros Island, he rushed for his binoculars and turned them on the shore before the fog returned. What he saw there caused the hairs on the back of his neck to raise. It seemed unbelievable—the trees were not mangroves at all, but tall swamp cypresses, with thick, green moss hanging from their limbs.

His hands were slightly shaking as he focused on a small collection of buildings set at the base of these trees. He knew that it wasn't possible, but spread out before him were the distinctive outlines of Port Mayaca, the town he had grown up in! And it was then he identified the familiar smells and sounds that surrounded him as belonging to Florida's Lake Okeechobee.

A disturbing question remained to haunt him. How in heaven's name did he ever end up in this landlocked body of water, along with the two ocean-going submarines, a good two hundred miles from the waters off Andros?